A Little Goodbye

Tender Blessings: Book 2

by

Teresa Slack

Library of Congress Control Number: 2018912696

Thank you for buying this book. To get to know me and my other titles better, I'd like to gift you with a free download of *A Promise for Josie: A Willow Wood Prequel*. Simply follow the link and sign up for my newsletter to get the free download of the story that started the best-rated *Willow Wood Series*.

Click here to pick up your free novella.

Also by Teresa Slack

Tender Blessings Series

Love Begins
A Little Goodbye

Stand Alone Novels

The Ultimate Guide to Darcy Carter
Runaway Heart
Joy Redefined

Nine Brides for Cowboy Creek

Rennie
Eliza
Carrie
Bridget
Katie
Marianne
Scarlett
Rachael
Amelia

Willow Wood Brides Series

A Promise for Josie: Willow Wood Prequel
(Available to Newsletter Subscribers)

A Lawman for Lisette: Book 1
A Love Letter for Jessa: Book 2
A Dream for Harper: Book 3
A Wedding for Felicity: Book 4
A Hero for Ellie: Book 5
A Cowboy for Meggan: Book 6

Jenna's Creek Series

Streams of Mercy
Redemption's Song
Evidence of Grace
A Jenna's Creek Wedding: *A Christmas Novella*
Legacy of Faith

What readers are saying about the Tender Blessings Series

"Infused with humor and practical insights, (Tender Blessings) and its characters will capture the hearts of readers who love children, understand their challenges, and appreciate the many definitions of family." —Aspiring Retail Magazine

"...Slack's feel for her Ozarks setting and her knack for drawing minor characters turns this romance into a fine realistic novel."
---Booklist

"I stayed up until 3 a.m. just so I could finish this book. Loved it! I love how Teresa incorporates the word of God into the lives of her characters. What perfect timing for me. I can relate with Michelle so much. You have no idea what similarities we have. Thanks Teresa Slack. Love your work."   ---Reader review

"Tender, heart wrenching story. Breaking your heart and bringing love full circle in the lives of small children and family struggles to overcome real life heartaches." ---Reader Review

"After reading the first book in the series, I had to know what happened to the kids, Aunt Shell and Pastor Kyle. So enjoyed both these books. Loved her approach to Christianity. So realistic." ---Reader review

"Read "A Little Goodbye" last week (for the second time!) I liked it even better this time! I would be up for a 3rd book in this series! Teresa's characters are very believable and interesting. I was entertained and inspired!!" ---Reader Review

"This series is wonderful...Slack puts into perspective real life troubles that we see in our world and sometimes our own lives. If you have children or irresponsible siblings, you can connect with this story for sure." ---Reader Review

"This book is all about its characters, including its setting. I would say this isn't a book any author could be successful at, but Teresa Slack clearly has the gift. This was a refreshing and heart warming read I can happily recommend. This was my first taste of Teresa Slack's writing and I look forward to reading more."   ---Reader Review

"Teresa creates a perfect blend of humor and humanity as she reveals the story of a young woman's struggle with in herself. She also addresses the feelings of men and their relationship with a woman who is already established in a career, something often not covered in the Christian writing world. Thank you Teresa for creating delightful characters in a relaxing setting. Great read!" ---Reader Review

Dedication

This book is for my beautiful niece, Cory Curtis, such a good mom, though she doesn't give herself enough credit.

Chapter One

I layered the last of the mozzarella cheese onto the pizza and then brushed my hands off on Grandma's old apron tied around my waist. I had perfected my homemade pizza recipe years ago, but living alone for so long hadn't required me to dust off my recipe box. Until now. I hoped I hadn't lost my touch. The pizza looked right, but I couldn't stop second guessing myself. Had I let the yeast rest long enough? Had I put too much oregano in the sauce? I always tended to season too much when I was in a hurry. Was the baking stone too hot? Too cold?

I wanted this pizza to turn out perfectly. Barry Schilling was bringing his daughter Caitlyn over to watch a movie that had just been released on DVD. Emma and Caitlyn were best friends at preschool. They wanted to see the movie. Barry and I wanted to see each other.

Most of our dates—if they qualified as dates—were spent with the kids. Barry shared custody of Caitlyn with his ex-wife. If it was one of his weekends with Caitlyn, our plans included her and my two.

Okay, so Emma and Jonah weren't technically my kids, but since I hadn't seen my sister Nicole in over a year, and it had been six months since she abandoned her kids under my lilac bushes, I had begun to think of them as mine.

Tonight Barry was about to discover I wasn't much of a cook. When Grandma was alive, she did all the cooking while I went out and earned a paycheck. She taught me the rudimentary skills necessary for anyone who raised part of their own food. While she lacked patience for teaching, I lacked patience to let yeast rise. The two of us struck a happy balance. Not happy maybe, but one that worked. She cooked. I worked. Now nearly seven years after her passing I still didn't cook.

Emma and Jonah's appearance into my life hadn't changed that.

Fortunately for their palates and growing bodies, they got most of their sustenance from Aunt Wanda who lived on the farm next door. I couldn't very well let Aunt Wanda cater dinner tonight, though the thought had occurred to me. Nor could I feed Barry and Caitlyn pancakes or macaroni and cheese, the only dishes I excelled at.

I thought of Barry and smiled. We had been on two grownup dates without the kids in the last month. Two weren't much for most people, but it was more than I'd had in nearly a decade. Barry was a great guy. He was funny and charming and he liked most of the things I liked. Like sitting at home on a Friday night eating homemade pizza and watching a DVD with the kids.

I went to the sink to wash my hands and then turned to survey the tired kitchen. As far as I knew it hadn't been updated since Great-Grandpa added running water before moving his bride into the house.

When I was in my teens, Grandma Catherine had supervised while Aunt Wanda painted the kitchen and mudroom. Other than that, no renovations had been made. The faded, cracked kitchen tiles were the kind that stuck to the floor with adhesive backing. The appliances didn't match each other, and the aluminum sink was ugly and too shallow for serious dishwashing. The cabinet doors sat a little crooked on their hinges. Some of them didn't shut all the way.

Funny how I barely noticed most of the house's flaws before the morning the kids came to live here.

According to the kids' account and Nicole's own words, she hadn't personally left them here, but she was in complete agreement with the boyfriend who did. I hadn't heard from her since Christmas. The kids still hadn't asked about her. I had nearly reached the point where I hoped she'd never come back. It was a complete one-hundred-and-eighty degree change from the way I felt the morning Gypsy woke me up barking at a delivery in the front yard that turned out to be my niece and nephew. I hadn't wanted them here. I hadn't wanted my well ordered life to change. Now I couldn't imagine my life without the kids in it.

Someday Jonah and Emma would bombard me with questions about their missing mother, especially as they grew older and began to recognize the uniqueness of their situation. For now we were getting along one day at a time with nobody mentioning Nicole or what we'd do when she turned up.

I looked again around the kitchen. Kids or no kids, it was probably time for some updated appliances. Especially a refrigerator that didn't sound like a jet engine preparing for takeoff every time the motor started during the night, and a microwave that wasn't big enough for one of the kids to climb into.

Tonight I didn't need to impress Barry with the condition of my kitchen, or even my cooking skills for that matter, though I had gone to great lengths with the pizza. We hadn't reached the commitment stage of our relationship. We were still just hanging out and getting to know each other while the kids played in the next room. No need to get carried away thinking about a future with the guy when I wasn't sure how I felt about him yet.

Gypsy let out a solitary bark from the front of the house. "They're here," Jonah cried out. Two sets of little feet pounded across the living room to the door.

I laid a paper towel over the pizza to keep the cheese moist before going to the mirror by the backdoor to check my hair and makeup. My goal was to look carelessly put-together and not like I'd spent thirty minutes after my shower getting ready to watch movies and eat pizza with three preschoolers and a man I insisted I wasn't trying to impress. My fine blond hair had frizzed a little in the heat from the oven. A sheen of sweat glistened on my forehead. At least the makeup designed to accentuate my blue eyes and high cheekbones was still intact.

I snatched a paper towel from the roll over the sink and blotted my forehead and the back of my neck. I lifted each arm and sniffed. My deodorant had held up as well. I took a deep breath and headed to the front of the house where I could hear animated voices welcoming our guests.

My pizza was the best he'd ever eaten outside a mom-and-pop pizzeria, Barry assured me later as we washed the dishes while the kids played in the living room.

"I was afraid I got the cheese too dark while waiting for the crust to brown," I said, secretly relishing the praise. I hadn't gotten a lot of that in my lifetime.

"It was perfect." He took the last plate out of my hand and dried it while keeping his eyes on me.

I let the warmth of his gaze wash over me a moment longer before I broke eye contact and pulled the stopper out of the sink. I focused on rinsing out the sink, another daily chore since the old kitchen was not equipped with a dishwasher, and I had never seen the need for one when it was just Gypsy and me living here. I tried not to feel too self-conscious, knowing Barry was still watching me. I wasn't sure why his attention was so disconcerting. He wasn't the only one in this picture with a bit of a crush on the other party. The more time I spent with him, the more obvious his redeeming qualities became.

But I hung back. I wasn't ready to put myself totally into a relationship. Too many changes had occurred in my life over the last year. I wasn't ready to add a man to the chaos as well.

I finally turned away from the sink. Barry was still watching me, a bemused expression on his face. Jonah appeared in the doorway. I nearly laughed out loud with relief.

"Are you coming?" Jonah's brown eyes shone with anticipation. "We're ready to watch the movie."

I turned back to Barry and hoped my smile looked apologetic. I moved past him, half afraid he'd take my arm and tell me he knew what I was doing and why didn't I let down my guard for a minute and give him a chance. I couldn't do that. I really liked Barry. He just wasn't…

I pushed those thoughts out of my head before they could manifest into a full blown pity party and followed Jonah into the living room where Emma and Caitlyn were waiting in front of the TV. I took my time putting the movie into the machine as I considered the seating arrangement in my head. Should I sit next to Barry? Should I put the kids in the middle of the couch with both of us on either side like bookends holding them in place? He would think I was nuts if I sat in my usual chair adjacent to the sofa.

I couldn't figure out why I was so uncomfortable. This wasn't our first date. We had shared a few kisses. For the most part we got along well. Was I nervous because our relationship was headed to a level for which I wasn't ready? Or was I afraid Barry was already there, and it wouldn't be long before he became impatient and started rushing me to join him?

While I agonized, Barry solved the whole seating issue by moving the coffee table and piling pillows on the floor for the kids. After they were situated, he motioned me to the center of the couch. I sat down, and he plopped down beside me with barely an inch separating my thigh from his.

He rested his arm across the back of the couch behind my head. He squeezed my arm with his other hand and then turned to the TV. It was a little awkward sitting there like I had in high school with a boy I wasn't sure I liked. The only boy I liked back then was Kyle Swann.

I groaned inwardly. Kyle. Always Kyle. Every time I thought he was completely out of my head, he popped in again to give me grief.

I had thought I put our high school love affair behind me until I discovered Kyle was the pastor at the church that sponsored the kids' preschool. I wasn't a total heathen. But I was definitely not the type of woman a preacher would ever date. I kept telling myself to forget Kyle and be happy I found Barry. It made sense in my head, but it wasn't always easy to do.

Emma, Jonah, and Caitlyn barely looked up from the movie as soon as the coming attractions began. Barry moved his arm off the back of the couch and snaked it around my shoulders. We had never shared physical contact in front of the kids before. I didn't want them to make assumptions, good or bad, about what was going on. They were too young for that when we hadn't decided where this was headed, if anywhere.

I got up once to refill the kids' drinks, and when I came back to my seat Barry took my hand. Jonah got off the floor and joined us on the couch. I almost pulled my hand free when he looked at my hand in Barry's, but that would be more conspicuous than leaving it where it was. Jonah had assuredly seen his mother in more compromising positions with God only knew how many men. But Aunt Shell? She didn't cozy up to anyone.

He paused for a moment in front of us like he was debating more over who to sit with than about Barry and me getting chummy. Then he jumped onto Barry's lap and leaned over to rest his head on my shoulder.

Barry and I shifted apart to make room for him. I kissed the top of Jonah's head and smoothed down his hair. Then we all went back to the movie.

The kids managed to sit still until the closing credits began to roll. Immediately they were up and off the floor, pillows flying. Gypsy jumped up with them.

"Help me put the pillows away, please," I said as they prepared to run upstairs. I looked at Barry. "You don't have to leave yet, do you?"

He smiled slyly up at me. "No." He drew out the word as his smile broadened.

I smiled back. He was really cute when he smiled like that. I wasn't sure if he had always been or if he was just growing on me. I stole a surreptitious look at the clock on the DVD player. It was only a little after nine. The kids didn't have school tomorrow. Neither Barry nor I had to work. He and Caitlyn could stay as late as he wanted. Or as late as I wanted.

He took a blanket out of my hands. "Let the kids go upstairs. I'll help you with this."

I smiled my agreement. The kids whooped in delight and thundered up the stairs with Gypsy panting in their wake.

"Things seem to be running pretty smooth around here," Barry said as the footsteps reached the second floor.

I knew he wasn't talking about day-to-day life on the farm. He meant with Nicole and the way I had adapted to having two kids in my house after a lifetime of doing things my own way.

"I like order."

I winced, recognizing the words as something Grandma Catherine would've said. But it was true. I liked order and routine and structure. I wouldn't apologize for it, even if I probably inherited the trait from her.

"I assume it was more orderly when you had the place to yourself."

I leveled a look at him. "That's an open ended statement if I ever heard one."

He smiled like he'd been caught with his hand in the cookie jar.

"Are you trying to ask how it's working out raising another woman's kids?"

He set a stack of pillows into the easy chair where I had considered sitting. I was glad I hadn't.

"I'll never forget the look on your face the first time you went on one of the preschoolers' field trips," he said.

We both laughed at the memory. "I was never so terrified of anything in my life. I was sure one of the kids would run into the street or get snatched by a psycho or have an allergic reaction to peanut butter."

"You're a nurse. Don't you deal with emergencies every day?"

"It's not the same."

He nodded. It wasn't the same. It was never the same when it involved kids, especially your own. Or even kids dumped on you by your irresponsible sister.

"I never thought I'd get used to the chaos of a hundred preschoolers in the same place."

"It showed."

"And now?"

"Now you act like an old hand at it."

I smiled as I plumped the sofa pillows into place, but part of me wasn't sure I wanted to become an old hand at taking care of Emma and Jonah. Sure, I loved my niece and nephew. I was so happy they were in my life. Thankful even, though I didn't know if I should be thankful to Nicole for leaving the kids with me or thankful to fate or a deity or whatever was responsible for things like that. I just didn't know if I wanted to do this forever. Wasn't I entitled to a life of my own caused by my choices, not the choices of others that kept kicking me in the throat?

I leaned over to straighten out the wrinkles in the rug where the kids had piled the pillows. "I guess everything gets easier the more you do it."

Barry tilted his head a little. The silence lengthened. I rethought my words and wondered if he was thinking about being with me. I hadn't been particularly attracted to Barry when we first met. Not because of anything personal. He was nice looking. I liked the way his eyes crinkled when he smiled, which was often. He had an easygoing appearance to go with his easygoing personality. He had grown on me. Or maybe the idea of dating and sharing my life with someone was what had grown on me. I doubted I ever would've reached this point if the kids hadn't shown up under my lilac bushes last summer.

I straightened and set my hands on my hips. "Nicole called me at Christmas. It was the only time I've heard from her except for when she called to explain why she needed me to keep the kids. I haven't heard a peep since. She was drunk."

I wasn't sure why I added that tidbit of information. He didn't need to know Nicole was a substance abuser or Grandma Catherine emotionally and psychologically harangued me from the moment we met or that I hadn't spoken to my dad since I was thirteen.

Barry sat down on the sofa and looked up at me as though drunken phone calls over the holidays weren't outside his experience. "What did the kids say?"

"Nothing. They were at the sitter's when she called."

"You realize someday she'll call and you won't be able to keep it from them."

I nodded gravely. "Hopefully it will be later rather than sooner."

"What are you going to tell Emma and Jonah when it inevitably happens? Kids aren't dumb. They know Nicole is out there somewhere. Even if she hasn't been in touch with them, they know she didn't drop off the side of the earth."

I exhaled and sat down on the ottoman. Our knees nearly touched. I resisted the urge to scoot the ottoman back. If we were technically dating I needed to stop being so uneasy about physical contact.

"We've had our bouts with separation anxiety," I told him, thinking of Emma's multiple meltdowns last month when she wouldn't let me out of her sight. "Sometimes Jonah acts out, but for the most part the biggest adjustment is on my end. The kids are much more resilient and handling the situation a whole lot better than I am."

He cocked his head. "Don't kid yourself. It won't go on like this forever."

Did he need to remind me? The last thing I wanted was for thoughts of Nicole to intrude on our nice evening. I got mad every time I thought about what she had done to Jonah and Emma—what she was still doing to them—and I didn't want to get mad tonight.

The silence lengthened, neither of us saying what we were probably thinking. I wanted to remind him our situations weren't that different. I was sure Caitlyn sometimes asked why Mommy and Daddy didn't live together. How did one explain to a five-year-old that the two most important people in her world couldn't stand the sight of each other enough to keep a marriage together? They hadn't been separated that long. Surely Caitlyn had memories of the good old days when Mommy and Daddy slept in the same bed and tucked her in at night. But maybe those days hadn't been so good, and she was better off now with them living apart but still loving and caring for her.

My thoughts concerning Barry and Sue's marriage weren't exactly charitable. I just couldn't help but resent the liberty he felt in asking how I would field questions or handle Nicole when he and Sue had put Caitlyn in nearly the same position. The only difference in me and Barry was I had never gone into a covenant agreement with Nicole to love and cherish her till death do us part like he and Sue had done.

I didn't ask any of those questions. Our relationship wasn't ready for that much gut-wrenching intimacy. If we even had a relationship.

"I just want Emma and Jonah to enjoy being kids," I finally admitted. "I don't believe they've had much time to do that. Whether it's another week or six months, I want to give them as much freedom as possible from worrying about grownup issues."

Barry nodded thoughtfully. "They're probably worrying even if they don't say so."

"I know, but if I can shield them a little longer, I will."

He smiled softly, and I think I saw affection in his gaze. I looked away sharply. I didn't want to say what I thought he wanted to hear. I didn't want him to develop feelings for me beyond what he already had until I knew how I felt about him.

"You're really good for Emma and Jonah," he said gently. "They've changed so much since they came here."

He wasn't the first person to tell me that.

"I've changed too."

"I noticed that."

He was looking at me again in that meaningful way like he was waiting for me to give him the green light. I picked at the pilled fabric on the ottoman. No matter how perfect Barry seemed for me, I couldn't stop comparing him to Kyle. There would never be anything between Kyle and me, even though we had professed our love for each other a few months ago. If I loved Kyle, was any of this fair to Barry?

Barry caught my hand and pulled me onto the sofa with him. I tensed, afraid he'd ask what was on my mind and I'd blurt out I was thinking about another man whom I could never have.

Instead he asked me about work. For the next thirty minutes I told him stories about patients and plans for my flowerbeds while he explained his wavering considerations on investing in a zero-turn lawn mower. Nothing serious or permanent or heavy. Just banter between friends who might become something more down the road.

The noise upstairs escalated, and Barry decided it was probably time to take Caitlyn home. There was no goodnight kiss. In the confusion of finding Caitlyn's shoes and the girls begging to spend the night and Jonah adding his own attempts at attention, we didn't have a chance to sneak one in.

It was probably better that way. I didn't know about Caitlyn, but Emma and Jonah were not ready to see me kiss someone. I didn't want them to think I was like their mother, and any attention spent on a man would mean there was less available for them.

Barry and I exchanged meaningful glances over the kids' heads as he slid Caitlyn's jacket over her shoulders. He wagged his eyebrows at me. I could tell he was disappointed we had so little time alone together. I probably didn't mind as much as he did. Deep down I figured it wasn't getting involved with Barry that bothered me as much as knowing he wasn't Kyle.

I wouldn't think too hard on that right now.

Chapter Two

Spring has always been my favorite season even though it brings a pile of chores to add to an already beleaguered list. When it isn't raining in northern Arkansas, the temperatures are typically perfect for getting outside to repair the damage done over the winter; clearing away fallen limbs and garbage that collected along the fencerows, cleaning out flowerbeds and designing new ones, tightening eave spouts and nailing down loose shingles.

When she died, Grandma Catherine left me the fifty-two remaining acres of the original farm bought by my great-grandfather over a hundred years ago. Even that small acreage was too much for me to handle with a fulltime job, a part-time job at the local hospital, and now two little kids. Uncle Jeb did most of the mowing and weed eating. Uncle DeWitt kept an eye on the fences and made sure the pond drained properly. Even though I wasn't a farmer by any stretch of the imagination and my uncles took care of the really unpleasant jobs, I loved living on the farm and pretending I knew what I was doing.

This year was the best of all. I missed most of March due to long hours at work, but things had settled down in my routine. I was finally able to enjoy the kids without worrying about Nicole barging in and upsetting our apple cart. I knew she would eventually, but I successfully pushed the possibility out of my head.

When things go without a hitch long enough, you begin to forget what a hitch could do to your life. I should know better than anyone yet I sometimes forget.

Emma had recovered from her separation anxiety and Jonah had grown into a big boy with big boy ideas. I often had to remind myself that seven months ago I hadn't wanted my sister's kids thrust upon me. I was perfectly content on the farm with nothing but Gypsy and the garden to occupy my time away from the hospital. Now my house was never quiet. Instead of dogging my every step, Gypsy preferred to run the fields with the kids and come home with her coat matted with burrs and sticks and pieces of brush. I was teaching the kids to brush her out and help with bath time. If they were going to have a dog—technically she was my dog, but her loyalties had changed over the last half year—they would learn to be responsible for her.

My phone chirped inside my pocket, alerting me to a missed text. As always when I received a text or phone call or simply caught sight of a black truck in traffic, my heart skipped a beat. Even before I looked, I knew the sender was not the person I longed for it to be.

Just a few weeks ago Kyle Swann had told me he loved me. He was the pastor of the church where I sent the kids for preschool. He was also an old sweetheart from high school. The only sweetheart from any time in my past. Besides telling him I loved him back, I had spilled my guts about how my parents' abandonment had totally screwed me up. I told him how hard it had been living with an old lady who hadn't loved me, or if she had, was sorely equipped to show it. I even told him all the conflicting feelings raging through me since Nicole dumped her kids on me and walked away.

Kyle knew it all, good and bad, yet he loved me still. But we both knew a relationship beyond pastor and intermittent, doubting churchgoer could never work.

Since those few tear-filled encounters, we hadn't had time for more than a passing nod every time we ran into each other at the preschool. I wondered if Kyle preferred casting a wide berth around me the way I did with him. Maybe he found it less painful, the way I did.

Regardless of the pain at keeping Kyle at a distance, I sure wished things could be different.

I drew the phone out of my pocket. As expected, Barry's number flashed at me. I exhaled, partly from relief since a relationship with Barry was relatively uncomplicated, but more because I wanted Kyle to want to hear from me as badly as I wanted to hear from him.

I enjoyed last night, Barry had written. *Let's do it again.*

Sounds good, I typed back.

Immediately it chirped again. I couldn't decide if I was annoyed or flattered.

When? he texted back.

The traffic light turned green. I dropped the phone onto my lap and moved forward, relieved at the interruption. This was why I didn't like texting. People expected you to be available at every moment of the day. They were almost offended if you were busy or preoccupied or in the middle of something. As if you had some nerve doing things other than staring at your phone all day.

The phone hummed again. I ignored it. Like a responsible driver, I waited until I pulled into the church parking lot before I turned the phone over to look at the screen. A number I didn't recognize displayed on the screen.

A number with a Tennessee area code.

My stomach dropped. Unknown numbers were never good. Especially numbers from the vicinity of your worthless sister's last known address.

I pulled into the first empty spot in front of the preschool doors. My heart thudded in my chest. It's a telemarketer, I told myself over and over again. Or a wrong number.

I went back to the home screen. A tiny red number one indicated Barry had sent me another text. I opened it with shaking fingers. Anything to delay finding out who had called from Tennessee.

Let me know when works for you, he had written.

He was letting me know the ball was in my court. I could get back with him for plans for another date or let it slide for a while. Whatever worked for me.

My heart warmed as I forget the other call for a moment. Barry really was a nice guy. Thoughtful. Whatever I wanted was fine with him. Always. What about what he wanted? If I said I didn't want to see him for a while, would he mind? Would he try to talk me out of it? Or would he lift a shoulder as though he didn't have an opinion either way and walk out of my life until I sought him out?

Whatever I wanted.

I thought of Kyle. It had been over fifteen years since we dated, yet both of us were still unmarried. Was that significant? I had never heard of a single pastor. They always married young and had a houseful of kids. At least the ones in my experience. Not that I had much experience with pastors.

What was wrong with him?

What was wrong with *me*?

I hadn't intentionally spent the last decade and a half waiting for him. I barely thought of him since high school. That was until the last few months when our lives intersected again.

Had Kyle been waiting for me? At our last meeting he said he still loved me, that he had always loved me. I wasn't sure what to make of that. I wasn't exactly loveable. And I wasn't pastor's wife material. I wasn't even a Christian.

I reread Barry's text. We were a better match. We both had kids—well, I had my sister's kids, and probably would for a long time unless the unidentified call was from Nicole telling me she was on her way to get them. We had preschool tuition and field trips and dinners to make after a long day at work. I wasn't sure how I felt about Barry, and I sure didn't know how he felt about me. But we had a solid foundation of commonality on which to build a relationship.

I took a deep breath and opened the info on my missed call. No message. A telemarketer, I was sure. Nicole would've left a message. She would've started rambling about how much she missed the kids and how much she appreciated my sacrifices to make Jonah and Emma happy. All of it would've been lies, of course, but it that never stopped her from saying it.

I thought of the phone call I received the day after Christmas. She had wished me a lackluster Merry Christmas before launching into a diatribe about depression, her uncertain future and why nobody loved her. I tried to be compassionate. Despite her narcissism and poor mothering skills, she was my baby sister. I wanted her to be happy.

She hadn't asked about the kids. If the last seven months was any indication, they seldom crossed her mind.

Had they crossed her mind today? Was she behind the mysterious phone call with the Tennessee area code? I needed to know. Was she suddenly ready to play the role of Mommy again? How would it affect me if she did?

My thumb hovered over the phone icon next to the unknown number. I should just call it back. If it was a telemarketer I would be rerouted and then cut off. I could find out just as easily if the call was a wrong number. What if it wasn't? What if whoever was on the other end had meant to call me and ruin my life?

I looked away from the phone and down the long expanse of brick to the portico and main entrance of the church. Kyle's truck sat in its usual spot in the parking lot. A fist of anticipation tightened in my belly. I moved my thumb away from the phone. I wanted to talk but not to the unknown person on the other end of my phone.

I stared at the double doors. If Kyle walked out this very moment I would take it as a sign that I was meant to talk to him. It had been over a month since I unloaded on him in his office about the kids and my past and abandonment issues with my parents. We had even kissed like we meant it, as if turning back the clock to a time before we got so burdened down with baggage that a life together was a possibility.

Then he fled to his side of the desk and slammed the door on those dreams.

I stared at the church doors a little longer. If he walked out by the time I counted to ten I would know it was fate our paths crossed today.

One, two, three…

By the time I got to seven, I was letting several seconds lapse between each number.

Another car pulled in beside me. A harried looking mother jumped out of her SUV and bustled toward the preschool entrance. I couldn't sit here all day and stare at the church doors like some kind of groupie. I swallowed my disappointment and got out of the car. At this time of day, right after naptime, the preschool was loud and raucous. I often wondered how the teachers survived each day. They looked as tired and frazzled as me after a long shift in ICU.

I waited my turn at the sign-out sheet as the mom ahead of me signed her name and headed toward the play area to gather her offspring. I had barely started scribbling when I heard my name. Jonah rounded the bank of cubby boxes just as I dotted my I and crashed into me. Emma was right behind him. It warmed my heart each time I entered the school and saw them playing and interacting with other kids. Emma was always in the middle of a bunch of girls when I came in, playing baby dolls, working puzzles, or tripping around the play area in cast off high heels from some member of the church.

Jonah had turned out to be a leader in his group. He liked to initiate games with the other boys, build things out of blocks, or career around on the carpeted floors pushing oversized plastic trucks. I sometimes forgot the two little waifs I enrolled in the preschool last August.

I wondered what Nicole would think if she saw them now. Would she be pleased at the independent secure children they had become? Or would she resent how they had grown and developed without her influence?

Amped up by the excitement of leaving for the day and the usual competition to get my attention, they jumped from foot to foot and pulled at my hands and shoved papers under my nose for my approval.

"Okay, okay," I said, trying to look calm and stern, but secretly relishing the warmth of love for them. "One at a time."

"Miss Jennifer brought in a turtle today," Jonah exclaimed.

I made an appropriately revolted face. "I don't like turtles."

Jonah wasn't fooled. "Yes, you do, Aunt Shell. This one was really cool. We got to hold it and feed it lettuce leaves."

"Amelia's mom is going to have a baby," Emma trilled.

My heart sank. Babies. Did that mean it was time to have the talk? It was actually overdue. I'd read somewhere the discussion of sex and reproduction and the differences between boys and girls should be a natural part of conversation, not a lecture administered at the onset of puberty and promptly forgotten.

Even though I was a nurse and totally comfortable with discussing where babies came from, I shuddered at the thought of broaching the topic with Emma and Jonah.

I forgot about the stressful day I'd had at the hospital and the message on my phone from the number I didn't recognize. I didn't think about my sore feet or the negative run-in with Joan in administration. Life was good and too short for regrets.

We waved goodbye to the teachers on duty as I held the door open for the kids to go out before me. They were still talking a mile a minute by the time we hit the parking lot, ping-ponging from one subject to the next so fast I could barely keep track. I herded them toward the car, nodding and trying to follow the flow of the conversation.

"Hey, Michelle, wait up," a masculine voice called out as I opened the car door.

Emma and Jonah threw papers and book bags into the back seat, then clambered in over them. The rugs on the back floorboards weren't doing much to keep the spring muck from getting tracked inside the car; a car I once kept immaculately clean. I reached down with one hand to straighten the rugs and ran the other hand through my naturally wavy, usually frizzy blond hair. A few minutes ago I had fantasized about running into Kyle. Now I was wishing I could hide long enough to freshen my makeup and make sure I didn't have anything stuck in my teeth.

By the time I got the rug and my hair straightened out, Kyle was right behind me.

"How's it going?" he asked. As usual he looked great. Jet black hair deliciously tousled. A late afternoon shadow darkening his jaw. His usual workday polo shirt straining against his wide shoulders.

He put a hand on the car door to hold it open for me and leaned forward to peer into the back seat. I resisted the urge to reach out and squeeze his bicep.

"How was school today?" he asked the kids.

"Fine." Emma responded.

"Great," Jonah said much more enthusiastically. "Look what I made." He held aloft a wrinkled paper with some unknown object he'd drawn. A muddy shoe print made the picture even harder to recognize. "It's a birthday cake," he explained, "on account 'a I'm four now."

Kyle looked at me for confirmation.

I nodded. "Last week."

"Wow," he told Jonah. "No wonder you've gotten so big."

Not to be outdone, Emma held a drawing of her own into the air as high as she could from the confines of her booster car seat. She and Jonah were balking the car seats more and more every day. I didn't care how much they complained. They weren't getting out of those seats until they could no longer physically fit into them. I saw too many children in the emergency room with injuries that could have been prevented if they'd been properly buckled into a size appropriate seat.

Kyle made the proper noises of approval over the papers the way I had inside. Then he turned his attention to me. "Where you headed?"

I cocked an eyebrow. "Home."

He smiled. If it were possible, I think he would have blushed. "Yeah, sorry. I guess that was a dumb question. Actually, I've been wanting to talk to you." He glanced at the kids again in the backseat. "We haven't had the chance to say two words to each other since…well, for a while."

I knew exactly what he was talking about. The last time we talked I had gone to his office for advice about Emma's sudden clinginess. Kyle's answers had been surprisingly spot on, considering he didn't have kids of his own, and I had never really told him the complete dirty picture of what Emma and Jonah apparently endured while living with their mother.

Of course we hadn't ended our conversation on the topic of Emma. It had gone from childhood fears to our past to my inability to trust anyone to us being locked in each other's arms. I was sure Kyle didn't want to talk about that now.

I fumbled in my purse for my keys as I tried to forget the touch of his lips on mine that day in his office.

"You know how it is. Busy, busy."

Kyle nodded, but I got the feeling he could see right through me. "I've missed you at church."

So that's what this was about. He hadn't come out here because he missed me or was tormented by thoughts of my lips on his. He was simply fulfilling his pastoral duties of keeping the flock in check.

I lifted my shoulders and reached for the car door Kyle was still halfway blocking with his body. "We'll be there at the next Preschool Sunday."

He didn't move away from the door. He looked out over the top of my car into the parking lot as if something heavy was weighing on his mind and he couldn't think of a way to bring it up. If he was going to give me a lecture about why church attendance was so important when kids were young, he could save his breath. I had moved past much of my animosity for church and churchgoers, thanks to my training at Grandma Catherine's knee, but I still wasn't sold on the importance of regular church attendance. The kids and I were getting along pretty well attending once or twice a month.

"If you're not in a hurry to get home," he began, slowly bringing his gaze down to meet mine, "how about going somewhere for a quick bite? I'd love to know how everyone is adjusting to the changes." His head made a subtle motion to the backseat out of the kids' line of vision. "It would give us a chance to catch up on old times, too."

"I don't know," I said, searching my mind for a plausible excuse, and wondering why I didn't want to give him one.

"It'll be fun." He gave me that grin of his that could always melt my insides. "Just someplace for a burger or something. It doesn't have to be a big deal."

Did he think I would make a big deal out of it and spend the rest of the week wondering what he really wanted? Maybe

I would. Maybe I wanted it to turn into something more than a burger and a chance to catch up.

Regardless there was no point in pretending I would refuse. "Sure. We can't stay out long though. I've been up since five and I'm beat."

Sounds of excitement started in the backseat as the kids realized something unplanned was happening in our usual mundane weekday routine.

"I wanna go to Burger King," Jonah said from the back seat.

"Yeah, Burger King," Emma repeated.

I looked apologetically at Kyle.

His smile widened. "I was hoping you'd say that. Do you want to follow me?"

"Yeah, that would be fine."

I tried not to ogle as he walked across the parking lot to his truck. I took a few cleansing breaths to remind myself he just wanted to talk about the kids, and he wasn't any more interested in me than he ever was. I wouldn't allow myself to forget the way he fled to his side of the desk after our kiss in his office.

I nabbed the lipstick out of my purse and did a quick pass around my mouth. I peeked in the rearview mirror to make sure the kids weren't paying attention as I checked to make sure I hadn't gotten any on my teeth. I sure didn't want them telling Kyle I was primping for him.

No worries. They were bouncing up and down in their seats, excited about the turn of events and not paying the least bit of attention to me. Even if they had, they would realize there wasn't a whole lot I could do to make myself more attractive to the opposite sex short of a major overhaul.

Chapter Three

At the restaurant I ordered the usual for the kids and me and let Kyle elbow his way in to pay. It took several minutes to stick straws into drinks and open ketchup packets and listen to the typical banter about who got the most fries. Kyle stood beside me being as helpful and understanding as I could hope for a man without children to be. Finally the four of us were seated around a too-small square table. The kids clasped hands and bowed their heads automatically over their food. I was glad they were used to saying grace before each meal, a habit they'd picked up at preschool and brought home to me. At least Kyle wouldn't think I was a total heathen.

We exchanged charmed glances over their heads as they recited a favorite prayer.

"Thank you for the world so sweet. Thank you for the food we eat. Thank you for the birds that sing. Thank you, God, for Burger King. Amen."

My eyes flew open and I jerked my head up, mortified. Right in front of a preacher! What must Kyle be thinking? Should I correct them right now? Should we discuss it later so they could understand that making a joke out of prayer was inappropriate? Emma and Jonah squealed with laughter and proceeded to dig into their kids' meals. I darted a scandalized look in Kyle's direction.

A grin split his handsome face. "I've often found myself thankful for Burger King too. I just didn't have the right words to articulate it."

I smiled in return and relaxed. As long as they meant what they said when they brought their petitions before the Lord, I supposed no prayer was inappropriate.

There wasn't much chance to catch up on lost time sitting at a table with two preschoolers, but I couldn't remember having a better time at Burger King. Kyle was funny and so obviously not trying to impress me. We talked and laughed, almost exclusively about or with the kids. They had a way of taking the pressure off a potentially embarrassing situation. I still had feelings for Kyle, but didn't know what, if anything, I wanted to do about them. Kyle was handsome, sweet and charming without effort, just as I remembered, only better with the passage of time.

I had worried neither of us would be able to get past what happened in his office when he kissed me and then obviously regretted it. Maybe it was due to the kids' cheerful banter keeping us preoccupied, but I had a great time.

I wondered briefly why I hadn't given myself time for a relationship in my adult life. I thought of Nicole's claims that I was cold and too controlling to allow myself to fall for a man. My reasoning was much simpler than that if I took the time to think about it. Relationships were too much work. I had dated a few times during college, but someone always expected something from me I wasn't willing to give. I didn't have female friends for the same reason. I was too busy, lazy, or selfish to invest the time necessary to build a lasting bond. With Kyle, I might be willing to take the risk.

I inwardly kicked myself. What was I doing? Kyle had given no indication he was here for anything other than a quick bite at Burger King in lieu of going home and eating alone. He could be just as busy, lazy, and selfish as me, and just as unwilling to invest time in a relationship. He probably thought God would send him a woman when he was ready for one.

I sure didn't need that kind of pressure.

Even if he was willing and I was the right woman to make him take the leap, what about Barry? We were sort of seeing each other. I really liked Barry, but he never put me as at ease the way Kyle did. Did that mean anything? Barry was great and he liked me. I just couldn't figure out what Kyle wanted.

Before I knew it the kids had finished their meal and were eyeing the indoor playground. I usually didn't let them go in, cautious about freak accidents that had been to known to occur in places like this. But it was presently deserted, and I wanted to prolong my time with Kyle. We could supervise while enjoying each other's company. At least, I was enjoying his. I had from the first time I laid eyes on him.

I had never been able to figure out what made Kyle Swann choose me out of all those girls in high school; girls much prettier, taller, richer, smarter than me. Even now, solidly in my thirties, I was gangly and clumsy, tripping over my own feet, or worse, my tongue. I would think something sounded clever in my head, but the instant it went from my mouth out into the world, it sounded stupid or banal or ridiculous. I had learned to keep my mouth shut as much possible and not draw attention to myself.

Growing up, I was a total loser. I couldn't do anything right. Not at home and not at school. Somehow I got Kyle Swann's attention. He thought I was funny and unusual. He didn't seem to notice I wasn't pretty or sophisticated. Around him, I developed a confidence I never had anywhere else. I opened up and said whatever was on my mind whether it sounded stupid or not. Talking to Kyle was easy. Natural. During our last two years at Winona High School, our friendship evolved into something more, almost without us realizing it.

High school couldn't last forever. Kyle's parents couldn't afford college, yet they made too much money to qualify for significant financial aid. Still, Kyle had his sights set on getting an education and maybe flying airplanes one day. When he told me the summer before our senior year that he was going to enlist in the Air Force after graduation, I smiled and told him what a practical idea that was. Deep down I knew he was making the right choice. The Air Force would solve all his problems. On a more selfish level, I was angry he was leaving Winona when he knew I wasn't free to go anywhere. Someone had to be here for Nicole. Dad had already deserted her. Mom was off and living her life who knew where, calling to check in every year or two. I was all Nicole had.

As angry as I was at Kyle for wanting to leave and make a life outside of Harrison County, I didn't let it show. During senior year we grew closer and closer, even though I knew I should distance myself from him. How could I let him go to San Antonio if I fell any further completely, madly, in love with him than I already was?

All my emotions came pouring forth the night of our graduation. Everyone was standing around outside the gymnasium after the ceremony, hugging, taking pictures, exchanging small gifts, tears flowing, knowing full well many of us would never lay eyes on each other again. Not me, of course. I would be right here in Winona where anyone could find me if they took a notion to look.

Kyle had laid a possessive arm across my shoulders and hammed it up for the camera. He was always popular and everybody wanted to get a shot of him. By association, they got one with me, too, whether they wanted it or not.

Throughout the night Kyle's arm grew heavier and heavier on my shoulders. I couldn't think of anything beyond him leaving for San Antonio in eight days. I knew I'd never see him again. Who in their right mind would come back to this little nothing place after seeing what the world had to offer? Whatever he learned in the Air Force, he couldn't parlay into an occupation in Harrison County. There was no reason to come back. Certainly not me. If I were so important to him, he wouldn't leave in the first place.

I was stuck and he was free, pure and simple.

The fight we had was a veritable free-for-all. It was easier to let Kyle go after getting every hateful, inconsiderate, jealous thing off my chest. He said if I cared for him, I'd support his decision. I told him if he cared for me, he would feel as rotten as I did. He called me spiteful and petty. I called him selfish and uncaring. He left me standing in Grandma Catherine's driveway that night, tears streaming down my cheeks, as he raised a rooster tail of dirt and gravel on our little country road. He left for Texas without a good-bye phone call. I hated him all the more.

"Do you remember the night we graduated?" I asked.

He barked out a laugh. "How could I forget? I'd never heard so many curse words come out of such a pretty mouth before."

It took me a moment to recover from the 'pretty mouth' comment. I laughed to cover my discomfort. "All those years living with Grandma Catherine gave me a bit of an acid tongue."

Thankfully Kyle laughed again. "I'll say." His face sobered. "But even then I understood why you felt the way you did. It wasn't easy for me either, you know. I wasn't sure what I was doing. I'd never been out of Arkansas. You were the only thing I was sure about."

Before I could ask what he meant by that, he turned in the chair so he could see the kids better. "It looks like everything worked out like it should though."

He watched Emma climb over a net bridge. She was laughing and hurrying to keep up with Jonah.

I nodded, though I wasn't sure I agreed. "I suppose. I wasn't really mad at you. You know that, right? I was angry I had to stay here when it seemed like everyone else in the county had a future to look forward to. As far as I was concerned, nothing was going to change for me. Just more school, looking after Nicole, and listening to Grandma's complaints every night."

Kyle turned back to me, his face filled with sympathy. "I hope it wasn't too terrible."

Was he trying to appease his conscience for leaving me here?

"No. I'd gotten used to the way things were long before graduation."

He nodded thoughtfully. The two of us watched the kids a few moments in silence.

"What about you?" I asked to shift the conversation away from myself. "You never did get to fly those jets."

He shook his head. "Wasn't up to the rigors of training. It wasn't as hard to accept as I thought it'd be. I realized before I was too far into the program I didn't have the right stuff. I ended up training soldiers who would be in the air instead. I enjoyed it though. Four years, but by the time it came to re-up, the Lord had already made his plans known."

"How do you know?" I asked icily. "What if you misinterpreted?"

"I didn't," he said with a confidence I'd never felt about anything. "I listened for a long time. 'Make your call and election sure,' the Bible says. I was sure. The Lord called me to preach and I never looked back."

"Haven't you ever wanted more? Like a family?" I hoped my expression wasn't too telling.

"Who says I can't have both? I'm not a monk or a priest. I can have a wife. I'm looking forward to it someday, if it's God's will, of course."

"Of course," I added absently.

He tipped his cup to catch the last of his milkshake. He smiled at me as his lips tightened around the straw. My insides turned to mush.

"You don't sound like you believe in that sort of thing," he said.

I picked at a French fry Emma left on her napkin, anything to keep my eyes off his. "Didn't God create us with a will so we could make our own choices?"

Kyle brightened, eager to talk about his passion. "Oh, yes, and my choice was to follow his will. He created me in his likeness, so I figure I can trust Him to lead me down the best path for my life. He holds me in the palm of his hand and has numbered every hair on my head. He knows my tomorrow, so I don't need to worry about the small stuff."

"I guess you think I should trust God with my future. Stop worrying about Nicole and her kids and put my problems in God's hands."

"That would be ideal. Your worrying isn't going to change the outcome one bit anyway, so why bother? Trust God. Let him work it out."

"Isn't that a pretty irresponsible attitude? I've got two little kids depending on me. Their mother obviously isn't concerned with whether they have a hot meal or a place to lay their heads. Somebody's got to see to all the boring details of taking care of them."

"They are so blessed to have you, Michelle."

I looked away from the tenderness in his gaze. "I guess some people would say that. Sometimes I wonder."

"Don't be so hard on yourself, Michelle." He looked pointedly at the top of the jungle gym. I followed his gaze and saw Emma and Jonah laughing and playing together. "I can't imagine a better place for those kids to be at this point in time." He covered my hand with his.

I pulled my hand away and dropped it inot my lap. The warmth stayed with me. Kyle looked a little disappointed by the break in contact, or it could've been my wishful thinking.

He recovered quickly. "How are the kids getting along? We haven't spoken since that day you came into my office to talk about Emma."

You mean the day you kissed me and told me you loved me and then ran away like a scalded dog?

Of course I didn't ask my question.

"She's doing so much better." I was actually relieved to shift the conversation to the kids and away from a relationship we may have shared. "Jonah, too. You knew exactly what you were talking about when you said Emma was worried about me leaving the way Nicole had done. Once we faced it, things got a lot better."

"I'm glad to hear it. I'm always here if you need to talk."

As a spiritual counselor, I thought bitterly. Never anything more than that.

"I appreciate the offer," I said instead. It wasn't fair to either of us to expect anything else from him. "Emma's back to sleeping in her own bed. And Jonah, well, he's just amazing. I keep telling myself not to borrow trouble."

"What kind of trouble?"

I looked at the kids to make sure they were still occupied and leaned into the table, closing the gap between Kyle and me. "I got a phone call today. A nine-oh-one area code."

"Nicole?"

"I'm not sure. Whoever it was didn't leave a message."

"It could've been anyone."

"It could've, but I'm pretty sure it wasn't. Nicole's in Memphis. At least I think she is." I sighed again.

His blue-gray eyes darkened with concern. I kept my hands clasped in my lap in case he wanted to take one of them again. His compassion could crack my fragile façade at any moment.

"She called me once already." I looked back at the kids. They were still on the top level of the play area and well out of earshot.

"The kids don't know?" he asked.

"I don't want her upsetting them. Mom used to do that to Nicole and me all the time. She'd call and make these big promises she had no intention of keeping." I shook my head. "I don't know. Maybe she meant to. Either way, it hurt every time she let us down. Of course I was a lot older than Emma and Jonah are now. It didn't take me long to learn her promises meant nothing. I don't want them to learn that lesson for a long time."

Kyle's face softened again. Every time he looked at me like that, I thought of the kiss we shared and then the deer-in-the-headlights look on his face afterward. The look that said it had been the biggest mistake of his life.

"You're a good aunt, Michelle."

"But not so good of a sister." At his questioning look, I continued. "Nicole sounded strange when she called. She'd been drinking, but that's a given. She kept saying how she was tired of the way her life was going. She needed to make changes. She didn't know how much longer she could live the way she was."

"That doesn't sound good."

I snagged my bottom lip with my teeth. "No, it doesn't. The whole time, all I could think about was how I didn't want her to come home. For the kids, of course. I didn't want her dragging them down with her drama. But just as much for me. I didn't want her messing up my life again."

I looked to the top of the play area and leaned even closer to Kyle. "I don't want her to come back. The kids and I are doing fine the way things are. If she comes back, she'll just mess everything up, and we'll all be right back where we were eight months ago."

I sat back in my chair and let out a slow breath. Confession apparently was good for the soul. I felt better already just saying the words out loud.

"Anyone can understand how you feel. You want to protect the kids."

And myself. I wanted to protect myself. So why was I sitting here adding insult to injury when I knew Kyle would never love me the way I wanted him to?

Chapter Four

A smile stretched from ear to ear across Jonah's face. "Miss Billie let me sing into the microphone today."

I gave him a quick glance before returning my gaze to the bank statement on my phone. "Uh huh."

My mind was still on the mysterious call yesterday. I hadn't worked up the nerve to call the number back. I should do it just to put my mind at rest since it was probably nothing. But I was almost afraid to find out. What if it was Nicole? Or something about Nicole? That would be even worse. What if she had been hurt?

I should probably worry about my sister more, but all I could worry about was how her reckless lifestyle could impact mine.

"I sang the whole song all by myself," Jonah continued. "The other kids had to sit in the pews and watch me. It was awesome."

His words finally registered in my brain. "You sang onstage? By yourself?"

"Yup, all by myself."

"Hmm."

I guess Billie knew what she was doing by letting a kid handle such expensive equipment. She was always telling me Jonah was gifted with a beautiful singing voice. Maybe he'd hit the big time someday. An image of Bones, Nicole's old guitar-mutilating boyfriend, flashed through my mind.

I studied Jonah out of the corner of my eye. He didn't look anything like the Bones I had met only once. I remembered straggly brown hair, a long wiry body void of muscle, a big nose and glazed over eyes. Nope. No Bones in Jonah's DNA, especially if Miss Billie was right and Jonah possessed actual musical talent. Bones certainly hadn't.

"Why were you singing by yourself?" I asked.

Jonah shrugged.

"'Cause he sings the best," Emma piped up from her end of the table, her blond head bent over a coloring book.

"He does?"

She nodded and chewed her bottom lip as she searched the box of crayons for the perfect shade of purple, her favorite color. "He's a good singer. Miss Mary says he's gonna sing by himself in church."

I remembered the way Jonah had belted out the songs louder and clearer than any other kid on stage during the Christmas program and at every Preschool Sunday. His talent had been obvious to anyone with two working ears, but he had been in a group then. What if he got nervous on stage all by himself? It was too much pressure for a little kid. "Are you sure Miss Mary said that? He can't sing all by himself during a service? He's only three."

"I'm four," Jonah countered.

"Oh, yes, that's right. You're four."

We'd had a birthday party at McDonald's on the last day of March with six little boys from preschool and Caitlyn in attendance for Emma. Barry had to work so Caitlyn's mom dropped her off and picked her up an hour and a half later. I was glad Sue didn't hang around like most of the mothers. I wasn't sure if she knew Barry and I were sort of seeing each other and that's why she didn't stay, or if she was just happy for a little time alone to run errands while Caitlyn was at the party. Either way, I was relieved when she left.

"But still, singing on stage by yourself at church in front of everybody," I said to Jonah.

"That's what she said," Emma repeated gravely.

"So when is this supposed to happen? Nobody said anything to me."

Both kids stared at me like I'd lost my mind. "Easter," they chorused. "It's this Sunday," Jonah added.

My heart fluttered in my chest. Easter. Already? How had it sneaked up on me? I looked at the calendar on my phone, which of course did not have holidays designated. I left my chair and went to the wall calendar hanging in its customary spot next to the refrigerator where it had been since before Grandma Catherine and Grandpa Walt took over the farm. A wall calendar was useless these days, but the pictures were so pretty and it brightened up the otherwise dismal room. It was cheaper and easier than painting the room.

I turned the page since the calendar was still on March and scanned through the Sundays. The kids were a little off on their weeks. Easter wasn't for another week and a half. Plenty of time to investigate and see if there was anything to my Jonah singing a solo in front of the congregation.

The next morning, we arrived at the preschool a few minutes early so I'd have time to talk to Billie.

"I've been meaning to talk to you, too," she said when she saw me coming her way. "I'm sure you saw the announcement by now about our Easter program."

I swallowed my guilt. "I saw it this morning."

Billie shook her head. Her loose, long curls danced around her shoulders. "You sure like waiting till the last minute."

I smiled. No use defending myself.

"The youth are putting on a program for the church on Good Friday at seven p.m." she said, probably figuring I hadn't read the announcement thoroughly enough to glean all the details. "The preschoolers will open the program with a few songs, a finger play, and a memory verse they've been working on the last few weeks.

"I want to make sure you'll be there. Did Jonah tell you we're planning for him to sing a solo? The other preschoolers will be on stage with him, and after he sings his part, they'll join in for the chorus."

"He and Emma told me about you letting him sing by himself with the microphones. They mentioned a solo, but I thought they were mistaken. I can't imagine Jonah singing in front of the whole church. Not by himself."

Billie's perennial smile widened. "I let him sing yesterday so we could see how he'd react with the other kids watching. Oh my goodness, Michelle, his voice gave me chills. He definitely has a gift, I'm telling you. We've never had a child Jonah's age show such potential."

I couldn't believe she was talking about my Jonah. What if he couldn't do it? What if he forgot the words and everyone laughed?

"Are you sure he's up to the pressure? He's so little. What if he freezes or misses his cue?"

"Then we'll sit in our seats and watch him standing up there looking handsome in his Sunday clothes."

I stared at her. Surely she wasn't serious.

"That's the thing about preschoolers. No matter how well or how poorly they perform, it doesn't matter. Even the criers are adorable. But I have every confidence in Jonah." She laid a reassuring hand on my arm. "I know he'll do his best. All we can do is make sure he knows when to start singing and when to stop. And pray of course."

I grinned at her like she possessed the wisdom of the ages. Secretly I worried she was out of her tree. Jonah singing a solo in front of the whole church, Kyle included. I didn't know what good prayer would do. Only Jonah could control his reaction once he looked out over the sanctuary and saw three hundred strangers staring back at him. I hoped he didn't wet his pants out of sheer terror.

I bought Jonah a new shirt in robin's egg blue to go with his black trousers. He was as ready for the Easter program as any four-year-old boy could be as far as I was concerned.

Aunt Wanda had other ideas. You'd have thought he was getting ready for an appearance on *The Voice* from the way she carried on when she found out about the solo. She picked the kids up Saturday morning to take them shopping at her favorite mall in Jonesboro. In the middle of the afternoon, the three of them burst through the back door bearing too many packages for one shopping trip and two small kids.

"Aunt Shell, look what I got," Jonah exclaimed. He tore through the packages looking for what belonged to him.

"Careful," Emma cried. "You'll tear up my dress." She snatched the largest bag out of his reach.

"I need that one. I want to show Aunt Shell what I got."

"So do I."

"Okay, you two." Aunt Wanda positioned her body between them and extracted the bag from Emma's clutching fingers. "We'll show Aunt Michelle our stuff together." She opened the largest bag and pulled out the frilliest confection of tulle I'd ever seen. "Isn't it gorgeous?"

She actually had tears in her eyes.

Aunt Wanda had lost her pea picking mind? A white dress trimmed in the subtlest blue piping—I'd never keep that thing clean.

"That's mine," Emma exclaimed proudly as if there were any doubt. A white straw hat with coordinating ribbons streaming down the back followed the dress. Jonah made an impatient grab for the bag, but Aunt Wanda held it out of his reach.

"Hold your horses, big guy." She winked at me, paused dramatically, then handed the bag to him.

He reached inside and pulled out a vest and tie to match the blue shirt I bought. I saw the receipt at the bottom of the bag but didn't bother to look at the total. It was probably more than Aunt Wanda and Uncle Jeb spent on groceries in a month. I had given up a long time ago telling her not to spend money on clothes the kids would outgrow after only a few wears. Every time I did, she'd jut out her bottom lip and lament that Violet and Cliff, that awful husband of hers, would probably never give her grandchildren, and must I deny her this one pleasure in life?

The Easter outfits came complete with new black slip-ons for Jonah and white patent leather pumps with a daisy on top for Emma. They were from the finest shoe store in the mall, one of the few remaining whose clerks still measured your foot with those cold metal slides and offered complete individualized attention.

At the look on my face, she held her hands out in front of her. "I know. I know what you're going to say. But I noticed Jonah's church shoes had some scuffs the last time he wore them." She turned the box around so I could see the size while keeping her thumb strategically positioned over the price sticker. "I bought one size larger so he can grow into them."

"Thank you, Aunt Wanda," I said graciously. "The old ones were getting tight."

After some more admiring of the new clothes, the kids lost interest and disappeared into the back yard with Gypsy.

I put my arms around her. "I appreciate everything you and Uncle Jeb do for the kids."

'I love you' lodged in the back of my throat. I couldn't remember ever telling her I loved her. I wasn't sure if I did. Not before...

Before the kids came, she and I had developed an adult relationship of pseudo-respect and mutual acceptance since we were related and neighbors and needed to make the best of a not-very-cordial situation. I never thought she liked me. She couldn't forget I was the burden who stole Grandma's chance at a pleasant retirement. I couldn't forget she was an extension of Grandma's loathing at having me around.

We lived side by side with a begrudging tolerance of the other. We shared too much baggage for two naturally stubborn women to form any kind of friendship. Over the past eight months the whole dynamic of our relationship had altered.

Had she changed—or had I?

All I knew was I no longer dreaded the sound of her tread on the front porch. I looked forward to sharing thoughts and concerns with her, and not just those concerning Emma and Jonah. I sought out her wisdom and advice on purpose. For the first time I felt like part of a family that wasn't all messed up, and Aunt Wanda played an integral role in it.

I dropped my arms and moved away before I said something that might come back to bite me.

Aunt Wanda cocked her head for a fraction of a second. Had she picked up on my emotional epiphany or was she experiencing one herself? She reached toward me but let her hand fall back to her side before she made contact.

"I know you do, honey." Her voice was soft and gentle.

To keep from looking at her, I rechecked the size of Emma's dress.

The moment passed. Aunt Wanda slid Jonah's shoebox back into the bag. "Believe me, Jeb and I aren't doing anything we don't want to do. In fact, while me and the kids were shopping for clothes, Jeb was out buying CD's and a back-up battery so he can video tape the Easter program with no chance of missing a second of it."

I laughed with her. "Why doesn't he just use his camera phone like everyone else?"

Aunt Wanda snorted. "Doesn't trust them. And forget about trusting the cloud." She laughed as she glanced toward the window at the kids in the yard. "Those two little ones have got him shopping for things he would've mocked a year ago."

"How about some tea?" I asked. "I just made a fresh pitcher."

"That'd be great." She pulled out a chair and dropped into it. "I have such a good time shopping for those kids. It reminds me of when Violet was little." She sighed wistfully as she brushed her hand across the multi-layered ruffles of the dress's skirt.

I gave her a smile before heading to the refrigerator. For the first time, I understood how difficult it was for Aunt Wanda to lose the close contact she enjoyed with her only daughter.

Violet moved away four years ago when the forestry service transferred Cliff to the western part of the state near Fayetteville. Aunt Wanda was an absolute nightmare to be around the entire three months leading up to the transfer, and for a couple of years afterward. Even Uncle Jeb couldn't make her see reason. Cliff, who up to this point had been a relatively decent son-in-law as sons-in-law go, instantly became the Devil Incarnate. I wouldn't have traded places with him for all the tea in China. It was difficult enough just being her niece, her butcher, her drycleaner or the new bagger at the A&P who set a dozen eggs on top of a loaf of bread.

I, on the other hand, felt the relief of a sixteen-year burden lift from my shoulders when Violet moved two hundred and fifty miles away. At times Violet had been my only friend, at other times, my nemesis. Ours was a love/hate relationship; the love more evident when Grandma and Aunt Wanda weren't around. In the clear light of adulthood, I could see Aunt Wanda had been threatened by any friendship between Violet and me. She had built her life on that little girl, while I was the tainted daughter of her wayward sister's dalliance with a worthless rogue. The threat she feared from me came instead from Cliff, whose name she still spoke with a sneer.

"I never realized how much I missed this," she said, stroking the dress fabric. I couldn't tell if she was talking to me or thinking out loud. "You don't...I guess...I mean you don't realize what you've got till it's gone." She looked from the dress to me, her eyes misty.

"I remember how you girls played around here when you were little. You made so much noise. This place was quiet before you and Nicole got here. Mom had no patience with kids. How she'd react to this." She chuckled.

I didn't know if she meant the amount of money she'd spent on Emma's dress, or Emma and Jonah being here at all.

"Mom always said Nicole was trouble with a capital 'T'. I guess she was right."

Question answered. I opened the cabinet door and took out two tall glasses that had been in the kitchen as long as I had.

"Jeb and I enjoy those young'uns so much," she continued. "They can be a handful sometimes, especially on those mornings we get 'em ready for preschool. But I do love it, Jeb, too. He always had a way with kids. You remember that, don't you, Michelle?"

I nodded as I poured the tea over ice.

"That's why I don't let myself get uptight the way I used to," she went on. "One of these days, we're going to wake up and they'll be gone, and I don't want to have the same regrets."

I hoped she was talking about Emma and Jonah growing up and moving away like Violet had done, and not about the inevitable day Nicole would return. Either way, I didn't want to think about it.

"Have you given any thought about what you'll do?" she asked. "I know you've gotten attached to the little buggers. A body couldn't keep from it. If they could soften an old bird like me, nobody else stands a chance."

I didn't want to talk about what I'd do when and if they left. The woman from Children's Services had called a couple weeks ago 'just to check on things', and she had alluded to the same thing. I didn't have an answer for her either.

I needed to tell Aunt Wanda about the phone call yesterday and the one from Nicole the day after Christmas. I knew how she'd react. It was why I hadn't said anything before. I didn't want to upset her or make her worry. Worse, I didn't want her to make me worry.

"I never expected it to happen so completely, but I have gotten attached," I admitted.

"You've done more than that. You've fallen in love with them as hard as the rest of us."

I didn't try to deny it.

She studied me another moment before asking, "So, what are you going to do about it?"

I knew exactly what she was asking, but I didn't have an answer. I really didn't want to think about what would happen when Nicole came back. Every time that little nagging voice started in the back of my head, I pushed it aside. I wouldn't stew on a problem that hadn't materialized.

I focused on my glass of tea and absently slid my fingers up and down the sides, leaving little tracks in the condensation. I shrugged. "I guess we'll cross that bridge when we come to it."

She shook her head sadly. "If it were only that simple. You've got to think about those kids, Michelle. How long's it been now, six months? Isn't that enough time to charge Nicole with abandonment? She's not coming back, and if she is, she's already proven to any court in this county she's not fit to be those kids' mother. You need to talk to that welfare lady about doing something legal. If you don't, Nicole can waltz in here any time she wants and take them away.

"What happens the next time she decides she's tired of playing Mommy? Where will they be then? She might be ticked off at you for any number of reasons so maybe she'll turn them over to foster care, a drunken neighbor, or leave them on the doorstep of a church. We can't trust her to consider what's best for Emma and Jonah. She's incapable of doing that. You've got to do something, Michelle. You can't let her take them to God knows where, where we might never see them again."

I suddenly had a pounding headache. To think this day had started out so good. "I know, I know, but this is really tricky. If I act in haste or do the wrong thing, I can do irreparable damage to the family."

"What a bunch of baloney. It sounds like a fancy way of saying you aren't going to do anything except dodge your responsibility. Nicole is not your concern anymore, Michelle. You need to think about Emma and Jonah. You're obligated to them. You do for family, that's all there is to it."

"Nicole is family," I reminded her.

She sniffed and took a sip of her tea. She made a face. I'd put in too much sugar for her taste. "Nicole is a big girl. She can take care of herself. Emma and Jonah need you right now. It's the right thing to do, Michelle, and you know it. Christian charity. You don't have a choice."

"There's no sense worrying about it now. Nicole isn't here. She hasn't given any indication she will be anytime soon. It could be another year before we hear from her."

I was glad I hadn't told her about the phone calls.

She sniffed again. "Well, somebody better worry about it because that girl will come back, and when she does, it's going to tear those two little kids apart. They need to know things are taken care of, that they're not going to get ripped out of the only home they know."

"Technically, this isn't their home. Nicole has more leverage, as far as the courts are concerned, than I do. There's nothing I can do to keep her from her kids if she wants them back."

"If you believe that, you're either terribly naïve or looking for an excuse not to keep them. Any judge in this county will find her unfit, especially after I take the stand. If you don't want the responsibility, well, Jeb and me haven't changed our minds. We've discussed it quite a bit in the past six months seein's how we don't know what your plans are. If you're not willing to fight for those kids, we will. I don't care how long or how much money it takes. Emma and Jonah don't need to go back with Nicole. God in heaven knows she has no business taking care of a dog."

The glasses of tea sat forgotten on the table in front of us. "I didn't say I didn't want the responsibility. I just said I didn't see any point in worrying about it when Nicole isn't even here. I don't want the kids to leave. As far as I'm concerned, this is their home. But Nicole is still their mother. I know for a fact the courts and social services do whatever they can to keep children with their biological parents."

"Well, not in this case. Nicole is unfit. You have turned your whole life upside down to accommodate those kids; everybody sees that. It would give me peace of mind if you'd just talk to that woman from the welfare and find out what to expect when Nicole shows her face."

I puffed out my cheeks and released a defeated sigh. There was no arguing with Aunt Wanda once she got an idea in her head. I even agreed with her to a degree. But if I went to a lawyer it would mean I was thinking about it, and thinking about losing Emma and Jonah was something I wasn't ready to do.

Chapter Five

After Aunt Wanda left, I went outside for a little yard work, I went outside for a little yard work, which always helped clear my head. Emma and Jonah spent the afternoon tearing around the yard after Gypsy, who kept taking sticks I threw onto the burn pile and running off with them. It was a favorite game of hers. She only wanted to be chased. If I ignored her long enough and let her steal a few sticks, she'd eventually lose interest and stop and leave me to finish my work in peace. The kids fell into her trap and gave chase until all three dropped from exhaustion.

By the time the yard was clean, it was time to think about dinner. I set Emma and Jonah at the table with a puzzle while I fixed macaroni and cheese and hotdogs. I opened a can of peas, knowing full well the kids would barely touch them. At least something green had been provided in case anyone asked—like a judge who wanted to return them to their mother.

A judge? I had no reason to impress a judge. Hadn't I looked forward to the day Nicole to come back and get her kids? They belonged with their mother. I didn't even like kids.

I thought of the aggravations everyone at work went through planning holidays, missing work for doctor appointments, or begging for overtime to make extra money for braces. Who needed it? I had Gypsy. All those years I had loved coming home after a long day and falling into my chair, fixing what I wanted for dinner, no demands for my attention, no bickering, no struggling to get a preschooler into the bathtub.

If preschoolers were difficult, what did I expect from the next few years? Starting school was when kids really began to cost money: new clothes, those outrageously overpriced name brand shoes, school supplies, field trips, extracurricular activities. The list went on and on, and money wasn't even the main issue.

What would I do when Jonah got into a fight at school? Or Emma came home crying because someone teased her? Or God forbid, she got a boyfriend?

I wasn't up to this. They weren't my kids.

When had my life gotten so complicated?

Aunt Wanda was right. I was beyond simple attachment. I was in love. There was no point in denying it. I couldn't imagine the day they would leave, whether with their mother or when they joined the Navy, if they stayed that long. I didn't want them to go away. I wanted them to stay with me forever. They were mine now, yet they weren't. No amount of wishing, praying or providing them with a good home would matter one way or the other when Nicole came back.

Regardless of what Aunt Wanda thought she could say on the witness stand to sway a judge, they belonged to Nicole. If she could prove she was repentant for leaving them with me and she'd turned her life around, she would probably win in court. Even if she didn't, was I up to a potentially bloody fight with my own sister?

In bed that night I tossed and turned, and then slept fitfully, wishing the alarm would hurry up and ring already so this night would end. I stared at the ceiling and thought of all the changes that had occurred in the past few months. Not only did I have two little people depending on me for food, shelter and everything else that came with parenthood, I attended a church semi-regularly for the first time in six years. Kyle was back in my thoughts, if not my life, and I had met many wonderful people. I tried to form a prayer in my head. I was so out of practice I couldn't think of how to begin. If God was up there and knew everything about the situation like Kyle and the teachers at the preschool believed, wasn't I wasting his time and mine anyway? He knew what was best for Emma and Jonah without me keeping him apprised of the situation. He knew I never wanted kids, yet my insides were all torn up over the thought of losing them.

"Go to sleep. Stop thinking about it", I chastised myself. "Nicole hasn't even called. You can obsess over it after she comes back…if she ever does."

But I kept thinking. Borrowing trouble.

It was hard to think of anything else around the house with Emma and Jonah talking about nothing but the Easter program. Jonah didn't act concerned about singing in front of an audience. Emma looked like she'd throw up every time he mentioned it, and she wasn't even the one doing a solo.

Aunt Wanda and Uncle Jeb picked us up in their minivan the night of the program. Uncle Jeb headed straight to the sanctuary to stake out the perfect spot to set up the camcorder, while Aunt Wanda and I herded Emma and Jonah down the hall to the classrooms. The teachers were already there, getting everyone organized.

A father was holding out his phone as his wife struggled with a lopsided barrette in their daughter's hair. The little girl's eyes glistened with unshed tears. "Tonight's the big night,

Trinity," Daddy said in a high-pitched voice designed to build excitement. "Our little girl's stage debut. Smile, baby—a big smile for Daddy. Let me hear your memory verse again."

The little girl shook her chestnut head, barely holding the tears in check. The barrette slipped farther out of place.

Mommy shot Daddy an evil look. "Troy, do you have to do that now?"

Daddy ignored Mommy's irritation. "Come on, Trinity. Right here, Dumpling. Give Daddy a big smile and say 'Happy Easter'."

Trinity shook her head more vehemently this time and turned into her mother's arms, dislodging another barrette.

"Troy, please. Leave her alone," the mother admonished. "She'll calm down if you get that phone out of her face."

Troy scowled at both of them and lowered the phone. "Excuse me for wanting to capture this moment in our daughter's life."

"You can capture it, just not in this room." The mother looked up and saw Aunt Wanda and me within arms' reach. She grabbed the little girl's arm and ushered her to a chair, away from us and away from Daddy, to finish her job on Trinity's beautiful long hair.

I had assumed life with children would be easier with a responsible father figure in the picture. Maybe it didn't always work out that way.

Aunt Wanda and I headed through the sanctuary to find Uncle Jeb. He had claimed an aisle seat in the front row. With the rapidly filling sanctuary, he couldn't hold our seats forever. I spotted Barry entering the room with his ex-wife and an older man and woman. A pair of Caitlyn's grandparents, I assumed. On which side of the family, I couldn't tell. The man was tall and broad like Barry but with faded red hair that reminded me of the hair Caitlyn had inherited from her mother.

The older woman was several inches shorter than Sue but also willow thin and sophisticated looking. I couldn't tell from this distance if she resembled Sue more or Barry. It didn't really matter. All that was important was they were here for Caitlyn. I could already imagine the bright smile in her green eyes when she looked out from the stage and saw them in attendance just for her.

I pushed down a nugget of jealousy that Barry had shown up with Sue. I was being ridiculous. I didn't have a claim to him. I hadn't even taken the time to get back with him to schedule our next date. It obviously wasn't that high on my priority list. If he grew tired of waiting for me and went out with any other woman, it would be my own fault.

I turned away before Sue could catch me looking. I didn't want her to get all territorial on me. Barry and I weren't really dating, but Sue may still have feelings for him, and she may not appreciate me moving in too soon. I didn't know if I wanted it either.

Barry spotted me just as I turned away. He lifted a hand in greeting and arched his perfectly shaped eyebrows. I waved back and then squeezed into the pew next to Aunt Wanda.

Eventually the music started, and the children filed in two-by-two up the center aisle. There were no bells like there had been at the Christmas program. This procession was sedate and orderly. I leaned forward to see around Aunt Wanda. The instant I caught sight of the procession, my vision blurred with tears. An idiot grin spread across my face. After some confusion getting everyone situated on the stage risers, Miss Billie stepped to the mic and made her usual welcoming speech.

One preschooler is a hard thing to tame. A whole pack of them in one place is impossible. Their portion of the program was markedly brief. A prayer from one of the teachers, a few words from an older gentleman I'd seen at church a few times telling us what a marvelous group of teachers we had caring for our children, and then a couple of memory verses followed by three songs.

Then came Jonah's solo.

Aunt Wanda tensed and my eyes misted anew before he even opened his mouth. He strode to the center of the stage somehow managing to look adorable and grown-up at the same time in his new blue suit. Miss Gail handed him a microphone, offered a smile of encouragement and backed away where she would be out of the way but available for moral support if he needed it.

He didn't.

Although Jonah knew the piece by heart, he watched Miss Gail for the cue on the correct note of music. Then he opened his mouth and started to sing. My heart soared as his tiny voice resounded through the sanctuary. By the time he got to the second or third word, all signs of timidity and uncertainty had vanished.

"The Power of your love is shaping me, molding me, making me into someone new. The power of your love is shaping me, molding me. Change me by the power of your love."

I didn't notice the tears streaming down my cheeks until Jonah repeated the opening.

I couldn't have said it better myself. The power of his love, and Emma's, had changed me over the past eight months without me realizing it. I was no longer the detached business professional married to her job, who was more aggravated than concerned to find two cold, scared little kids under her lilac bushes. Now I was a mother who felt pride in their accomplishments and grief over their pain. Little things that had previously gone without notice suddenly had meaning because I shared them with two people I loved. I wasn't the aloof girl Kyle dated in high school. I wasn't alone in the world either. Two special, wonderful people needed me, and I needed them right back.

I wasn't the only one who'd changed. Emma and Jonah were different too. They knew they were loved. They slept through the night without fear of something horrible or unexpected happening before they awoke. Emma was no longer afraid of her own shadow. She talked and smiled all the time. She didn't suck on her fingers. The confident, intelligent little man inside Jonah had blossomed.

Jonah sang the stanza again, and then a little girl in a yellow dress stepped to the mic beside him and started to sing. Jonah looked out over the crowd while he waited for his cue to join back in and spotted us in the front row. He raised his hand and wiggled his fingers. His grin of elation said it all.

I grinned back and mouthed, "Good job."

His grin broadened. Aunt Wanda nudged my ribs. She was beaming through a veil of tears.

I scanned the risers for Emma and gave her an encouraging smile. While she didn't look as comfortable as her brother, she managed a tremulous smile in return. My heart swelled with love. When had the scales tipped in their favor? When did I stop seeing them as a curse and realize what a blessing they were? I didn't deserve their love. I was afraid of it. Afraid of being hurt again. I held the world at a distance. Yet somehow my life had turned around when these two amazing little people entered it.

Chapter Six

Tears of joy streamed down my cheeks. It took me a moment to realize I wasn't just crying out of love for the children. I was crying for what had happened in me. I felt like the Grinch whose tiny heart had grown three sizes in one night.

The music built in crescendo, and the rest of the children joined in the song. The entire sanctuary went wild. They were no longer proud parents but the body of Christ touched by the Lord's presence. It was obvious to everyone. Even I could tell something had changed as a hundred little voices rose in praise.

Amen's rang out around me. Hands lifted toward Heaven. Tears flowed freely. The children continued to sing, emboldened by the crowd's reaction.

My own heart swelled like I never experienced before. It wasn't the children's love that had changed me, or even my love for them. It was God's love that had changed me from the scared, closed-off woman I had been my entire adult life. I was finally free of judgment and condemnation. My Creator loved me. Not because I deserved it. Not because I worked for it the way I did with every other person in my life who I wished would care if I lived or died.

I could never deserve this love. I had it because God was a merciful, loving God, and I mattered to Him.

"Forgive me, Lord," my spirit cried out. "Forgive me for ignoring you all these years and blaming you for what I didn't have. I'm sorry I wasted so much time trying to create something out of my control. I know I'll never be good enough on my own or worthy of your love. Emma and Jonah are here for a reason. To teach me of your blessings. I want to serve you, Jesus. To live for you. Come into my heart and begin a new work in me. Start me over again, fresh and new."

Without even realizing it, my hands lifted in worship along with half the congregation. The music faded and the crowd rose to their feet in applause. I joined in. As proud as I was of Jonah, it was the Lord I praised. He did love me. He accepted me just the way I was. Kyle had been right the day he talked with me in his office. Nothing I could do would ever win God's favor. He loved me simply because He did.

Aunt Wanda knew something had happened—something beyond the expected pride over the kids' performance. She pulled me against her. I sank into her softness. A love I never knew I possessed for this woman poured out of me. At this moment I wanted to show every person in my life how much I loved them. I almost wished Grandma were here so I could tell her I appreciated the sacrifices she made for Nicole and me. As bad as things were, they would've been much worse if she hadn't taken us in. I had never thought of it that way before.

Aunt Wanda pressed a tissue into my hand as the last strains of the song died away. She brushed a tear from my cheek as we took our seats.

The program continued and I listened with a new intensity. The preschoolers left the stage and were replaced by the Youth Choir. Each song seemed to have been chosen specifically for someone like me who wanted to praise the

Lord but didn't have the words or capacity to do it. More tissues were passed my way, and I used every one. Uncle Jeb reached around Aunt Wanda and patted my knee. I squeezed his hand as fresh tears flowed down my cheeks.

I felt like I wanted to wrap my arms around the whole world and hug it. Then I felt like an idiot for being so ridiculously sentimental.

After the choirs exited the stage, Kyle stepped behind the pulpit to thank everyone for coming.

"We often forget at this time of year just how important our Savior's death on the cross was. His sacrifice was the only thing that could reconcile us to God. It wouldn't have been possible had Jesus not been willing to give Himself in our place. When I was a kid, I didn't understand the significance of that sacrifice. I thought that was what Jesus was supposed to do; the whole reason He'd been born. I didn't understand He was flesh just like us, yet He was willing to pay the ultimate price that we might live."

I listened earnestly. Why had I been fighting this for so long? God did love me. He wasn't responsible for my misinterpretations of faith. He wasn't responsible for Dad taking off, Mom leaving, or Grandma not loving me. The Christian charity I'd grown up with had nothing to do with true Christianity. Jesus never made anyone feel indebted to Him. True Christians who wanted to follow His example wouldn't either. They lived and behaved in a way pleasing to Him. Not to fulfill some distorted sense of Christian duty.

I felt sad all over again for Grandma Catherine. She had missed the whole point. She thought she was serving God through her begrudging good works. She would've been a whole lot happier if she had let God do the work and accepted His gift of mercy for what it was. A gift. Not something she had to sweat and labor to earn every day of her life.

After their portion in the program, the preschoolers followed the teachers to the classrooms to wait for us. After

Kyle dismissed the assembly with prayer, Emma and Jonah ran up to us waving treat bags. They were so full of energy and excitement over the program they barely acknowledged our compliments on their performance. I took my phone from my bag and snapped some pictures and then posed for a few.

I kept an eye out for Kyle. As excited as I was over the kids' performance, I couldn't wait to tell him I had accepted Christ. For the first time since seeing him after all these years, I wasn't thinking of him in a romantic sense. I wanted him to know I finally understood what he'd been talking about a few months ago when I spent the afternoon in his office—the day of our kiss. It didn't matter how handsome he was, how I wished things could have worked out differently between us or that I regretted all those wasted years. I had finally accepted into my cold stone heart that God loved me and always had. I wanted to let Kyle know.

We followed the crowd to the fellowship hall for refreshments like always after a church function. I'd never met a group of people more dedicated to finding an excuse to eat cake.

I offered to stand in the cake line for Aunt Wanda and Uncle Jeb while they claimed chairs. I was too excited to think about cake. I smiled greetings to parents and spoke to a few as I made my way through the crowd to the front of the room.

As I took a place in line, someone grabbed my elbow and spun me around. It was Angie, the woman who babysat the kids when I worked late nights or weekends. She pulled me into an embrace.

"You must be so proud," she said after releasing me. "Jonah did beautifully." She put her hand to her chest. "His little voice just went right through me. I was bawling my eyes out by the time he finished."

"Me too," I managed before she went on.

"Chris got a bunch of pictures. I'll post them online so you can see. Emma did wonderful too. She looked like such a doll.

She has really come a long way, you know. I can just imagine how proud you are of them."

Finally she stopped talking long enough for me to do more than smile. "I am proud of them, but I have something else to tell you."

Angie's eyes widened in anticipation. Suddenly I felt self-conscious. What if no one else thought it was a big deal? Or worse, I had done it wrong, and God hadn't accepted me like I thought or I hadn't gone through the proper channels? What if there was more I needed to do before I was worthy enough? What if I had fallen too far? Spent too many years scoffing at Christianity?

I pushed aside my doubts. I knew in my heart what happened to me, and no one could take it from me!

I took Angie's hand. "I accepted Jesus as my Savior tonight." I blinked away tears. "He saved me, Angie."

Tears sprang to her eyes. She threw her arms around me and squeezed me like Aunt Wanda had done. "Oh, sweetheart, how wonderful. I'm so happy for you."

"Thank you. So am I."

She hugged me again. "This is what the whole resurrection story is about. Death to the old fleshy ways isn't an end. It's a beautiful beginning. After we die to the flesh and are born again spiritually, we have the promise of reigning forever with our Father in Heaven."

I nodded. I understood the semantics. It was the getting it through to my heart that had taken so long—too long.

"There's Kyle." She grabbed my elbow and jerked me out of line.

Aunt Wanda and Uncle Jeb were never going to get their cake and punch. I stiffened, no longer sure I wanted to tell Kyle, especially in front of Angie.

"Pastor, Pastor," Angie called out as she dragged me across the fellowship hall. "Praise the Lord, Pastor," she said when we caught up with him. "Our sister accepted the Lord tonight during the service. Isn't that wonderful!"

Kyle turned his gaze to me. I blushed under his smile. "Well, glory to God." He grabbed my shoulders and pulled me into a chaste, one-armed, pastorly hug that knocked the wind out of me. "That's so exciting. I'm happy for you, Michelle. I'm happy for the Kingdom."

I didn't know how to respond. I wasn't sure what kingdom he was talking about, but from the look on his and Angie's faces, I assumed it was a good thing. This church was nothing like the one I attended with Grandma Catherine. I hoped he wasn't going to make me testify or something in front of all these people enjoying their cake.

"Um, thanks." I looked around and realized it was just Kyle and me. Angie had disappeared into the crowd.

He squeezed my elbow. "I could see the Lord working in your life from that first day you came to the preschool."

"I guess I can too. I'm glad He was patient with me."

"He's patient with all of us, and it's a good thing. I don't want to overwhelm you right off the bat, but I'd really like to see you in our New Converts Class. You may be interested in joining some small groups, too, where you'll find wonderful godly mentors. Women like Angie who've been where you are now."

I nodded, still smiling. I imagined I'd be smiling for a long time. "That would be great. I'd appreciate it."

"This Sunday's Easter, so we have our early morning service. Maybe Sunday afternoon I could squeeze in a brief counseling session for you. You're welcome to bring the children along."

"No, you don't have to do that. Aunt Wanda is having a big dinner at her house after church and they're hiding eggs for the kids." Realization hit, late again, as usual. "You should join us. They would love it."

He was already shaking his head. "I have plans."

Disappointment flooded through me, along with a nugget of jealousy. The vague answer made me wonder if he had plans with someone other than his parents and sister. I forced myself to focus on the conversation. Where Kyle spent his time and with whom was no business of mine.

"Okay. Well, if anything changes…"

"You too. We'll definitely plan on getting together to talk as soon as possible. Whatever makes you comfortable." He pulled me into his arms for a final brotherly, pastoral hug. "This is wonderful news, Sister Hurley."

My smile widened. Sister Hurley, my new identity.

Chapter Seven

The kids and I colored eggs Saturday evening, loaded them into two empty ice cream buckets, and carried them across the field to show Aunt Wanda and Uncle Jeb. Earlier in the week I'd bought baskets and filled them with every chocolate, candy-coated, marshmallow confection they carried at the Genoa Wal-Mart. I wrapped the final products in clear plastic gift-wrap and hid them in the mudroom. I'd bring them out after church so Emma and Jonah's minds would be on Sunday School and not the Easter bunny.

There was an Easter egg hunt on the grounds outside the church after service. Even Uncle Dewitt, dressed in his circa 1990's coat and tie, joined Aunt Wanda, Uncle Jeb and us at church. Neither Aunt Wanda nor Uncle Jeb had said anything, but I think they were planning to change churches. They'd been attending the same church since the day they married, but now it seemed like the whole family should worship together.

Years ago I would have done anything to remove myself from family and tradition. My way of thinking had changed significantly over the last eight months.

Another wonderful thing I hadn't noticed in church services past was the Easter message. It didn't even matter that Kyle looked beyond handsome in his immaculate navy blue suit that brought out his gray eyes. I listened intently to the message as if hearing it for the first time. Maybe I was.

Like every year, Aunt Wanda went overboard on the ham and fixings at her house after church. Along with the usual assortment of desserts, she bought one of those grocery store cakes shaped like a rabbit covered with white frosting and coconut. We ate until we could barely move and then went outside to hide eggs in the tall grass.

Uncle DeWitt sat on the porch and watched the proceedings. Jonah went to him to show off his full basket. I wasn't close enough to hear the exchange, but Jonah explained something with great intensity, and Uncle DeWitt seemed to pay attention. To my amazement, Jonah climbed into his lap to continue the discourse. Uncle DeWitt draped an arm over the little boy's shoulders as he nodded and smiled. He must have sensed me watching because he looked up and winked. I smiled back and turned away, a strange knot in my throat.

The words from the song Jonah sang the other night at the program filled my head. "Your powerful love has changed me into someone new."

Love had changed me all right. My life suddenly had meaning. It was still important to me to be needed, and I was. I was in love with two wonderful little people, and I was a child of the King.

How could things get any better?

"Whose car is that?"

Gypsy noticed the car in our driveway the moment the words left Jonah's mouth. She lunged forward. Her deep-throated, don't-mess-with-me barks shattered the afternoon stillness. Emma reached out and took my hand. Jonah ran ahead after Gypsy, the basket of eggs he'd gathered at Aunt Wanda's swinging precariously in his left hand.

"Gypsy, no!" I shouted. She was full of bravado. I didn't think she'd bite anyone, but I wished she didn't have to act so fierce every time she saw someone she didn't immediately recognize.

"Jonah, wait for us," I called though, like Gypsy, he chose to ignore me.

I tried to get a better view of the car on the other side of the fence but could only make out a blue, older model vehicle. The only family who ever visited was back at Aunt Wanda's. It was probably someone from church. I envisioned Gypsy jumping up on a dear sister in the Lord who had come all this way to invite me to a Ladies' Meeting, only to have her new Easter dress ruined by dirty paw prints.

I picked up my pace, wordlessly urging Emma forward. "Gypsy, stop. You come here right now. One of these days I'm going to wring that dog's neck," I added with a smile for Emma, who recognized, like Gypsy, the emptiness of my threats.

Jonah reached the gate that separated the field from the yard and began the climb to the top. Always climbing over something. It was a miracle he'd never fallen on his head and broken something important.

Gypsy slithered through the slats in the gate and disappeared. Jonah balanced at the top. He held on with one hand and clutched his Easter basket in the other. I could see the wheels turning in his head. The Easter basket was slowing him down. He swung one leg up and over the gate but couldn't get the other leg over without holding on with both hands.

My heart leaped into my throat. "Jonah, stop! Wait for me to open the gate."

He decided he wanted over the gate more than he wanted to save the Easter basket of eggs and candy. He let go of it, swung his other leg over the gate, and climbed down far enough to jump the rest of the way to the ground. He gathered a few things back into the partially spilled basket and took off toward the house.

I shook my head at the futility of trying to keep the boy in one piece. When Emma and I reached the gate, I lifted the latch to open it wide enough for us to squeeze through. I went first and turned to wait for Emma, who didn't want to get rust from the gate on her clothes.

Jonah's voice split the warm April air.

"Mommy!"

Emma turned wide sapphire eyes up at me, and I stared down at her for a fraction of a second. Then her face lit up, and she tore around me and disappeared after her brother. She no longer cared what the rusty gate might do to her clothes.

My heart plummeted. Not Nicole. Not today. I wasn't ready. But I knew Jonah wouldn't have made that mistake even after all this time.

Wasn't this what I'd been waiting for for eight months—my family together again? My sister accepting her responsibilities like a mature adult? My life back?

I replaced the latch to keep the gate from swinging open where it would inevitably catch on a rut in the ground and be impossible to close again without the help of three men and a mule. I took a deep steadying breath. I adjusted my blouse on my shoulders, smoothed my hands through my hair and turned toward the house.

Gypsy was circling the car, still barking, but no longer menacing. She loved everyone, even ratty sisters and their loser boyfriends. Nicole was squatted on the ground next to the car. Emma and Jonah were locked in her arms. There was no mistaking the rapture on all their faces.

A rough looking character about my age, dressed in faded jeans and an old tee shirt, stood next to the driver's side door. His arms rested on the roof of the car while he watched the reunion. His face was a study in complete disinterest. Was this the infamous Dean I'd heard so much about? The kids and Nicole seemed to have forgotten he was there.

Nicole saw my approach and disentangled herself from the Jonah and Emma. Even standing at her full height she was several inches shorter than me. "Michelle."

"Hey," I said, trying to sound as detached as the man watching us. "Long time, no see."

Nicole lifted her chin as she rested each hand on top of the kids' heads. "I tried to call you last week."

As if that would undo eight months of no contact.

To avoid offering anything resembling an explanation or apology, she squatted before Emma and Jonah again and put her arms around them. "I missed you guys so much. Look how big you are. I can't believe how much you've grown."

I resisted the urge to remind her that's what kids usually did over an eight-month span. Gypsy stopped circling the car and sniffed the man's feet. He looked down at her but didn't move. I always heard dogs were excellent judges of character. I wondered if he had heard it, too, and expected her to attack any minute.

I took my eyes off the man I supposed was Dean to look at my sister. She looked like she'd lost weight, but it was hard to tell. She had always been willow thin. I noticed bags under her eyes. Her long brown hair hung loose and unkempt around her shoulders. Her high cheekbones and narrow chin were pronounced, but she was still pretty. I was amazed at how I could see both the kids in her face. For a reason I couldn't explain it made me envious. I wanted her to get back in her car and go away. These two little kids who looked nothing like me belonged here.

She took Emma and Jonah's hands and straightened.

Jonah gazed adoringly up at her. "I sang in church the other night, Mommy. All by myself."

Nicole gasped. "You did? Oh, Jonah, how exciting. I'm so proud of you."

Jonah beamed.

Possessiveness got the better of me. *Don't tell her, Jonah,* I wanted to say. *She doesn't deserve to know one thing about you and Emma. If she wanted in your lives so badly, she wouldn't have left you in the first place. You're too good for her.*

"I had my own birthday party," Emma piped up. "Uncle Jeb made games and all my friends came."

"How fun!"

My hand itched to reach out and smack her. She had plenty of birthdays for which to throw cool parties, but she never did. It was all me. Me!

Who did she think she was? Why was she here? What did she want? Aunt Wanda's words had proven prophetic. Just when I fixed the problems Nicole created, she waltzed in and threatened to mess everything up all over again.

I swallowed my jealousy and indignation. I wasn't that person anymore. I was compassionate and loving and patient. At least I really wanted to be.

Chapter Eight

This was how things were supposed to work. Children belonged with their mother. I was here when they needed me, and now my job was done. I could go back to my life, and they could go back to theirs. I should be relieved. My precious freedom was within reach after eight long months.

"Let's go into the house," I said. My charitable tone belied the feelings thundering around in my chest. "There's lemonade and iced tea in the fridge," I added for the benefit of the man leaning on the car.

The corners of his mouth twitched as though trying to smile for the first time in his life. It was plain to see he didn't want to be here. He heaved a sigh and trudged after me.

The kids led Nicole ahead of us, chattering like magpies. Had they forgiven her already? They hadn't asked where she'd been. Of course they probably knew how this game was played. They didn't ask, and she didn't offer information. They still hadn't acknowledged Dean, if that's who he was. I was sure they hadn't purposely excluded him. They were too young for spiteful behavior. They were just too excited over Nicole's appearance to notice anyone else. Even me.

I had turned down Aunt Wanda's offer of leftovers after Easter dinner, so I didn't have much in the kitchen to offer our guests.

"Are you hungry?" I asked nevertheless. I went to the freezer and pulled open the door. "I can pop a pizza in the oven. Or I can cook something."

Nicole shook her head and continued to gaze lovingly at the kids. "No, thanks, we're fine. We ate on the way. Right, Dean?"

He gave a stiff nod and sank uninvited into a kitchen chair. I wanted to hate him after everything he'd done. My sister wouldn't walk out on her kids for eight months without someone like him influencing her. But the new me wouldn't hate anyone. The new me would show him charitable kindness even though he didn't deserve it.

I walked over and stuck out my hand. "I've heard a lot about you, Dean. I'm Michelle."

He took my offered hand only because he had no choice. He gave it a half-hearted shake. "Mmm," he mumbled.

"Where are my manners?" Nicole tittered. "I always forget introductions."

She forgot a lot of things.

"Don't worry," I said, amazed by my diplomacy. "If you're not hungry, I'll pop a casserole in the oven in a few hours. The kids and I had dinner at Aunt Wanda's so we won't be hungry for awhile."

Nicole laughed. "Michelle, what's happened to you? You don't cook."

I looked pointedly at Jonah and Emma. "A lot of things have changed around here, I guess."

My sarcasm was lost on Nicole. She looked at Dean and laughed again. "My sister could never boil water. Grandma Catherine went to her grave lamenting Michelle's inadequacies in the kitchen."

"It wasn't that I couldn't cook. I didn't have time. I was too busy getting an education and a job."

I bit my tongue. Why did I let her pull me into defending myself so quickly?

Nicole rolled her eyes. "Well, that didn't take long." She directed her comment to Dean, whose focus was on Gypsy still sniffing at his feet. "I'm not in the door five minutes and she's reminding me how she's the perfect one, always improving herself, while I'm the slacker."

"You started it."

Good grief. I sounded like a five-year-old. The last thing I wanted to do was let her draw me into a disagreement in front of Dean and the kids that would make her look like the victim and me the cold, unfeeling tyrant. I'd been down that road before.

She continued her one-sided conversation with Dean as if I hadn't spoken. "My sister has never made a mistake in her life. The rest of us can never measure up to her." She put her hand on her hip and glanced over her shoulder at me before looking back at him. "I was always the screw up in the family. Just ask Michelle. She had everything together while I made one mistake after another."

I glanced anxiously at the children, who had grown quiet and pensive. I forced a smile. "Really, Nicole, Dean doesn't want to hear about our dysfunctional family. Emma, Jonah, where are the pictures you made in Sunday School this morning? I bet Mommy would love to see them."

Their faces lit up. "Okay." They took off toward the staircase at the front of the house. As soon as I heard their footsteps thundering on the stairs, I glared at Nicole. "Why do you have to do that? Start something in front of the kids? Don't you think they've been through enough?"

Nicole rolled her eyes yet again. "Of course, Michelle. You're right as usual. You know what's best for *my* children. You know what's best for everyone."

Now was not the time to lose my temper. I didn't want this to turn into a shouting match. I simply wanted her to see what was so obvious to anyone in possession of a few functioning brain cells.

"I'm not saying I know what's best, Nicole. I just don't think it's a good idea for them to hear us bickering. It's the first time they've seen you in eight months. I'd like it to be a nice afternoon."

"So would I, Michelle. You just know how to push my buttons. Don't pretend you don't do it on purpose."

"I'm not pushing your buttons. The kids and I were having a wonderful afternoon until you showed up out of the blue and started in on me."

"I know. I know. It's my fault your afternoon is spoiled. I wanted to see my kids, or don't I have the right to do that anymore?"

The muscles tightened at the back of my neck. I couldn't believe she was actually miffed about her parental rights after months of no contact. There was so much I wanted to tell her, so much I wanted to ask. Like who did she think she was walking into my house after all this time and accusing me of trying to make her look bad? Where had she been? How long did she plan to stay? Was she taking the kids with her when she left?

Instead I watched Gypsy tire of sniffing Dean's boots and flop down on the floor at his feet. She sighed and rested her chin on her paws. Had she decided he was not a threat and she could let down her guard, or did she realize he wasn't going anywhere and she may as well accept it?

The kids charged back into the kitchen and went straight to Nicole. She dutifully took the Sunday School pictures offered her and squealed approvingly. When she turned Emma's over, the smile froze on her face. With a sinking heart I remembered what Emma had written on the back of her paper.

She was just learning that stringing letters together made words, and words turned into sentences.

I could picture her in Sunday School this morning, her tongue protruding out of the corner of her mouth as she carefully wrote each letter the teacher dictated to complete what she wanted to write. In oversized, lopsided script that ran to the edge of the page and down one side, were the words; *I love Aunt Shell.*

Nicole's knuckles whitened on the paper. She stood up abruptly and glared at me as if I had intentionally insulted her. While Jonah and Emma were stung by her rebuff, they had no idea what caused the sudden shift in tension.

I couldn't take much more of this. I hated seeing the confusion and helplessness on Jonah and Emma's faces. It had taken months of living here to lose those looks, especially for Emma. I wanted to scream at Nicole to open her eyes, to look at what she was doing. She was upsetting everyone. We were happy to see her as long as she was here for the right reasons. If she had actually learned something in the last eight months and gotten her life straightened out and was ready to be a responsible parent to these two kids, then we were thrilled she was back. But if she was only here to upset the fine balance we'd struck, she could get on down the road this minute.

Of course I couldn't say any of that. I would have to surreptitiously figure out what was going on in her head without coming out and asking. Even if I had the nerve, I was almost afraid of what I'd hear.

I would be patient with Nicole. Patient and compassionate like I wanted people to be with me. My flesh wouldn't rule my actions. No matter what my mouth wanted to shout, I would behave like Christ.

"Lord, help me control my tongue," I prayed silently. "Let me put the needs of the kids first and also those of my sister. She needs you in her life. Give me the words to say. Words that will help and not hurt."

The quick prayer offered no comfort. I may as well have been talking to the ceiling. If only Kyle or Angie were here. They would know how to ask Nicole lovingly and without guile what we all wanted to know. They would empathize with her pain. They could explain in words she could understand that God loved her and wanted to reach out to her where she was. All I wanted to do was wring her skinny neck for all the trouble she'd caused.

Nicole still clutched the Sunday School paper in her hands. Her jaw worked back and forth in an attempt to control her anger. Maybe she was thinking up the perfect slur to throw at me about how I stole her child's affections or something equally ridiculous.

I had to diffuse the situation before she upset the kids more than she already had.

"Would you like to see the kids' rooms? Jonah has your old room and Emma is in the one that used to be mine. We painted and changed the linens. It's totally different upstairs from what you remember. You are spending the night, aren't you? We can put Emma and Jonah in one room and you and Dean can have the other."

I was rambling, but I had to keep talking. Putting two unmarried people in the same room was something Kyle or Angie would never do. I wasn't that strong. I was too desperate to make Nicole happy and get those cold angry eyes off me.

Jonah grabbed her hand. "Come see, Mommy. We painted my room yellow and blue. Emma's is pink and green. Aunt Shell let us help. Uncle Jeb painted Violet's old toy box and let me have it. It's big enough to climb in if I take most of the toys out. Gypsy and me hide in there from Emma sometimes. Gypsy's so big I can't close the lid. It's okay on account 'a I'm kinda scared to close the lid all the way anyhow."

With Jonah prying at her hands and talking a mile a minute, Nicole had no choice but to look away from me.

"All right, all right, Jonah. Would you let me think for a minute?" She made a visible attempt to quell her irritation. "What do you think, Dean? Would you mind staying here? I hate the thought of staying in a motel when my kids are here."

Dean shrugged, and a glance passed between them. A glance that said they'd discussed it already in the car and had every intention of staying with us and foregoing the cost of a motel room.

I clasped my hands in front of me. "Then it's settled. You two go on upstairs and enjoy your tour and I'll put out something to thaw for dinner."

Nicole shot me another blistering glance that said this wasn't over before allowing the kids to turn her around and lead her from the room. Dean wearily pulled his legs in and rose from the table to follow them. I headed for the mudroom and the deep freeze and tried to squelch the dread rising up in me.

Surely this was God's plan. Nicole needed her kids back. I needed to get back to my life. How peaceful it would be to come straight home from work without swinging by the preschool first to pick up the kids, and then trying to plan dinner while they chattered incessantly in the backseat. I could put in for overtime and start saving money again. I wouldn't work as much as I had in the old days. Just whenever it suited me. If I'd learned anything in the last few months, it was there was more to life than work.

I thought of Barry. Handsome. Funny. A devoted dad. But would we have anything in common if Emma and Jonah moved back to Memphis with Nicole?

What about Kyle? He was single and available, too, unless he considered himself married to God. Was there a chance of something developing between us? Now we'd have all the time in the world to pursue a relationship if that's what both of us wanted. Not that I had any idea of how his brain was working. He said he'd know if and when God sent him the right person. He was still a pastor, whether I was born again or not. The wife of a pastor would have to be the second worst position in the world, the first being the pastor himself.

Wife! Good grief. Where had that come from? I was staring down the barrel of getting my old life back for the first time in eight months, and my mind was suggesting marriage, or even a relationship with two men who hadn't expressed any serious interest in pursuing one. I definitely needed to get hold of myself. I was too stubborn and set in my ways to think about becoming anyone's wife.

Freedom. I opened the freezer and let a sigh escape my lips. What a beautiful word.

Buried under the frozen pizzas, chicken nuggets and fish sticks I found a pack of boneless chicken breasts. If Nicole took the kids, she could take all the junk food with her, and I could go back to eating like a normal childless person. I lowered the lid and headed back into the kitchen, trying to ignore the heaviness that settled into my chest.

Chapter Nine

"Aunt Shell."

I was instantly awake. I hadn't been awakened in the middle of the night in weeks. The kids had outgrown many of their childish fears and mannerisms. I couldn't help blaming Nicole's presence for bringing them all back. I opened my eyes and saw Emma's face inches from mine. She'd given up the worn 'blankie' with the row of ducks along the hem she found in Violet's room months ago, too, yet there she stood with it clutched against one cheek. She rested her free hand on my bare arm. I propped up on one elbow and rubbed my face.

"What's the matter?" I mumbled through my sleep-fogged brain.

"I can't sleep."

I knew what that meant. I slid over to make room. She scrambled up beside me, immediately turning away and curling into the curve of my body. She hadn't gotten into bed with me in ages either. It was a habit I rigorously discouraged. I figured I knew what was keeping her awake.

"Did you have a bad dream?" I asked the back of her head.

In the pale moonlight through the window, I saw her shake her blond head no.

"Just couldn't sleep, huh?"

She nodded. I put an arm around her middle and snuggled against her. I lowered my head back on the pillow and breathed in the scent of her freshly shampooed hair. The springs creaked at the foot of the bed as Gypsy's weight settled against my feet.

"Gypsy? Is that you?"

Emma giggled. Within minutes, all three of us were asleep.

It took a moment to remember why my bed was so crowded and how my body had come to be twisted into such an uncomfortable position. During the night, Emma had worked herself down to the center of the bed and Gypsy had maneuvered her way up so they met in the spot where I usually slept. A bony knee jabbed my lower back, and the blankets were pulled off my legs. I disengaged myself from a web of twisted sheets, arms and dog parts, and slid out of bed. I twisted to work out the kinks. Gypsy raised her head and glared at me, clearly annoyed by the racket my bones and joints made as they popped back into place.

There was no point in trying to go back to sleep. It was nearly five, almost time for the alarm to go off anyway.

"Dogs don't belong on the furniture," I hissed at Gypsy in Grandma Catherine's raspy voice. She responded by stretching out on her side next to Emma. Emma reached out in her sleep and put her arm over Gypsy and snuggled against the dog's broad back. She looked like an angel lying there, a tangle of blond hair across her face, her jaw relaxed and lips parted.

I checked on Jonah on my way to the bathroom. He was sound asleep in what used to be my room, recently renovated per Emma's preferences, unaware he had slept on the double bed the last few hours without his sister. The two of them spent the night there last night while Nicole and Dean occupied Nicole's old room. After straightening the covers and kissing Jonah's downy cheek, I went to the bathroom for my morning ritual.

The night before had gone relatively well, considering. After a dinner of oven-fried chicken and rice pilaf, we spent the evening in front of the TV watching the kids' favorite videos. Nicole popped popcorn and had the kids laughing and carrying on about every little thing. Dean sat apart from the rest of us, still detached but warming up as the evening wore on. Jonah sat on his lap a few times, and Emma showed him some of her books from the bookshelf. I spent the evening quietly in my chair, part of the group but not intrusive. Maybe that was the balance Dean was shooting for.

I finished in the bathroom and went downstairs to the kitchen. I hit the button on the coffeepot and sat down on a kitchen chair. I opened the novel I had been reading for the past week and a half. It was due back at the library in a day or two, and I was only halfway through it. Though I loved to read I never found the time, now more than ever. With Nicole and her sudden appearance on my mind, I couldn't even remember the struggle my heroine was facing.

"I thought I smelled coffee."

Nicole stood in the doorway, uncertainty all over her face. She was dressed in the baggy tee shirt and cotton shorts she slept in. Her hair had been hastily combed but not much else by way of making herself presentable. Regardless, she looked rested and pretty. Go figure. I had forgotten how young my sister was. She had done so many things and made so many major mistakes in such a short amount of time, it was easy to forget she was only twenty-three.

I needed to give her a break. Extend a little charity. It was hard to do with her standing there looking so much like the little girl upstairs in my bed I had come to love so much.

"Got enough for two?" she asked.

"More than enough." I replaced my bookmark and closed the book.

"What are you reading?" she asked as she approached the table.

I slid the book across the table to her. I knew she didn't really care. Nicole hadn't read a book of her own volition in her life. She was making conversation to prevent me from asking questions she might not want to answer.

She glanced at the cover and nodded thoughtfully as she'd been meaning to read it as soon as she got the chance. Then she lowered herself into a chair. "I checked on the kids on my way downstairs. Jonah was alone in the bed. It took me awhile to find Emma." Her voice took on an accusing tone.

"She came in and got in my bed during the night," I said.

She sniffed. "I never thought it was a good idea to let kids get in the habit of switching beds during the night."

She had to be kidding.

"Yesterday was a pretty stressful day. She couldn't sleep."

Nicole actually looked wounded. "I don't understand why it would've been stressful. I would've thought it was the best day of their lives. Seeing me after all this time."

"Nicole, they're little kids. Your disappearance scared them half to death. They didn't see or hear from you for eight months. Then you breeze back in here like nothing's out of the ordinary. They don't have any idea what's going on."

She exhaled and looked away like I was the most obtuse person she'd ever come across. "I did them a favor by leaving them here."

I agreed with her on this point, but I wasn't about to admit it. We were talking about two totally different things.

"I couldn't take care of them properly at the time," she continued. "I'm the adult and I make the tough decisions. I did what had to be done…for their sakes."

I wanted to grab her by the throat and give her a good, hearty shake. I took a deep breath and hoped the anger and frustration wouldn't sound in my voice. "You could've explained it to them first. Even if they had hollered and begged you not to go, at least they would've known what was happening and that it wasn't their fault."

"I handled things the best way I knew how."

"By taking the path of least resistance."

The coffeemaker sputtered and hissed, its ancient mechanism going through the motion of making coffee. I got up and took two mugs from the cupboard. I filled the mugs and replaced the pot under the drip. I took the milk out of the refrigerator and added a splash to my cup. I set the jug on the table next to Nicole. I couldn't remember how she took her coffee. At this moment I didn't particularly care.

I sat down and took a cautious sip of the hot brew. "We are glad to see you, to know you're all right. I just can't help but wonder what you've got on your mind. I'm sure Emma is wondering too. That's why she couldn't sleep."

Nicole added milk to her coffee and let out a belabored sigh. "I wish everyone didn't feel the need to analyze everything I do and second guess me all the time. Maybe I miss my kids. Did you or Emma ever think of that? Maybe I miss my sister. Maybe I just wanted to come home."

Her voice cracked appropriately on the word 'home'.

I bit my tongue and took a deep breath. Speaking my mind would only make her resentful, and it would accomplish nothing. "I'm sure you miss the kids," I said instead. "They miss you too."

"You sure couldn't prove it by the way they're acting." A tear glistened in the corner of her eye. "Emma didn't even come to me when she couldn't sleep. How do you think that makes me feel, Michelle? I'm her mother."

Again, her voice cracked in all the right places.

With great effort, I kept the condemnation out of my voice. "You should be more concerned about how they feel, Nicole. You are practically a stranger to them. Eight months is a long time in the life of a five-year-old. They've both had birthdays since the last time they saw you. Emma's reading. Jonah's turned into a little performer. They've grown up a lot and you haven't been here."

Nicole slapped the table, rattling our cups. "See? I knew you were blaming me. I knew you couldn't understand. You're so perfect."

"I've been here, Nicole, raising your kids. Just look at how they've blossomed in the last eight months."

"You mean how they've blossomed with you in charge." She snorted. "Not all of us are as put together as you are, Michelle. Some of us are mere mortals who sometimes need a little time to get our lives worked out."

My patience was wearing thin, especially since I was somehow at fault for behaving like a responsible adult.

"Come off it, Nicole. No one expects you to be perfect. But when you bring two complete people into the world, you have to put your own needs aside for theirs. The world is no longer about you. It's about them. It's all about them. You need to stop worrying about all the crap going on in your own life and consider how your actions affect your kids."

"You know so much about what you're talking about," she retorted scathingly.

"I've never had children of my own, if that's what you're getting at. I've just had other people's thrust upon me."

"Michelle, I needed you. I didn't think you'd hold it over my head for the rest of my life."

"I wasn't talking about you."

I forced myself to stop shaking. I was losing control, something one shouldn't do when talking with Nicole. I took another sip of the coffee and sent a quick prayer heavenward. "I was talking about Mom and Dad."

"Here we go again."

I ignored her sarcasm. "I was fourteen when I started raising you. Grandma made it plain she wasn't going to do it. I couldn't participate in anything after school or have a boyfriend because I had to come straight home to take care of you."

"You never had a boyfriend because you acted snotty and had no clue about how to have fun. Men don't like an ice princess, Sister. Yes, you came straight home from school every day, but you loved it. You loved playing the martyr. You could blame your evil grandmother and me for making you cold and distant and incapable of loving anyone. We were your perfect alibi."

"Aunt Shell?"

Our heads snapped in the direction of the voice.

Jonah stood in the doorway rubbing the sleep from his eyes. "Why's everybody yelling?"

Remorse washed over me. What kind of a witness was I creating for my lost sister? I could just imagine her snide comments about hypocrites who preached one thing and lived another when she found out I had become a Christian in her absence.

"We're sorry, honey. We didn't mean to wake you up."

Nicole jumped up from the table and scooped him into her arms. "It's all right, darling, Mommy's here." She gave me a dark look over the top of his head. "Come on, I'll take you back to bed."

After they left the room, I put my elbows on the table and rested my chin in my hands. That went well. Why couldn't I learn to keep my mouth shut? What a mess everything was. Aunt Wanda was going to throw a fit when she found out

Nicole was back. I never had gotten around to talking to a lawyer. Too late for that now. I drained my coffee cup and set it in the sink. I'd have to hurry if I was going to get to work on time. I still had no idea what Nicole wanted by being here.

Chapter Ten

I needed to let them know at the preschool the kids weren't coming in today. Then I had to text Angie and tell her she didn't have to pick them up there at four o'clock like she ordinarily did on my long workdays. I had suggested last night to Nicole that Emma and Jonah should go to preschool as usual while I was at work. She wouldn't hear of it.

"I'm here now," she'd said. "There's no point in having strangers baby-sit them when their own mother is perfectly capable of doing it."

I didn't bother to tell her the teachers were neither strangers nor babysitters. But I didn't plan for one minute to leave her and Dean here alone with them while I worked a twelve-hour shift twenty miles away. After calling the preschool, my next call would be to Aunt Wanda. I was sure she wouldn't mind spending the day here to keep an eye on Nicole. I knew she and Uncle Jeb would move heaven and earth to make sure she didn't high tail it out of here with the kids the second my back was turned.

I carried my phone out on the front porch for privacy, but instead of dialing the preschool's number, I dialed the church instead. I wanted to leave a message for Kyle to call me on my cell phone as soon as he got a chance.

He picked up on the first ring. "Abundant Life Fellowship."

I knew he stopped by his office early most Mondays before heading to the hospitals to visit those whose family had requested visits on Sunday, but this was early, even for him.

Relief flooded through me at the sound of his voice. "Kyle, it's Michelle," I said in a hushed voice. "I can't believe I caught you."

"Michelle." Surprise resonated in his voice. "Shouldn't you be getting ready for work?"

I was suddenly dangerously close to tears. I cleared my throat. "I have a feeling I'm going to be late. Nicole showed up yesterday."

There was a short silence. "Is she staying with you?"

I glanced toward the door to make sure no one had discovered me. It was a shame I had to hide to use my own phone. "Yes," I whispered. "For the time being anyway."

"Has she said anything about her plans? How long is she going to stay?"

"I have no idea. She hasn't said a word about anything."

"I'm so sorry, Michelle. I know how hard this is for you."

My throat thickened at the sympathy in his voice. It took a moment of deep breathing before I could respond. "You know what they say, the Lord works in mysterious ways."

"I guess the kids are happy to see her."

I had hoped he would tell me this wasn't God's plan; that the kids belonged with me, not Nicole. My heart sank even farther. "Yes, well, I think so," I managed. "They picked up on the tension between us even though I'm trying hard not to get into anything with her. Emma got in bed with me last night. She hasn't done that in ages."

"How's the rest of the family taking it?"

"No one else knows yet. I'm going to call Aunt Wanda and Uncle Jeb after I hang up from you. I can imagine what their reaction will be."

"I am sorry. Is there anything I can do?"

"Could you let Miss Billie and the rest of the teachers know what's going on? Nicole wants to keep the kids home with her today while I go to work. I have to tell you I'm not thrilled about it, but regardless of what her plans are, I can see a lot of adjustment problems down the road for the kids. I can't imagine what's going through their heads."

"It has to be strange for them. Don't worry. I'll let everyone here know what's going on. We'll pray for you."

"That's probably a good idea. I think I lost my religion when I saw Nicole standing in the driveway yesterday. Anyway, tell Billie I hope to have the kids back at preschool tomorrow. I'd better get back in the house before she comes looking for me. I'm hiding on the front porch."

"Michelle? Hang in there, will you? Remember God is with you all the time. He'll see you through this. He already knows the outcome."

"I know. I wish I had a little insight of my own."

I ended the call, braced myself, and dialed Aunt Wanda's number. I still needed to call Angie, but I wanted to get my other phone call over with first. Aunt Wanda was going to be fit to be tied.

Dean had barely spoken a word to any of us. He sat up late watching TV while Nicole and I gave the kids their bathes, and was still in bed when we had our encounter in the kitchen. By the time I finished making all my calls, spent some time in prayer and went back into the house, he was in the kitchen with Nicole. She was rummaging through the kitchen cabinets for something to fix for breakfast. Emma and Jonah were at the table, oblivious to the activity around them.

"Everything's where it's always been," I said when I realized what she was doing. "You know me. I never change anything."

"You got that right," she said with a chuckle. "I found a box of raisins that I think was here before Grandma died."

I took no offense. She was probably not exaggerating. "There's cereal in the pantry and plenty of eggs in the fridge. The kids love scrambled eggs doused in ketchup."

The playfulness fell out of her gaze. "I know, Michelle."

"Sorry."

Her face softened. "I know. So am I."

Emma sat on her knees on one of the kitchen chairs coloring. She was still wearing her pajamas. She looked at me. "We're gonna be late for school."

Nicole and I exchanged glances.

"You're going to stay home with Mommy and Dean today while Aunt Michelle goes to work," Nicole announced with a big grin. "Won't that be fun? You can take me for a walk to the creek and we can watch more of your movies."

"We're 'posed to go to school on Mondays," Jonah declared from the other side of the table. "That's when Miss Jennifer goes over the calendar and tells us our letter for the week."

It was immediately apparent Nicole wasn't happy Jonah hadn't reacted the way she thought he should. "It doesn't matter if you miss one Monday, Jonah. She can tell you your letter tomorrow."

"But all the other kids will already know. Their papers will be hanging on the bulletin board and mine won't."

Nicole set a carton of eggs on the counter and slammed the refrigerator door shut with her foot. "Knock off the whining, Jonah. You know I can't stand that. She can hang your Tuesday paper on the bulletin board."

He hadn't been whining before, but he was now. "But it won't be the same paper as the other kids'. Mine will be different and I'll look stupid."

"You won't look stupid. Now stop acting like a baby. You're not going to school today, and if you don't shut up, you won't go tomorrow either."

Jonah slammed his fist onto the table. It was the closest I'd come to seeing easy-going Jonah throw an all-out temper tantrum. "I hate Tuesday. I wanna go today. Aunt Shell, tell her we gotta go today."

His bottom lip quivered. He was close to losing control and bawling in front of everyone, but his pride wouldn't allow it. He crossed his arms over his chest and glared at Nicole. Emma looked as close to crying as he did.

I wanted to tell Nicole the kids weren't used to raised voices or having their concerns dismissed as trivial. The teachers at the preschool treated them with respect while still maintaining authority. I tried to do the same. She was already mad enough. I knew any parenting advice from me would not be appreciated.

I went to Jonah instead and put my hand on his head. "Jonah, you don't have to go to school today. I already called the preschool and told them you and Emma aren't coming, so you may as well stay home and have fun with Mommy."

He slumped forward on his elbows on the table and blinked hard to keep from crying. He didn't complain any further.

Nicole slammed the cabinet door and set a skillet on the stove with a bang. She spun around to face us. She set one hand on her hip and glared at me. I knew immediately what was wrong. She didn't like that Jonah had listened to me instead of her.

I prayed she wouldn't make an issue of it. Jonah hadn't done anything wrong.

A range of emotions flitted across her face as she made an effort to regain composure. She picked up the egg carton. "Who wants eggs?" she sang out.

Aunt Wanda chose that moment to stick her head in the back door. "Yoo-hoo, anybody home?"

I saw the irritation flash across Nicole's face and then disappear behind a wide smile. "Aunt Wanda!" she called out. She set down the eggs and hurried across the kitchen to embrace our aunt.

I had to hand it to Aunt Wanda. She had great timing. She managed to look duly surprised by Nicole's presence in the kitchen. "Nicole, child, is it really you? Where'd you come from?" She loosened her arms from around Nicole and pulled back. "Well, honey, you're melting away to nothing. You need some meat on your bones."

"All in good time," Nicole said playfully. "Seems to me you were a tiny little thing back when you were my age."

Aunt Wanda's cheeks turned pink. She dropped her arms from Nicole's waist and patted her own hips. "I suppose I was. Been so long ago, I didn't even remember."

She turned her attention to the rest of the room. In an instant her eyes registered the hard set of Jonah's jaw and Emma's tearfulness, Dean seated on the opposite side of the table where it butted up against the window, and my own cautious presence.

"What's the matter with everybody? Jonah, you look like you've been sucking on a sour pickle. And, who might you be?" She approached Dean and stuck out her hand.

He managed a sort of smile and shook her hand. "I'm Dean," he said before Nicole could do it for him.

"Well, nice to meet you, Dean. I'm Michelle and Nicole's Aunt Wanda, their mother's sister. I presume that's your car in the driveway. You're the fella who brought our Nicole home where she belongs."

Nicole's smile faltered. "Aunt Wanda," she cautioned.

"What? I'm just asking the young man a question."

"Nicole is fixing everybody breakfast." I glanced at my watch. "I've got to be getting to work, but you're more than welcome to stay and eat."

"Lands, no. I ate with Jeb already, but I wouldn't mind cooking for everybody else." She turned back to Nicole. "You're not just going to have eggs, are you?"

"Well, whatever everybody wants."

Aunt Wanda headed to the refrigerator. "Michelle, surely you have some bacon or sausage in here. How about some homemade biscuits? Nicole, you haven't had my biscuits in ages. It'll only take a minute to whip up a batch. Michelle, you run along and I'll take care of breakfast. Are you kids hungry?"

"I can fix breakfast," Nicole said meekly, though she was clearly pleased the job had been taken out of her hands. She went to the coffee pot and poured herself another cup.

Aunt Wanda took the cup away from her and poured the coffee down the sink. "That's old. Let me make a fresh pot. Now, go sit down and relax."

Nicole didn't have to be told twice. She settled into the kitchen chair against the wall next to Dean. "You don't come over here and fix breakfast every morning, do you?" Her question was directed at Aunt Wanda, but she eyed me suspiciously.

Aunt Wanda was already poking through cabinets rounding up the ingredients for biscuits. "Lands sakes, no, girl, but I pop in from time to time, especially when Jeb has a slow day on the farm and hangs around the house driving me crazy. That's what he's doing today, so when he turned his head for a minute, I made a beeline out the door. I'll call him after I get the biscuits in the oven and tell him you're here. He'll be so excited. Do you have any plans for today? We'd love to catch up with you. We never get to visit since you moved off after little Emma here was born.

"Jeb and I are so happy about getting to know these two. It's been the most wonderful time for us. Jeb's just taken to the kids like a duck to water. It's not all him, though. I'm having the time of my life too. I don't think our Violet's ever gonna give us grandbabies, so these two've filled a void in Jeb's and my heart."

Emma had gone back to scribbling furiously in her coloring book. Jonah sat beside her with his shoulders hunched, looking resigned now more than belligerent. Aunt Wanda beamed lovingly at the backs of their heads. She didn't ask about the altercation she had obviously walked in on.

I eased out of the kitchen. Aunt Wanda had everything under control. In her mildly manipulative way, she had ingratiated herself and Uncle Jeb into Nicole's day. She'd make sure Nicole and Dean were not alone with the kids for a minute. She'd probably have Uncle Jeb keep Dean busy somewhere on the farm while she talked Nicole's ear off in the kitchen. Nicole would be too relieved she didn't have to cook or entertain her own kids to get mad they were here. I could go to work in peace without worrying that I would come home to an empty house.

Chapter Eleven

The first thing I noticed when I got home that evening was Aunt Wanda's car still parked where it had been this morning. Dean's battered car was missing. My heart leapt to my throat. I scanned back to the old barn where I sometimes parked the Mazda on stormy nights. Had Aunt Wanda left for a little while and Nicole and Dean seized the opportunity and packed the kids into the car and gone? Surely Aunt Wanda would've called me at the hospital if that happened. I made sure I was easily accessible all day in case anyone needed to contact me during my shift.

I pulled alongside Wanda's car so my headlights shone all the way to the barn. Dean's car was nowhere on the property. Maybe he went into town for cigarettes or something. I could imagine him going stir crazy trapped in this house all day with Nicole, Aunt Wanda, Uncle Jeb, and two kids. Just thinking about it almost made me want to take up smoking myself.

I grabbed my purse, exited the car, and hurried around the house to the back door. Aunt Wanda was at the sink finishing up the dinner dishes. Uncle Jeb sat at the kitchen table, leafing through the Sunday paper he must not have had time for yesterday.

"Evening, Peanut."

Aunt Wanda turned halfway from the sink and gave me a smile in greeting. My heart rate returned to normal. They wouldn't be so calm if Nicole had taken off with Emma and Jonah.

"Where is everybody?" I asked, just to be sure.

Aunt Wanda wagged her head toward the living room. "Nicole's watching TV. The kids are upstairs. Nicole told them they could go to preschool tomorrow. I think she gave in so they'd quit pestering her about it."

"Rough day?" I asked in a stage whisper.

She shrugged. Uncle Jeb chuckled from his place at the table. "No more'n any day when you got two bored kids under your feet."

I went to him and patted his hand. "I appreciate you two sticking around."

He stood up and kissed my cheek. "You need to go talk to your sister," he said gravely.

My heart sank. "What's the matter?"

Aunt Wanda let the stopper out of the sink and dried her hands on a dishtowel. "I'm ready to go home, Jeb. My feet are plumb wore out."

"Mine too, dear. Good thing the car's here."

"What's wrong with Nicole," I hissed again. They weren't leaving without giving me some kind of heads up.

Aunt Wanda rolled her eyes. Uncle Jeb leaned in close. "Trouble in paradise."

"You mean Dean? Where is he?"

Uncle Jeb shrugged. "Don't know, but Nicole's been upset all evening."

Aunt Wanda put her hand on my shoulder and kissed my cheek. "They spent a lot of time talking in private this afternoon. From the sound of things they were having a good old fashioned fight. Finally he took off and she came stomping in here like a thundercloud. The kids knew to stay out of her way. She's spent most of the night staring at the television."

I didn't know if this was good news or bad. Without Dean, Nicole would have a hard time making a living to support two kids, and I'd be stuck supporting all of them. Nicole had hardly shown responsibility when it came to earning a living. I didn't want her and her kids living here and sponging off me indefinitely. I couldn't afford it. Nor did I want to. But if she was financially dependent on me, she would have a harder time taking off with the kids.

Dean had obviously played a part in Nicole leaving the kids here in the first place. He couldn't be a good influence on her. He was a partier, and according to Nicole's earlier claims, he had been physically abusive. She was better off without him in her life. What about the kids and me? So far, it didn't look like Nicole's patience and compassion with Emma and Jonah had improved much in the last eight months.

Part of me—a very big part—wanted to hear Dean's car in the driveway and an announcement that he and Nicole were headed back to wherever they came from.

Nicole appeared in the kitchen doorway. Her eyes were red and puffy. She looked like she could use about sixteen hours of sleep. She crossed her arms over her chest. "You can leave now," she said with a tired smile for Aunt Wanda and Uncle Jeb. "Michelle's here to keep an eye on me."

Uncle Jeb grinned. "Good. It's past my bedtime."

"We weren't keeping an eye on you, honey," Aunt Wanda told her, in spite of the fact even Gypsy could've figured out our scheme. "I was happy to spend the day with you and the kids. Like I said, I haven't seen you in a coon's age."

"Seriously, Michelle," Nicole said as soon as the door slammed shut behind Aunt Wanda and Uncle Jeb. "You don't need to send a babysitter over every time you leave the house."

"That's not what I was doing."

"Whatever. I'm just telling you it isn't necessary."

Her face softened and her stance relaxed. We smiled at each other. "You want me to fix you a plate?" I asked gently. "Are you hungry?"

She shook her head. "Always the big sister."

I raised my hands in surrender. "I can't help myself."

She smiled again. "You've been on your feet all day. I should be the one fixing you a plate."

"In that case, I'll have a steak, medium well, baked potato, and a huge chef salad with tons of fresh—"

"Easy now. I meant I should heat you up a plate of Aunt Wanda's leftovers. I didn't say I would."

We laughed easily. It felt good. There were times I loved being in my sister's company. She was funny and smart. She was also self-absorbed and flighty, but she was my sister and I loved her, faults and all.

I went to her and linked my arm in hers. "Let's go sit down. I am dog tired." We moved into the living room. "Anything on TV?"

"No." I let go of her arm, and she reached out and clicked off the old set. "I just came in here to avoid Aunt Wanda. She has talked nonstop all day."

I laughed. "She means well."

"Maybe, but she's exhausting."

I sank into the easy chair and propped my feet on the ottoman. Nicole sat down across from me on the couch. I had to ask. It would look suspicious if I didn't. "Where's Dean?"

She sank back into the couch cushions and sighed. I could see she was fighting tears, tears she'd probably been shedding all night with just the TV to hear her. "He's gone. We had a big fight and he left."

"I'm sorry, honey," I said, though I wasn't sure if I was or not.

She stiffened and crossed her arms over her chest. "I don't care anymore. I'm sick to death of him. It's his fault my life is in the mess it's in right now. I just hate him. Maybe he'll drive that old clunker of his off a cliff."

"Nicole!"

"Give me a break, Michelle. You don't like him either."

That was neither here nor there, but I wouldn't debate it with her. "What did you mean by it was his fault you're in the mess you are now?"

She swept her arms away from her in a large gesture. "This—leaving my kids with you. No job, no home. I guess I'm better off without him. But we've been together so long, it doesn't seem right that he take off as if I don't mean anything to him. He knows how much my kids mean to me."

I resisted the impulse to roll my eyes.

"You're not homeless, Nicole," I said instead. "You always have a place here." I wished there was something I could have said besides that.

"You don't mean that, Michelle. If you did, you would've invited me to stay here a long time ago."

She had me there.

"I didn't think I had to say it. You're always welcome."

She arched her eyebrows. "But not if I keep living the way I want to live."

"Well, um, I can't have drinking in the house. Or you coming and going at all hours. Especially with the kids here."

"You mean my kids?"

"It is my house. I don't drink and I don't want anyone else doing it either. In fact, if you have to smoke, it needs to be done outside too."

Nicole didn't bother to hide her eye roll. "That's what I mean. No one's welcome here unless they're willing to abide by a rigid list of rules and regulations. You have to control everyone and everything, Michelle. You've always been that way."

"I'm not saying that, but since I am the one who pays the bills, I guess I'm entitled to make up the rules."

There I went again, throwing my weight around because I had a good paying job and Nicole probably never would. I took a deep breath, determined not to turn this into a money and power issue. Maybe she was right, and I was some kind of control freak. But was it my fault everyone else was always wrong?

I began over again. "Nicole, you're my sister and I love you. You're always welcome here. But it isn't fair you come into anyone's home, not just mine, and expect to have things the way you do in your own house. It's only common courtesy you respect your host's wishes. You'd do it anywhere else. I know you would."

"You're right, I guess. But you forget this was my home once too. I was raised here like a lot of other people. So it isn't just your home alone. It's mine too. And Aunt Wanda's and Mom's and the whole rest of the family's."

"Then where are all of you when the taxes are due? How about pitching in on replacing these drafty, old windows?"

"Oh, Michelle, everything with you is either white or black. Nothing in between. I'm not saying I'm a partial owner. I just think I should feel welcome here, whether I'm willing to live by your rules or not."

"I'm sorry if I made you feel unwelcome." I really meant it. "I thought you were living the life you wanted. Every time I talked to you, you were in a relationship, telling me how happy you were and how excited you were about a new job. How was I supposed to know you were miserable and wanted to come home if you didn't speak up and tell me?"

Nicole hung her head. "I didn't mean I wanted to come home. Oh, I don't know what I want. For the most part, I was happy. But sometimes I'd stay with someone simply because I didn't think I had any other options."

I pulled my legs off the ottoman and rested my elbows on my knees. "That's no way to live, Nicole. You have a lot to offer. You don't have to settle for some man simply because he's there. You need to decide what you want to do with your life and then do it. You're young. You can go back to school. I'm sure you have interests. A vision of what you want your life to be like ten years from now."

She shook her head. "I'm not like you, Michelle. I didn't like school. I was never happier than the day I walked out of Winona High School for the last time. I don't have some fancy career in mind. I want a man in my life. Not just for security. I couldn't stand living like you out here all alone with just a dog and farm chores to keep me company. I'd go stir crazy. I have needs."

I definitely didn't want to discuss her needs. Nor was I going to open up about what I wanted and needed.

"I'm not suggesting you become a nun," I told her. "I'm sure there's a man out there who would treat you decently. You shouldn't put up with some low life because you don't think you have any other options."

"You don't know how it is out there."

"I'm out there every day."

"But you're not looking."

An image of Barry and Kyle flashed through my mind. I thought of my jealousy of seeing Barry with Sue the other night, and of the futility of harboring feelings for Kyle. One thing I'd learned by having the kids here for eight months was that I didn't want to be alone. I didn't want to go back to Gypsy and me alone on the farm. Or a distant relationship with my aunt and Sunday dinner at her house now and then. I wanted to belong somewhere.

"It's a jungle out there, Michelle, full of creeps, jerks and users. At least Dean treats me good most of the time. He works steady and we have a good time together."

"Isn't he the one who influenced you into giving up your kids?"

"It wasn't like that. We were having problems. He'd been out of work for a long time and we got evicted from our apartment. He was always saying things like how much easier it would be to find a place if it was just me and him with no kids. We'd have more money too. Everything he said was absolutely true."

"But they're your kids. They're not to blame for your money problems."

"I'm not saying they are. They're great kids and I love them more than anything in this world. But Dean was on me constantly. I'm weak and he knows it. He knows how to wear me down."

Blood rose in my cheeks. "And you put up with that?"

Nicole raised her hand to silence me. "You don't know what it's like, Michelle." She snorted derisively. "How would you? A relationship takes work and compromise on both sides."

"That's not compromise," I interrupted again. "You're talking about giving up your own kids because some man knows how to take advantage of your weaknesses."

She shook her head wearily. "Are you going to listen or are you going to keep insulting Dean?"

I sat back in the chair and gave her the go-ahead with a wave of my hand. While she was totally wrong and Dean was obviously pond scum, I did want to hear what she had to say.

"I know I shouldn't've given into Dean. That was wrong, but he kept hounding me. He wouldn't let up. He always waited until I had a headache or didn't feel well before really letting me have it."

"You mean when you were hung over."

"Not all the time." She gave me a warning look not to interrupt again. "Finally I couldn't take it anymore. I gave in.

It was just supposed to be for a few weeks until we could work things out. He had some job opportunities lined up…"

She paused when she saw me roll my eyes toward the ceiling in spite of my best efforts not to.

"Sorry," I said. "Go ahead."

"He was trying to find work for me too. He said no one would give me a job if they knew I had two kids at home to worry about. Once we were working regularly, we'd look into daycare and come take the kids off your hands. I was really hesitant about bringing them here. Frankly I didn't want a lecture from you or Aunt Wanda. You always make me feel like such a failure, even in the best of circumstances. When I explained that to Dean, he said, 'No problem, I'll take them for you'."

I was sorry I made her feel like a failure, but I couldn't keep quiet. "Did you also discuss leaving them so close to the road where a car might run over them? Did you tell him about the snakes we've seen under the lilac bushes? Did you worry at all about their safety?"

Nicole straightened her spine. "I did not know about that for a couple of weeks. He told me he was going to go to the front door and face you and tell you this is something we had to do and here they were. We knew you wouldn't turn them away. I just couldn't make myself come along. The whole thing had me very upset. I stayed at the motel on Highway 92 while he dropped them off. I couldn't bear the thought of giving up my babies. Besides, I was a little hung over."

I clenched my teeth to keep in the retort. How could she sit there and act like she'd done nothing worse than forget Aunt Wanda and Uncle Jeb's wedding anniversary?

"Dean said he left them at the house, and I didn't really ask for details."

"At six o'clock in the morning with barely anything more than the clothes on their backs?"

"I told you, I didn't know about that. I was sound asleep."

"I'm amazed you could sleep at all with all the grief you were going through."

"Not all of us can be as perfect as you, Michelle."

"This has nothing to do with perfection, Nicole. This is about being a responsible adult. Most people wouldn't leave a dog on the side of the road, let alone a child."

"You are so dramatic. Nothing happened, did it? They didn't wander into the road. Not that any traffic ever comes past here anyway. They are well-behaved children. If Dean told them to stay put, then they would stay put. No snake slithered out of the bushes and swallowed them. They were fine. Dean said that dog of yours started barking as soon as he pulled up to the gate, so he knew you'd be down in a matter of minutes. It wasn't like they spent the night out there."

"Did you bother telling Emma and Jonah what was going on? That they were going to live with an aunt they didn't know until you and Dean got jobs?"

Nicole pursed her lips thoughtfully. "They probably overheard some of our plans. They're smart kids. I'm sure they figured most of it out."

"Jonah was three. How much should he be expected to figure out?"

Nicole exhaled wearily and stood up. "Just forget it. I'm going to bed." She headed for the stairs but turned back. "You know, I am really sick of your holier-than-thou attitude. We all know the great Michelle would never make a mistake raising her kids. I'm sure they'd be as perfect as you are. But we'll never know, will we? You'll never have kids. You need a man for that, and you're incapable of giving a man what he wants."

I jumped to my feet and clenched my fists at my sides. If I seemed cold and aloof, it was because I'd been programmed that way. I'd put up with plenty in my nearly thirty-four years of living that earned me the right. I couldn't say any of that to

Nicole. She only heard what she wanted to hear and understood what she wanted to understand.

"If it makes you feel better to turn this around to be about me, go ahead," I said through clenched teeth. "But don't make excuses to my face about why you left the kids here. You were about as serious about getting your life together as you were about becoming a brain surgeon. You left the kids with me for no other reason than you're lazy. You and Dean didn't want to be bothered with your own flesh and blood. I don't want to hear one word about how it was for their good and they understood. They didn't understand. Emma didn't speak for weeks. When she cried, it was for Carrie, whoever that is. She didn't even ask about you. She just wanted Carrie."

I said it to hurt her. I was mad over her calling me holier than thou. I was mad because she said I couldn't give a man what he wanted. I wanted her to feel some of the pain she put her kids through. But as soon as I saw the look on her face, I knew I had gone too far.

A real tear formed in the corner of her eye. The first genuine one I'd seen in years. "She wanted Carrie?"

I felt like a jerk. I should've kept my mouth shut. "Yes." I couldn't look at her.

As suddenly as the contrition appeared, it was replaced by anger. "See what I mean? Those kids are ungrateful brats. After everything I do for them, all they see is how much fun they have at Carrie's."

She threw up her hands and stalked a few feet away. "I am so sick of this. Nothing I do makes anybody happy. Dean's gone. Now that he's not getting his way, he throws me aside. My own kids don't even ask about me when I'm gone. All I heard today was how great Aunt Michelle is. 'Aunt Shell does this.' 'Aunt Shell buys us that'."

She turned to face me, her venom again directed at me. "Well, I'm sorry, Michelle, if I can't show my kids the good time you can. I don't have a good paying job and a farm left to me by a bitter old lady. But kids don't understand that. They just know who throws them cool birthday parties and drives them around in a flashy sports car."

I took a deep breath. I wanted to set her straight, but I didn't want her to hurt anymore.

"I worked hard to get the job I have. The only reason Grandma left me the farm was because she knew I'd never leave it or sell it to an outsider. None of that is the kids' fault. The only thing you have to do to make kids love you is for you to love them first. Be there for them. Tuck them in at night. Wash off their scrapes and listen when they talk."

"You're giving me parenting lessons?" she shrieked. "Well, isn't that priceless. What do you know about anything?"

I hadn't meant to be condescending. "Nicole, please." I glanced toward the ceiling and purposefully lowered my voice. "There's no sense fighting about this. I'm not trying to give you parenting tips. I just wanted you to see what kids really want. They're not impressed by what kind of car you drive or how many toys you buy them."

"That's easy for you to say. Your life is perfect and mine is anything but. Well, believe me, I don't need advice from an old spinster who can't buy a date. So mind your own business."

My temper flared in spite of my determination to remain calm. "You made this my business, Nicole. I never wanted those kids, but you didn't give me a choice, did you? Your loser boyfriend dumps your mistakes in my front yard and once again, old Michelle is left to clean up the mess."

"Aunt Shell?"

Nicole and I snapped our heads toward the stairwell. Emma stood halfway down with her hands wrapped around the banister. Her blond hair was tousled and her eyes clouded with sleep. Gypsy sat on the step below her, reproving me with her eyes. If she could, she would probably click her tongue at me.

My breath caught in my throat. What had I just said? I was so mad, I couldn't even remember. I just knew it wasn't good. Something about Emma and Jonah being mistakes I had to clean up.

Emma buried a hand in Gypsy's red hair, searching for the collar the way she used to when she needed a lifeline to hold onto. She hadn't done it in months. She had come so far out of her shell. A few careless, angry words out of my mouth, and I shoved her right back in.

"Why are you yelling?" Her voice was barely audible.

Nicole recovered quicker than I did. She rushed to the bottom of the stairs. "Oh, baby, did Aunt Michelle scare you?" She started up the stairs. "Everything's all right. Mommy will take you back to bed."

Emma kept her eyes on my face like she didn't hear Nicole. Gypsy sensed the tension and stood up, blocking Nicole's path. Nicole stopped climbing and stared wide-eyed at Emma and the dog.

"I'm sorry, Emma," I said from my position on the floor. "I didn't mean to wake you. Let Mommy take you to bed so you can get some sleep. You've got school tomorrow."

"Gypsy and me woke up and went to your room, but you weren't there."

"I know. I didn't get off work till late. But everything's okay. I'm home now. I'll be up in a little bit."

"Will you come in and kiss me goodnight?"

"Sure."

Emma looked at Nicole for the first time. Nicole pasted a bright smile on her face. "Come on, sweetie. Time for bed." She stepped cautiously around Gypsy and scooped Emma into her arms. She grunted audibly as she straightened. "Oh, my, when did you get to be such a big girl? Before long you can carry Mommy."

She shot me a look of pure venom before heading up the stairs.

I winced inwardly. I knew that look. Nicole would make me pay for taking her place in her kids' eyes.

Chapter Twelve

As mad as Nicole was last night, I didn't know if she'd stand behind her word and let the kids go to the preschool while I was at work. As quietly as possible I got them ready to leave. They seemed to sense the need to be quiet and cooperative, too, and not wake their sleeping mommy. It was a little after six when we left, both kids strapped into their booster seats in the back, their heads bobbing from side to side as they dozed in the car. I dreaded facing my sister that afternoon. She'd probably accuse me of avoiding her on purpose or kidnapping her kids. But I had neither the time nor the desire to wake her and get into another fight.

Only one car was in the parking lot when I arrived at the church. Miss Donna usually opened the preschool at six-thirty before the other teachers started arriving at seven. I knew Kyle wouldn't be here this early, but I looked toward his end of the building anyway. I swallowed my disappointment at the sight of his empty parking spot. I needed to talk to someone. My stomach was in knots over Nicole's animosity and accusations, and not knowing what she would do.

I signed the kids in and got back in my car for the twenty-minute drive to the city. I drove on autopilot, unaware of the exits I took or the traffic around me. My day was quiet and routine. I spent most of my eight-hour shift monitoring Mr. Hooley who had undergone six-way bypass surgery yesterday. Tomorrow I'd get him out of bed for the first time. Today he was only capable of sitting up and holding a heart-shaped pillow against his chest while he coughed as I instructed. He whined and called me a sadist. Between visitors, we chatted about the construction company he owned and the trip we'd take to Hawaii if I promised to stop causing him pain.

I managed to push most of my concerns about Nicole to the back of my head until the drive home. As soon as I was on the highway, I called Angie to fill her in on Nicole. As far as I knew she'd pick the kids up tomorrow from preschool while I worked my Wednesday twelve-hour shift.

"I'm glad you called," she said. "I've been praying for you ever since you called yesterday. How's it going? Are the kids okay?"

"As well as can be expected. Nicole and I got into a shouting match last night and woke Emma up. She wanted me to tuck her back into bed. Needless to say, Nicole didn't appreciate it at all."

"Poor thing."

I couldn't tell if she was talking about Emma or me.

"Do you have any idea what Nicole plans to do?"

"No. Her boyfriend took off yesterday. I don't know if that's good or bad. Without him, she doesn't have a car and can't afford to go anywhere. I don't have to worry about her leaving with the kids. But that also means I could be stuck with her forever."

"You don't think...hold on a minute." I heard some moving around and children's voices in the background. Then all was quiet. "Okay, I'm back." Angie said in a softer tone. "I'm in the bathroom where no little ears can overhear. Where was I? Oh, yeah. You don't think Nicole's actually considering leaving with the kids, do you? She has to realize they're better off with you."

"I don't know. Maybe—maybe she's the best thing for them." I really wanted to believe it. "She is their mother. Aren't all kids better off with their mothers? Maybe this is God's plan."

Angie didn't reply right away. "It's possible. If Nicole's turned her life around and accepted her responsibilities, then yes, it is God's plan that she raise her kids. But if nothing's changed, and she's only here for convenience's sake, then no, I don't think it's God's plan."

I was quiet while I considered her words. I wasn't sure how I felt about it. Didn't I want my freedom back? Wasn't this what I'd been wishing for all along?

"Michelle, are you okay?"

"Um, yeah, I'm fine. I have to go. I'll call you if I don't need you to pick up the kids tomorrow night."

As soon as I clicked off the phone, it vibrated in my hand. I didn't take my eyes off the road as I hit the on button with my thumb. I was pretty sure I knew already who it was.

"Michelle?"

"Barry. Hi." I hoped my voice sounded normal.

Obviously it wasn't normal enough. "Are you okay? I haven't heard from you in a while."

I exhaled. I thought of telling him everything. Nicole was back. She was upsetting the equilibrium of my home. Bossing me around. Making a complete nuisance of herself. And, yeah, did I mention I got saved at the Easter service?

Had it only been five days ago? So much had happened since then.

"I'm fine," I said instead. "Just a lot going on at home."

"Oh." His end was quiet for a long moment. I heard voices in the background. He was still at the office. Preparing to leave for the day and thinking of me. I should be flattered.

"I didn't know if..." He paused.

I nearly spoke to fill the gap when he continued. "I thought maybe you were mad about..."

I realized where the conversation was going.

"...Sue and I going to the Easter program together."

"Why would I be mad about that?" I recognized the snap in my voice, but it was a dumb concern. Did he think I was that shallow?

I softened. "I'm glad you and Sue are able to put your differences aside for Caitlyn's sake."

He exhaled loudly enough for me to hear it over the road noise. "I'm glad. You and I have been spending some time together. I don't know. Maybe it's going somewhere."

He paused long enough for me to agree if I wanted to. I didn't have the energy to boost his ego right now.

"Anyway, I miss talking to you."

"I miss talking to you too, Barry. I'm sorry I haven't been in touch. There's just a lot going on."

"Yeah, you mentioned that."

I know he was thinking I was giving him the brush off. "We probably won't have time to get together this weekend, but I'd love to talk more. Maybe tonight after the kids are in bed?"

"That'd be nice."

"Do you have Caitlyn?"

"No, she's with Sue this week."

"Okay. Can I call you later if I get a chance before bed? I hate talking in the car when I should be paying attention to the road. Even with Blue Tooth it's a little distracting."

"Sure. Sure. I get that. I'll talk to you later then."

"Thanks, Barry. I'll talk to you tonight. If at all possible," I added as I hung up. I really wanted to talk to him and share my frustrations over the last few days, but I wasn't sure if he possessed any wisdom to help me put things in perspective. I supposed I'd find out soon enough.

"I don't like staying here alone all day," Nicole announced as soon as the kids and I walked through the door a half hour later. "I want the kids to stay home with me tomorrow."

Why did she have to bring this up in front of them? Emma and Jonah turned expectant faces toward me. They loved school, but they also missed their mother. They wouldn't be totally against sleeping in and spending tomorrow doing whatever suited Nicole. Jonah had already seemed to have forgotten his frustration over missing Monday.

"There's only a little over a month to go of school before Emma graduates. Why don't we keep their regular schedule till then?"

Nicole planted her feet and glared at me. "Because I'm bored. I want them here."

"Come on, Nicole. It's only four days a week. You shouldn't upset their routine just so they can entertain you. Tomorrow's Wednesday. Two more days and they'll be home the rest of the week."

I could see she didn't appreciate my logic no matter how…logical. "They're my kids, Michelle. That makes it my decision."

I gritted my teeth. She had a point as much as I hated to admit it. All the logic in the world didn't change that, and I didn't want to be the one to keep Emma and Jonah from spending time with her. What could I do?

"What if Aunt Wanda lets you borrow her car tomorrow?" I said. "You can drive the kids to school by nine and then pick them up after lunch. That way, they'll have class time, and you can have the morning to yourself. It's a shame for Emma to come so far and not be ready for the graduation ceremony. They're already practicing for it."

Emma and Jonah turned to Nicole. Nicole exhaled and looked from them to me. Her inner turmoil was obvious. She saw giving in as a small victory for me, but she did like the idea of mornings to herself.

"All right," she conceded, "but only if you ask Aunt Wanda if I can borrow her car."

"Great. I'll take care of it after dinner."

I hadn't smelled anything cooking when I came in so I figured I might as well get to that too. For someone who was so bored all day, Nicole sure didn't entertain herself with housework or food preparation.

I called Aunt Wanda while I cleaned up the kitchen after dinner. Nicole had gone upstairs to give the kids their bathes. Her maternal moments usually didn't last long so I was taking advantage of the respite to make my phone call in private.

"What's Nicole up to anyway," Aunt Wanda demanded after granting permission for the use of her car the following morning, though she was none to happy about it. It probably crossed her mind, the way it had mine, that Nicole might steal it and the kids as soon as she had the chance.

"I don't know. Dean's gone for the time being, but I don't have any idea what her plans are. I don't know if she's thinking of staying around here and getting a job, taking the kids back to the city, or what."

"That's why I tried to get you to take some kind of legal action so this sort of thing couldn't happen. She don't have no rights to those kids and you know it. Now here she is, making demands, turning things upside down. She don't care one thing about those poor babies. She just ain't got nowhere else to go right now, so she's messing up our lives."

"I know, Aunt Wanda, but she's family. You're the one always telling me we do for family. I can't very well turn her out. The kids are hers to do with whatever she wants."

Before she could interrupt I hurried on. "Did you ever think this is exactly how God has it planned? Maybe he's using Dean's exit and the kids to light a fire under Nicole. What if she's finally ready to turn her life around and we do something to sabotage it? We've got to give her all the support and understanding we can."

"That's hogwash and you know it, Michelle. She ain't never thought of nobody but herself, and that's exactly what she's doing now."

"God can change anyone's heart, Aunt Wanda."

"I think I know better than you what the Lord will and won't do. You've only been back in church a week, missy. That hardly qualifies you to go preaching at me when I've lived my whole life according to Scripture. It sounds to me like you want rid of those kids so you can go back to doing things the way you've always done."

"That's not it at all," I exclaimed, hurt she would even think it.

"Oh, isn't it? Don't tell me you haven't thought about how nice it'll be when your duties as benevolent aunt are over. You've done your part. Providing them with a good home this past year. But I think you're glad Nicole's back. She can take them off your hands and you'll be free to hole yourself up in that house again, hiding from the world. Well, let me tell you, missy, I am sure disappointed in you. I thought you had a changed heart. I thought you fell in love with those kids. Now you're ready to give them up without a fight."

"No, I…"

"Well, Jeb and I aren't willing to give up that easily. If you won't fight for them, we will. I'll lose everything I own to some high priced attorney before I let Nicole take off to God only knows where with those kids. Talk about doing for family. Emma and Jonah's family too. They're innocent in all this. I, for one, won't let them down. Yes, I feel sorry for Nicole, and I'll pray for her. I'll even help her out financially if she needs help getting an apartment or something. But I will not help her ruin those poor babies' lives anymore than she already has."

I sighed and clutched the phone. I couldn't dispute one thing she said. Was I being lazy? Did I want my own life back so badly I was willing to sacrifice the kids' safety and well-being?

"I hadn't thought about it like that," I admitted. "I don't want her taking the kids someplace where we don't know if they're safe either. I suppose something should be done."

"You're darn right I'm right. You tell Nicole she can come over tomorrow morning and pick up the car. In the meantime, Jeb and I will be online searching for lawyers in the area who specialize in custody or family disputes or whatever this is."

"You don't have to do that," I told her. "This is my problem and I'll take care of it. I'm going to do everything else, though, before I bring lawyers and courtrooms into it. This is how families get torn apart. If I can convince Nicole this is the best situation for everyone, then maybe we won't have to go to court. That would only cause more problems than it solved."

"You're not going to convince your sister of anything unless she's already made up her mind. You know how hard headed she is. It would be wonderful if she agreed to stay here and get her life straightened out. Or if she left town to get a job, and let the kids stay here. We all know neither of those things are going to happen as long as she has those kids for leverage to get her way. I don't want to take her to court either, but I don't see another way around it."

I massaged a pain in my left temple. "There has to be, Aunt Wanda. I can't sue my own sister. I just can't. She already thinks I've taken her place in the kids' eyes. If I take her to court to get custody, she'll never forgive me. I have to do this with her best wishes."

"Well, you're wasting your time. This is Nicole we're talking about."

"I don't know. She might see reason. She misses Dean, and she never has been satisfied to live on the farm for more than a month or so. All I need is for her to realize it won't only be the kids who benefit by them staying here. If she thinks it's in her best interest too, maybe she'll give me permanent custody."

"Oh, Michelle, I think you're setting yourself up for a disappointment. You go ahead and do what you think you have to do. Just don't take the rest of your life figuring it out. Emma and Jonah need stability now."

"They also don't need their mom and aunt tearing each other apart. I'll know when the time's right to approach Nicole."

"Pray, dear, and let the Lord guide you. Just be quick about it."

I clicked off the phone under the assault of a massive headache. Aunt Wanda was right about the kids needing someone to take care of them now. Freedom was an ideal lost to me as long as my niece and nephew were too young to take care of themselves. Like it or not, I needed to intervene on their behalf and do what was best for them. I just couldn't stop wondering what would happen to my sister if I took her to court to get custody of her kids. She wasn't the most stable person on the planet. Would this push her over the edge? What would happen to our relationship? We barely had one now. There had to be a way to reason with Nicole. Surely she wanted the same things for her kids as I did.

Unfortunately, her idea of what was best differed greatly from mine.

How could I get Nicole to agree? What if she never did?

God help me.

Chapter Thirteen

My conversation with Aunt Wanda took too much out of me to rehash the whole thing over again with Barry. Instead of a call, I texted him and wrote I was tired and would get with him after work the next day.

In the morning, I found a text from him asking if we could grab a coffee or something on our way home from work that evening. He didn't have Caitlyn this week. Emma and Jonah would be on the farm with Nicole so it really wouldn't matter if I was a little late getting home. I got off work earlier than Barry, but by the time I drove to Genoa from the city, he should be able to get away from his office as well.

Barry knew I only had a short window before I had to get home, so he suggested a cup of coffee at the local café. I arrived before he did. I checked my email and direct deposit balances while I waited.

A few minutes later his car pulled up next to mine. We waved at each other through the windows and then climbed out of our cars. He came around the front end of my car and gave me a quick kiss on the lips. It took me aback. He'd never been that forward before, but I supposed our relationship was progressing. He missed me. Or maybe he was showing me how he preferred my company over Sue's.

We went inside and he ordered two coffees. I turned down his offer of a big cookie. Hopefully dinner would be waiting fo Michelle would never make a too many big cookies led to a Big Michelle.

We took our drinks to a tiny table in the corner and sat down. "Rough day?" he asked.

I wrinkled my nose. "Is it that obvious?"

He smiled and touched my hand on the tabletop. I let the contact linger a moment before wrapping both hands around my Styrofoam cup.

"You look stressed," he said. "More stressed than usual anyway."

"I guess I am."

His gaze never left mine as he took a sip from his cup. Men generally preferred to talk about themselves, so I was heartened that he was taking such strides to let me say what was bothering me.

"Nicole is back," I blurted.

He nearly choked on his coffee. "Seriously? When did this happen?"

"Sunday. She showed up out of the blue. Can't imagine why we're not all thrilled to see her."

He nodded knowingly. "So where's she been? Did she say? Did she apologize for leaving you to babysit her kids for a year?"

"No to all of that. She hasn't given us a word of explanation except to say she couldn't provide a proper home for Emma and Jonah and they were better off with me."

He snorted. "We knew that already."

Even though Aunt Wanda and I believed basically the same thing, I sort of resented hearing it from Barry.

I took another careful sip of my coffee. It was cooling down but still too hot for a long d mistake raising her kids. I'm su and caffeine was just what I needed before going home and facing whatever waited for me there.

"I don't know what she's up to. The kids are stressing out. They don't know how to behave around her. She's so volatile. You can see them trying to gauge her moods or reactions before they make a move. It's pitiful."

"Well, at least it's almost over."

My cup was halfway to my mouth. I set it back on the table. "What do you mean?"

He made an expansive gesture with his hands. "This rollercoaster you've been on. None of it has been fair to you. Nicole is obviously a piece of work."

"She's a piece of work all right," I said warily, waiting for the rest of what he had to say.

"You'll be better off when it's over and she takes all her drama back to Memphis or wherever she came from."

"That's just it. I don't know if she is going back to wherever she came from. I don't know what she's doing. I can't talk to her. She twists every word out of my mouth to make it look like I don't care what she's going through."

"You don't care, do you? I mean about whatever she's going through. She sounds like a spoiled kid who's made all these wrong choices and now she expects you to clean up the mess."

"That's exactly what's happening."

As soon as the words were out of my mouth I remembered last winter when I met Barry's ex at the Christmas program. She had known too much about my situation with Nicole's kids because Barry had told her. I told him then I didn't appreciate him discussing my business with his ex-wife or anyone else. I didn't want Sue feeling sorry for me or for Emma and Jonah. And I didn't want the whole county knowing what went on in my house. Had I just made a big mistake by confiding in him again?

I dipped the stir stick into my coffee and stirred it around. The soothing aroma of coffee beans and cinnamon wafted up out of the cup. "I shouldn't have made it sound like I don't care about Nicole," I said. "I do. She's my sister and I really want to see her get her life back on track."

"Not everyone wants help, Michelle."

Frustration bubbled up inside me. "Well, Nicole does or she wouldn't have come to me."

"Maybe she came to you because she knew you were too soft hearted to say no. She knew she could manipulate you into doing what she wanted."

I started to defend Nicole, but then I realized that was exactly what she had done over and over again. Even now, she was sitting in my house, letting me pay the bills and wash the dishes and provide for her kids while she demanded I back off and stay out of her life. Any reasonable person would realize they couldn't have it both ways.

I dropped the stir stick into the coffee and took another sip. "I just don't know how to handle the situation. I want to get along with her, but I'm sick of her disrespecting me when all I'm trying to do is help."

I hated that I sounded whiny. Or worse, like I was complaining.

Barry set his cup on the table and sat back in the chair. "You can't let it bother you. It sounds like it's pretty much over anyway. Nicole will take her problems and issues back to Memphis, and you can put this whole mess behind you."

I felt my forehead crease. "What mess behind me?"

"The kids. They're not your problem anymore. You did your part. I mean it's a shame the way the whole thing worked out, but nobody can expect anything more out of you."

"Barry, I…"

He leaned forward and reached around our cups that sat in the middle of the table to entwine his fingers through mine. "I hate to see what this is doing to you, Michelle. You deserve better. Then again, if Nicole hadn't dumped the kids on you, we never would've met."

I pulled my hand free. "I used to feel like she dumped the kids on me, too. Not anymore. Getting to know them and having them in my life has been the best thing that ever happened to me."

"Of course it is. They're great kids. Caitlyn sure is going to miss Emma."

"Who said they're going anywhere?"

He blinked. "You did. I thought you said Nicole is here."

"She is. But she's not taking my kids."

Confusion clouded his handsome features. "Your kids? I'm afraid I don't follow. Isn't this what you wanted?"

Anger reared up inside me. How could he be so cavalier about Emma and Jonah leaving when it was breaking my heart?

But what right did I have to be mad at Barry? It was my own fault if he misinterpreted my feelings about the kids and thought I was eager for Nicole to take them and leave. Hadn't I intimated that very thing several times over the past few months? I made no secret of the fact I wasn't a mother. I never wanted kids and I wanted my life back the way it was. My beliefs and desires had made a complete one hundred and eighty degree turn since the first time I saw them under the lilac bushes. I couldn't expect Barry to understand it if I didn't tell him.

I took a deep, calming breath. "Sending the kids off with Nicole is not what I want. Not anymore. Emma and Jonah belong with me and that's where they're staying."

He held up his hands in surrender. "My bad. I didn't realize you felt that way."

Why didn't you, I wanted to ask. *Don't you know me at all? Can't you see how I've changed these last few months? Everyone else does.*

"Well, I do," I said instead.

It was his turn to study his cup like it held all the answers. "I'm sorry, Michelle, but I don't see how you can change things if Nicole insists on leaving with the kids. It's really hard to convince a judge you're a better choice than a kid's biological mother, even a bad mother. As long as she's not using or beating them senseless every minute of the day—and sometimes, even when she is—courts always rule in favor of keeping a family together."

I wanted to remind him I was Jonah and Emma's family. Me and Gypsy and Aunt Wanda and Uncle Jeb.

I couldn't say anything. Tears of realization clogged my throat. Barry was right. What hope did I have convincing a judge otherwise when Nicole was here demanding what belonged to her? There was no proof of drug use so there wouldn't be any mandatory drug testing. There would be a hearing if I pushed the issue, but I wouldn't stand a chance in court. When Nicole got them back to Memphis or wherever she planned to take them, she would be ordered to check in with Children's Services a few times. Like every other one in the country, the department would be busy and overworked. As long as the home had food and running water, and a social worker didn't find drug paraphernalia on the floor, Emma and Jonah would stay with Nicole. It wouldn't be long before they forgot all about life on the farm with me.

Barry and I didn't have much to say after that. He could see the wheels turning in my head as I mulled over his words. I kept wondering if he was more concerned about how this development would affect him and me than how it would affect the kids.

I told him goodbye and dropped the remainder of my coffee in the trash on my way out of the café. I was completely defeated. It might not happen today or next week, but sooner or later, Nicole would leave and she'd take Emma and Jonah with her.

Chapter Fourteen

I peeked at Nicole's phone before leaving for work the following Monday to make sure her alarm was set early enough to get the kids to preschool by nine. Fortunately for me, she still slept like the dead. Emma and Jonah were snuggled in bed beside her. I guess it only bothered her when kids shared beds with adults if I was the adult in question.

I put the situation out of my head and went to work. I understood why Nicole wanted to spend time with them and spoil them a little. I had done my own amount of spoiling the last few months.

I had spent the weekend rehashing Barry's words and ignoring his texts asking how I was doing. I didn't want to talk to him. I had no right to be ticked, but I was a little bit anyway. None of this was his fault. All he'd done was spell out the inevitable without painting a rosy picture like everyone else did.

My only hope to retain custody of the kids was for Nicole to get itchy feet. Maybe Dean would come back and the two of them would ride off into the sunset. I hated to think of how the kids would suffer by losing their mother all over again. For my sake and their own good, I wanted Nicole out of here before Aunt Wanda made good on her threats to hire a lawyer.

Maybe Aunt Wanda was right and that's what I needed to do before Nicole disappeared. But I hated to think of the harm it would do to my sister and me.

As far as I could see, it was a lose/lose situation.

Even though Nicole probably didn't see it, without Dean around to distract her, thing were beginning to change for the better. She didn't go to church with us yesterday morning as I hoped she would, but there was a hot dinner waiting on the stove when we got home. She was smiling more often, and some color had returned to her cheeks. After dinner she played on the floor with the kids while I cleaned the kitchen. Maybe our arrangement would work out after all.

At church on Sunday, I saw Kyle for the first time since the Easter service. We didn't have time to do more than exchange a few pleasantries. He asked how Nicole was doing and if the kids needed anything. I told him we were fine and everything was under control. I didn't burden him with the questions and worries whirling around in my head, like why was Nicole back after I had finally started serving the Lord and everything was going so well? What did she want from me? What did God want? Was I supposed to eat my words about Grandma Catherine and her Christian charity?

God was testing me. I just didn't know exactly what he required or if I'd pass or fail.

"How was school," I asked Jonah Monday evening when I got home from work.

He was on the front porch with an army of tiny green plastic soldiers positioned around him, prepared for battle. He set one on the top of a stack of wooden blocks and aimed the soldier's rifle into the air. "We didn't go today."

My purse slid off my shoulder and banged against my leg. "What? Why not?"

He shrugged and made shooting noises with his lips. "Mommy didn't get us up."

I headed into the house without another word. I didn't want to risk yelling at my innocent nephew when it was his mother I was angry at. I found Nicole in front of the TV.

"There's frozen pizza on the stove if you're hungry," she said without much enthusiasm.

I positioned myself between her and the TV so she would have to look at me. "Why didn't you take the kids to preschool today? Jonah said you didn't get them up."

She gave me a dirty look and leaned to the left to see around me. "I tried but they wouldn't get out of bed. I got tired of begging them. When they finally did get up, they said they didn't want to go."

"They're kids. You don't ask them what they want. You tell them."

She finally gave up watching her program. She sighed and focused her attention on me. "You know I'm not a morning person. I can barely get myself out of bed without worrying about getting two whiny kids up. I don't see why you're getting so excited. It's just preschool."

"Preschool that I'm paying a fortune to send them to."

She raised her hands in front of her. "Ooh, sorry. Put it on my tab."

"It's not the money, Nicole. It's very important for them to go. I don't know what I would've done if it hadn't been for the teachers at that school. Jonah and Emma have learned a lot and have really grown spiritually and emotionally since they've been there. I told you Emma graduates next month. Her class has already started practicing for the program. I don't want her to miss out on it."

"I'll send them tomorrow. Just chill. Now will you please get out of the way? You're going to make me miss the end."

"I'm not moving until I make you understand how important it is for the kids to get up and go to preschool. They are building discipline that will be with them the rest of their lives. If you can't get them up now, what are you going to do next year when Emma is in kindergarten? If you don't make her go then, they'll put you in jail."

"All right, all right. I said I'd send them tomorrow. You're right, as usual. I'm a terrible mother and I don't deserve to live. I promise I won't waste anymore of your precious money. I'll have them up at five a.m. and ready to go out the door. Is that what you want to hear?"

I wanted to kick in the TV screen, snatch Nicole up by her hair and make her listen to me. Instead I turned and went upstairs. She wasn't going to listen to a word I said. As usual, she saw me as an anal retentive bully and herself as the victim. Maybe I was making preschool attendance more important than it was. Millions of kids didn't go to preschool and they were fully prepared for regular school. I would definitely save a small fortune in tuition fees if I withdrew them and let Nicole keep them at home every day. When it all boiled down, it wasn't my decision to make. Before I got myself worked up, I'd see how things went tomorrow.

The kids made it to school on Tuesday and Wednesday, though things didn't go smoothly. On Tuesday, Nicole picked them up during lunch, forcing the cooks to bag what they hadn't eaten yet and send it with them. Wednesday, she lost track of time and didn't go after them until after Aunt Wanda called to ask about her car. It was nearly five o'clock before they left the preschool that day.

I didn't like the irregularity of their new schedule, but I decided worse things could happen to a kid. Such as living alone with Nicole in the city somewhere without me knowing where they were and if they were eating three times a day. I needed to relax and not imagine the fate of the world hung in the balance if they were late for school once in a while. Everything didn't have to work out the way I thought was best every single t

I didn't want to get into a custody battle with her. I knew exactly how she'd react if challenged. Like a she-wolf protecting her cubs. It was best for the kids to remain here with me, but I didn't know if I had the nerve to take a stand, especially if it meant threatening her with litigation.

I prayed every night she'd realize she needed a job and stability here on the farm. Deep down, though, I knew it wasn't going to happen. I braced myself for the storm just beyond the horizon.

"No! I don't have to."

Jonah stared up at me, his eyes defiant.

"Pick up those toys right now," I repeated. "I'm trying to cook dinner and you're in my way. Toys don't belong in the kitchen anyway."

"Mommy lets me play in here while she's cooking." Jonah gave the army men scattered at his feet an angry kick. Several skittered across the floor. One slipped under the refrigerator and disappeared. Perfect. Gone forever since I never bothered to clean under there.

"Jonah, I'm not telling you again. You can't play in here while I'm cooking. Someone could trip over a toy and get burned on the stove. Now get these toys out of my way. I've got things to do."

"I don't have to listen to you. You're not my mommy."

The attitude that had pervaded the house the past two weeks had not been put into words…until now.

"I may not be your mommy," I said, struggling not to give into the emotions warring inside me, "but this is my kitchen and you'll do as I say when I say it."

"You're mean." The little boy sat down among his toys, crossed his arms over his chest and glared at me.

"So you're not going to pick up these toys?"

"Nope."

"Fine."

I went to the mudroom and got the broom. Jonah bent his head over his toys, but I could see him watching me through the blond fringe of hair hanging over his forehead. I brought the broom and dustpan into the kitchen and began to sweep. I started near the refrigerator where the farthest army men had landed and worked my way toward Jonah. I moved slowly and deliberately, carefully reaching under the table and along the counters. Finally I swept against Jonah's backside.

He whipped his head around to stare at me. "Hey! What are you doing?"

"I'm cleaning up the kitchen so I can start dinner. Are you sure you don't want to help?"

Without answering, he spun around on the floor to face me and re-crossed his arms. He didn't say another word when I knelt down to sweep the army men and an alarmingly significant amount of dirt into the dustpan. I went to the trashcan and dumped the contents inside.

That brought a reaction. Jonah was on his feet in an instant. He ran to where I stood next to the trashcan and peered inside. Tears formed on his lashes. "Hey! Those are my toys. You can't throw them away."

I snapped the lid closed. "I can and I did. I gave you more than enough chances to pick up your toys. You chose not to help so I had to do it myself."

"But you can't throw my stuff away. Now what am I supposed to play with?"

"You should've thought of that when I asked you to pick them up."

"You're mean, Aunt Shell," he reiterated. "I hate you! I wish we didn't have to live here." He hollered for Nicole as he ran from the room.

My satisfaction over finding a practical solution to the problem of a preschooler who wouldn't pick up his toys vanished with him. He hated me, or at least he claimed to for the moment. In an hour he'd forget why he was mad and try to warm up to me.

For the past nine months, we'd been best friends. He made me cards and tacky presents at school. He curled up against me at night to watch television. The bond we'd formed had seemed indestructible. Now I was hated and evil, much like I had always thought of Grandma Catherine.

I returned the broom and dustpan to the mudroom and started dinner. Everything was falling apart. Nicole had only been here two weeks, and she was wrecking it all. If only things could go back to the way they were before she came.

I thought back to last summer before Emma and Jonah came. It seemed like a lifetime ago. Ah, how peaceful life had been. Dinner out of the microwave or a paper sack. No toys on the floor. No arguments that always served to ruin my appetite. Just Gypsy and me, happy as clams in our big old empty house. Even Gypsy had turned her back on me. She wasn't my dog anymore. She belonged to the kids. She was happy and fulfilled. She had no clue we were being used and mocked behind our backs.

I had become a guest in my own home, and I hated it. I had to do something. If I didn't want toys littering the floor and a fresh-mouthed kid spouting insolence, I shouldn't have to put up with it. Things were going to change, starting now. When Nicole came in to find out why I threw Jonah's toys away she was going to get an earful. If she didn't like it, she could find the door. Maybe it wouldn't be the end of the world if she left and took those kids of hers with her.

Chapter Fifteen

Generally I wasn't much of a crier. I couldn't remember the last time I'd had a good, old-fashioned, throw-yourself-across-the-bed-and-wail session, but I sure felt like it now. The night had gone from bad to worse with Jonah whining and Nicole accusing me of overreacting by throwing his toys away. Even Emma ignored me and sat next to her mother on the couch as I squirmed against their onslaught.

It was only eight-thirty when I went upstairs to my room. I lay across the bed and took my Bible from the nightstand. I felt more alone than I had back when Grandma Catherine was my only housemate and I would hide in my room to escape her constant picking and complaining.

Things didn't have to be that way now. I knew there was one who sticks closer than a brother. I flipped the Bible open to the Psalms and started to read. Unfortunately I had opened to the part where David cried out to God because his enemies besought him on every side. That made me even more depressed. I flipped over another fifty pages and landed in Proverbs. Somewhere in here was the assurance that if you beat a child with a rod, he would not die. That's what I needed. Confirmation I had done the right thing by throwing the army men in the trash.

I tuned out the noise drifting up through the old fashioned heating grates and read. When the phone next to my elbow rang, I nearly jumped out of my skin. I pounced on it without checking to see who was calling.

"Hello?" I practically gasped.

"Michelle? Is that you? Everything okay?"

I exhaled, more relieved than I had a right to be at the sound of Kyle's voice. "Yeah, I'm fine." I took a deep breath to slow the hammering of my heart in my chest. Heat had rushed to my cheeks. If Nicole or one of the kids came into the room right now, they would wonder why I was sitting here all red-faced like a lovestruck schoolgirl. I was sort of wondering the same thing myself.

"I was reading and the phone startled me."

"You've been on my mind lately."

My enflamed cheeks grew hotter. "I have?"

"Of course. I noticed you haven't attended any of the New Converts Classes."

My heart crashed around my feet. So that's why I'd been on his mind. He was worried about my soul, not the rest of me.

"I know you're going through a lot with Nicole and the kids right now."

"Yes, I am."

"I just hope you don't let that keep you from developing your relationship with Christ. As we go through the trials of life, it's imperative that we learn to lean on Jesus."

I'd never heard him sound so much like a pastor.

"There are a lot of wonderful brothers and sisters at the church who would be more than willing to give you some personal attention," he continued. "A listening ear. Anything you need."

"I appreciate that," I said flatly.

"Michelle." His voice lost its pastor-ly edge. "I'm serious. You have a lot of people who care for you."

The tears from earlier threatened again. *What about you, Kyle?* I wanted to ask. *Are you one of those people?*

Of course he cared for me. He was a pastor. He was *my* pastor. But I couldn't stop wanting him to care for me differently than the other members of his flock. I was sure he had feelings for me. I was also sure he would never compromise his faith for the sake of his heart. No matter how much he cared for me—even if he loved me or at least loved the woman I was fifteen years ago—we were simply too different. Too much had changed since we were kids and thought there would never be another one for us.

"Thanks, Kyle. I needed to hear that just now."

"Michelle, I want you to be honest with me. That's what I'm here for. I wouldn't be calling if the Lord hadn't put you on my heart."

Hope rose in my chest. "He did?" Had God answered my prayer by having Kyle call me even if he wasn't calling for the reason I hoped?

"I've been praying for you all evening. Is there anything you need to talk about? And I mean really talk. I don't want to just offer platitudes that sound nice, but don't really serve to help your problem."

This was uncanny. How could he possibly have known I had come up here just a little while ago wishing I could talk to someone? I studied the ceiling. Was this how God showed love to his people? Or had Kyle simply called to remind me of the New Converts Class and hit the nail on the head by chance?

"I wouldn't even know where to begin."

"Why don't we get together somewhere for lunch tomorrow? You don't generally work on Fridays, do you?"

I was flattered he knew so much about my schedule. Then I remembered he knew my schedule because the kids didn't go to preschool on Fridays. I tightened my grip on the phone wishing I was holding onto him instead. "No, I'm free."

"Good. Why don't we meet for lunch around noon at Giovanni's in Winona? We'll have the whole afternoon to talk. Unless you'd rather discuss things over the phone now."

I was getting that breathless feeling again. A lunch date with Kyle. Well, maybe not a real date, but he wouldn't have invited me if he didn't want to spend some time with me too. "Tomorrow will be fine. I'll see you around twelve."

We said our goodbyes and hung up. I lay back against the pillows and hugged the open Bible to my chest. Kyle had been praying for me. I was touched. Touched that he cared about me even if he didn't love me, and touched God had taken the time to put me on my pastor's heart. It had been so long since I believed anyone cared for me in any capacity, I almost didn't know how to feel.

I continued to look at the ceiling through a sheen of tears. I wasn't alone anymore. Regardless of what happened with Nicole and the kids, I wouldn't have to go through it alone. God loved me enough to put me on the hearts of people like Kyle.

And I was having lunch with Kyle tomorrow. Surely that explained the butterflies flitting around in my stomach.

Kyle's not interested in dating you, I reminded myself a hundred times as I drove the five miles into Winona for our lunch at the pizza place. One kiss a few months ago wasn't enough to indicate his feelings ran any deeper than friendship and normal male/female attraction.

The waitress recognized both of us when we went in and waved her indication that we seat ourselves. We exchanged pleasantries while we waited to place our order and for our food to arrive.

Kyle told me about a few of the people he'd visited at the hospital this morning. He definitely had a pastor's heart. It wasn't just the members of his own flock he visited regularly. While moving down the hall to the room of a patient he knew, he often stopped in other rooms for a quick hello to the occupant. Before leaving the hospital, he always stopped in the chapel to offer to pray with anyone there. If the chapel was empty, which was often the case, he prayed alone. He cared for everyone, and it made me love him all the more.

Love?

How was it possible after all our years apart? We didn't even know each other anymore. Looking across the table at him, I realized why I had never been all in on a relationship with Barry. I still loved Kyle.

The thought scared and thrilled me at the same time.

It wasn't until we had nearly polished off every pepperoni and bread stick on the table before he asked about Nicole.

"Has she given any indication about why she's here?"

I shook my head. Everybody asked that question and I still didn't have an answer. "We barely talk. She spends her time with the kids, which is good. I'm always at work so there's been few opportunities for a heart to heart. When we do talk, we end up arguing."

He blew out a puff of sympathetic air.

"I don't know any more about her plans than I did when she first showed up." I continued. "I don't think she even has plans. She's always been that way, living each day as it comes."

"Sounds good in theory, I guess, but not very responsible."

"Well, that's our Nicole." I took a sip of water and played with the straw. Kyle didn't speak. He just watched from his side of the table.

"I am totally losing control," I admitted finally. "The kids fight with me about everything. They don't go to preschool half the time. Nicole says I'm too controlling. I don't want to control anybody, but some things have to be done, right? Emma starts kindergarten next year and we don't even know if she'll be living here. I saw a sign in front of the elementary school the other day about kindergarten registration. I don't have the nerve to mention it to Nicole. I know it will lead to another argument."

The waitress approached and asked if we wanted her to clear away the dishes. Kyle and I waited while she took our empty plates and refilled our water glasses.

When she moved away, I started in again, barely giving Kyle a chance to breath.

"Aunt Wanda wants me to get a lawyer and take Nicole to court. Maybe that's best for the kids, but what if Nicole's really changed this time? Shouldn't I give her a chance to prove herself before I hire a lawyer? Any influence I have on her will be lost once I take that step. I almost think she wants the kids to hate me too. You should've seen the look she gave me the first time Emma wanted me instead of her. I don't know what to do.

"All I do know is I'm losing it big time. Everything I believe is suddenly insignificant. I tell Nicole something and she gives me this look like, 'Michelle thinks she's so perfect. Look at what a mess her life is.' I hate how she makes me doubt myself. Sometimes I think it would be so much easier if she left and took the kids with her. Isn't that awful? Aunt Wanda would hate me if she knew I was thinking this way."

I realized my hands were clenched around my glass. "Sorry, I didn't mean to get carried away like that."

"It's fine. You need to talk."

His voice was so gentle, so full of compassion, I nearly cried right there over the red-checked tablecloth.

"Do you think I'm terrible? I know the kids are better off on the farm with me, but it's taking everything out of me to have them there."

"Them or Nicole."

"Nicole, of course, but they're a package deal."

He pushed his glass aside, leaned his elbows on the table, and gazed into my eyes. "I don't think you're terrible, Michelle. Nicole is using you. She knows you care too much about those kids to risk saying anything to her. I also think she knows exactly what she's doing."

"Which is…"

"She's sponging off you until something better comes along. Do you think she'd hesitate for a minute to leave if that boyfriend of hers came back? For the time being she doesn't have any options so she has to put up with you." He sat back and leveled a serious look at me. "Something will happen and you need to be prepared."

Dread punched me in the stomach. "That's what Aunt Wanda tells me."

"You have to decide what you want. Do you want to keep Nicole's kids? If you do, then you need to talk to her about it."

"I know I do, but right now she's staying put and the kids need her. I hate to rock the boat."

"She's counting on that. She knows you won't kick her out as long as she can use the kids for leverage. You said yourself you can't keep living in limbo, not knowing what's going to happen tomorrow. You need to confront her."

I shook my head. "I can't do that. Emma's graduating from preschool in a couple weeks. Jonah's been acting out ever since Nicole came home. I can't throw the kids into more turmoil than they already are."

"What about you? What about the turmoil your life is in?"

I blushed over my water. If he only knew.

"I didn't expect this, Kyle. I figured you'd give me one of those turn-the-other-cheek lectures and tell me I need to be patient and understanding and compassionate while my sister works through her problems."

"You should do that, of course. But your top priority is those kids."

"I wish we could have one conversation that wasn't about my messy life."

"Oh, we will." He arched his eyebrows playfully.

Heat rose in my cheeks. "What's that supposed to mean?" I blurted out before I lost my nerve.

He reached across the table and put his hand over mine. "Please, Michelle, one problem at a time."

What was he doing? Did he have any idea the affect his physical contact had on me? I gazed into his blue gray eyes. No doubt about it. He knew. I swallowed. This was so hard. I had always known what Barry wanted from me, but with Kyle, I was lost. Even though I was now a Christian, we were still on polar ends of the spectrum.

"After all this is over with Nicole, you're going to start giving me trouble?"

I hoped he wouldn't notice the tremor in my voice.

He smiled. "I might. But you can't handle it right now."

He didn't give me time to process the meaning behind his words before he switched gears. "If anyone else came into your house and turned your routine upside down like Nicole has, you wouldn't stand for it. You would recognize it as totally unacceptable behavior in a houseguest and probably do something about it."

"She's not a houseguest, she's my sister."

"She's still a guest. You have certain rules and expectations for what can and cannot go on under your roof. As any decent human being, she has to respect that. It's time you stood up for yourself."

When I said nearly the exact thing to Nicole the other day, she had turned it around to make me sound like an unreasonable ogre. "I guess," I muttered, "but I've never been strong when it comes to my family. Every one of them has always rolled over me."

He squeezed my hand again. "You can do whatever you need to do, Michelle."

"I wish I had your faith in me."

"My faith is in the one who saved you from your sins. Trust him, Michelle, He promised to never leave you or forsake you. You're not going through this alone."

Chapter Sixteen

I arrived home with a new determination. I had to get over my fear of what Nicole planned to do. Kyle and Aunt Wanda were right. Nicole was taking advantage of her hold on me. She knew I couldn't stand up to her as long as I let her use the kids to control me. I could no longer overlook the way she and the kids were ruling my house. I wouldn't let her intimidate me one more minute.

I parked in my usual spot next to the kitchen door and marched into the house as though I owned the place. All was quiet except for the muffled sound of the television in the living room. I headed in that direction. The shades were drawn against the afternoon sun. The room was cloaked in shadows. It took a moment to make out the shapes of my niece and nephew asleep on the couch. Gypsy raised her head and looked at me from her position on the floor below them. I gingerly removed the remote from Jonah's open hand and clicked off the TV. The kids didn't stir.

I looked around the quiet room and cocked my head to listen. Where was Nicole?

I left the room, dropped my car keys on the sofa table in the foyer and headed upstairs. She had probably set the kids in front of the TV and went upstairs to take a nap or a bath. Typical irresponsible, Nicole behavior.

As suspected I heard movement coming from her room when I reached the landing. I pecked on the door lintel with my knuckles and stuck my head inside. She had just sat down on the bed when I looked in. She held something in her hands. It looked like she'd been crying.

My resolve to confront her crumbled onto the creaky floorboards.

"Nicole, are you all right?"

She jerked her head up. "Oh, it's you. I didn't hear you come in."

"I just got home." I came the rest of the way into the room and pushed the door shut behind me. "What's the matter?"

Her shoulders lifted slightly. She stared at the object in her hands. "Nothing."

By now I could see what had held her attention. It was a ceramic ballerina that used to sit on the shelf in her room. Mom had sent it from where she was living somewhere in Texas a few weeks after Nicole's tenth or eleventh birthday. At the time I remembered thinking it was too childish a gift for a girl Nicole's age. But who could expect Mom to know either of us well enough to send an appropriate gift?

The gift came with a card that didn't apologize for being late. The inscription read something like, *Love, Mom. Wish I could be there.* Of course, there had been no explanation as to why she couldn't. No 'I miss you', 'Here's my number' or 'I'll be there as soon as I can get some money together.'

Nicole had cherished that ballerina. Anytime she was feeling particularly low, she'd take it off the shelf and stare at it and caress it. Sometimes for hours.

I sat beside her on the bed and took the ballerina out of her hands. I smoothed my fingers over the line-splayed porcelain.

The blond hair and pink tutu had faded over the years. The seam that held the thing together was now wide enough I could feel it with my fingers. A cheap trinket that brought a little girl so much comfort over the years. I doubted Mom remembered sending it even though she only sent three or four packages during the years we were growing up without her.

"Do you remember when Mom sent that to me?" Nicole asked.

"I was just thinking about it."

She sighed wistfully. "I used to lie here in bed and stare up at her on the shelf and imagine her coming to life and dancing in some big auditorium. Of course, in my fantasies I was the ballerina. I would pretend Mom helped me style my hair like the ballerina's and made the costume for me. Then I would go to my dance recital and Mom and Dad would be sitting in the front row watching me dance to Swan Lake. When the music ended the audience would go wild with applause and everyone would stand to their feet. I would bow and people would throw roses onto the stage. I'd look out at the audience and Mom would be clapping hardest of all and crying her eyes out. She'd smile and nod and give me this little wave and keep right on clapping. Dad's face would be wet with tears too. He'd lean over and kiss Mom's cheek, and the two of them would be so happy."

I sat quietly beside her for a few moments, letting her remember. "Then what happened," I asked.

She took the ballerina out of my hands and stood up. "Nothing."

The wistfulness had disappeared from her voice. "That's where the daydream ended. Mom and Dad clapping and crying and being proud of me." She set the ballerina back on the shelf. "It's all I ever wanted. It was just a dream. A dream that never came true."

I suddenly felt very depressed. I wondered what got her thinking about that, but it seemed cruel to ask.

She ran her fingers over the front of the doll one last time and then turned to face me. "Why couldn't they love us, Michelle? What did we do so wrong that our own parents didn't want to live with us?"

If she only knew how many times I had asked myself the same questions.

I jumped off the bed and went to her. I put my arms around her and smoothed her blond hair behind her shoulders. "There was nothing wrong with us. We were kids. They were the ones…"

I almost said, "They were the ones who were horrible and selfish just like you're being now with Emma and Jonah."

I put my head on her shoulder and kept smoothing her hair with my hands.

She stepped away from me. "Dean called while you were out."

My stomach knotted.

"We talked for over an hour. He said he made a big mistake by leaving. He can't stop thinking about me. He told me he's sorry and wants me back."

"What about the kids?"

"He's sorry about that too. He says he was wrong to hassle me so much about them. He wants to come get me and move all of us back to Memphis."

My heart sank even farther. Here it was, the moment I'd been dreading but knew would come nonetheless. I sent a silent prayer heavenward.

"Don't take the kids, Nicole," I cried. "Let them stay here with me until you and Dean get on your feet." Even as I said it, I knew I didn't mean it. I never wanted her to take them from me. "Or they could stay here indefinitely," I said carefully. "I love having them here. It isn't like they're—"

"They're mine, Michelle. I can't live without them."

You did for eight months, I thought. But I didn't say it out loud. I took a deep breath. "What happens when Dean gets tired of them again or you two get in another fight? It would be so much easier if they just stayed here."

"Better for you maybe. You've always been jealous of what I have. You can't have children of your own to control so you think you can steal mine. I see how you are with them, Michelle. Everything has to be your way. Throwing Jonah's toys away because he wouldn't pick them up the instant you asked. That was cruel and childish. Is it so important for you to be right, you're willing to break the hearts of everyone around you?"

I couldn't believe she was attacking me. "I told him several times to pick up the toys. He wouldn't and I had work to do."

Now I did sound childish. I took a deep breath and started over.

"Nicole, I don't want to defend my child-rearing methods with you. I'm not an old pro at this. I'm learning as I go and I'm sure I make mistakes. The important thing is the kids are happy. They're going to school. They're involved in church. This arrangement is good for them." I prayed again for strength. "I think we should think about making it permanent."

Her mouth dropped open and her face flushed scarlet. She took another step away from me. "You've got to be kidding. You want my kids? No way." She sliced at the air with her hand. "No way."

"Come on, Nicole, think about it. This is the kids' home now."

"No, it isn't. This is your home. You make that evident every minute of the day. It's your house, your way. I know you don't want us here and you resent the way the kids disrupt your precious routine. There's no way I'd leave them here so I'd be indebted to my big sister the rest of my life."

"This isn't about you and me, Nicole. It's about the kids. I admit I did resent them here at first but not now. I can't imagine my life without them. At least think about it. Think about what's best for them. It isn't fair to uproot them after they've finally got some stability in their lives."

She set her fists on her hips. "This is what you always do. You make everything my fault. If I don't take them, I'm a terrible mother for abandoning my kids. If I do take them, I'm robbing them of the only stability they've ever known. God knows I never gave them any stability, isn't that right?"

I clenched my fists, burying my fingernails into my palms. "I'm not trying to make this anyone's fault. I just want you to see they're settled here. They're doing great in preschool. Emma starts kindergarten in the fall. If you take them away, it's only going to upset them and make it that much harder for you to get settled with Dean in the city. Isn't that why you gave me custody to begin with?"

Nicole shook her head. She didn't like what she was hearing. "I gave you temporary custody to help me out of a tight spot. We've already discussed this, Michelle. Dean is coming to get me. I know what I'm doing. I'm ready to be a mother to my kids."

"You just said he called. You never mentioned anything about agreeing to go with him."

"I didn't think you were interested in hearing a replay of the entire conversation. But, yes, we made up. We're going to be a family. We might even get married."

I slapped my forehead. "Nicole, no. Think about what it will do to the kids. This isn't fair to them."

"And think about what it will do to them if we do it your way. They'll grow up thinking their mother deserted them just like Mom and Dad did to us. They'll forever wonder what's wrong with them. I'm not doing that to my kids, Michelle. Look what it did to me and you. I can't keep a job or a man, and you've turned into a bitter old shrew just like Grandma."

"I'm nothing like Grandma."

She snorted derisively. "Yeah, right. Keep telling yourself that, Sis. Anyway, I don't want my kids growing up with the same feelings of inadequacies that we had. Do you think if Mom or Dad had put one ounce of energy into making me think I was special or they loved me, I'd be so quick to take the word of the first worthless man who showed me any affection? Of course not. I knew the guys I chose were no good. I figured I didn't deserve anything better because nobody ever told me I was worth more than them."

"Is that why you're settling for Dean?"

Her jaw clenched. "We're not talking about Dean. Yes, he's made mistakes. We all have. I'm giving him a second chance."

"Nicole…"

She slowly shook her head, warning me to shut up. "Mom and Dad leaving messed you up as badly as it did me. Instead of choosing losers, you went the safe route and avoided men altogether."

I had to hand it to her. She was dead on about that. I had realized years ago I wasn't worthy of anyone's love. Rather than think about it or chase after love where I wouldn't find it, I buried my head in my work.

"You're right," I admitted. "We both have some major issues to work through. Just don't make the situation worse by leaving with Dean. You know he isn't interested in playing Daddy."

"Maybe he's not my knight in shining armor, but he's here. I think he cares enough for me to build something together. I'm not so stupid I think it'll be perfect, but I want to try. What else have I got?"

"You've got your kids, Nicole. You need to think about what's best for them."

"I am thinking about them. They need a daddy. Heaven knows they'll never have a male role model as long as they're living here. I want my kids to have what we never did."

I wanted to tell her they'd be better off with no role model at all than with one like Dean. I kept my personal opinions to myself. I had to make her see reason before this situation escalated into an all-out battle neither one of us could win.

I spoke as calmly as I could, sort of the way you do when facing a dangerous and potentially unstable animal. "We're not talking about you and me, Nicole. We're talking about Emma and Jonah. They know they're loved here. They've got me and Aunt Wanda and Uncle Jeb and their teachers at the preschool. We could explain that while you still love them, we decided as the adults in their lives, it's better they live here for the time being. It wouldn't be like it was when Mom and Dad dropped out of our lives and never looked back. You'd still come by to visit and be part of the family. When they got older, if they wanted to spend a week or two with you over summer vacation, they could. They wouldn't have the same baggage we do."

Nicole clenched her jaw so hard I thought it might pop out of joint. "Why are you trying to live my life? This is my decision. It has nothing to do with you. They're my kids and they're moving back to Memphis with me. Whatever it takes to raise them, I'll be the one to do it. I won't have them thinking I abandoned them."

My patience and good intentions could only go so far.

"They already think that," I spat. "Your most recent loser boyfriend dumped them under my lilac bushes and drove away. They didn't even know who I was. Emma didn't speak for weeks. Jonah, your three-year-old, had to be the adult and comfort his big sister. Now you decide you're ready to play Mother of the Year. Forget it! You're not taking those kids anywhere."

Nicole's sapphire eyes flashed. Part of me wished I could take my words back. The other part wished I had the nerve to say what I really thought.

"I'd let Children's Services have them before I ever come to you for help again," she shrieked. "You sanctimonious toad! What do you know about being a mother? What do you know about caring for anyone? You're the coldest, most self-righteous hag I've ever met. No wonder Grandma hated you. No wonder Mom couldn't stand the sight of you after Dad left. All you did was remind her of how much she failed as a woman."

Blood surged in my ears. "What are you talking about?"

I knew I should lower my voice so we wouldn't wake the kids, but I was nearly as out of control as Nicole.

"You can't remember what it was like back then," I said. "You don't know what I did for Mom. If it wasn't for me, Grandma and Aunt Wanda would've—"

"Would've what? I know all about it, Michelle. Grandma told me everything. She told me how you babied Mom and talked to her late into the night after Dad left. How she always went to you for solace when life got too hard. She tried to lean on you and you failed her."

"I was fourteen. What was I supposed to do?"

"You were supposed to be there for her. To shut your face for once and just listen instead of trying to fix everything. You never knew how to shut up long enough for someone to tell you how they really feel. You assume you already know, and you belittle them for not being as perfect as you. Spouting your stupid and sanctimonious advice. You've always been that way. That's why no one can stand to be around you for more than two minutes. I'll leave my kids in foster care before I let you ruin their lives and turn them into closed-off, ice cold reflections of you."

"Then why'd you leave them here in the first place?"

"Because I had no choice. I know what I'm doing now. Believe me, I won't make the same mistake twice."

I'd had it. Any reservations about taking her to court and destroying what remained of our relationship went out the window.

"Then you better prepare for a fight, sweetheart," I raged. "I'm not letting you walk out of here with those kids. I'll hire the best lawyer in this county. No judge in his right mind would let you have them after what you've done."

Nicole smiled wickedly "So this is what it's come down to? My own sister taking me to court to get my kids?"

"You bet it is," I said with a sneer. "You don't deserve kids. I wouldn't trust you to take care of Gypsy. No one else in this county will either."

"I'm not a kid anymore, Michelle. You can't bully me around. I'm leaving and I'm taking what's mine with me."

I couldn't seem to stop losing my temper. "Over my dead body."

"That won't be the hardest thing I've ever done," she challenged.

I wasn't behaving in a very Christ-like manner, but I couldn't get hold of myself. "Just go, Nicole. Go back to Memphis or whatever hole you crawled out of and leave us in peace. Your kids are happy and stable for the first time in their lives. Do them a favor and leave and don't come back. You won't be missed."

"Don't worry, when I leave you'll be the first to know."

Chapter Seventeen

I blew it, I blew it, I blew it! The situation couldn't have gone any worse if I had choreographed the entire thing with a Hollywood stunt team. Nicole would never speak to me again. She'd never listen to my advice. More importantly, she'd never agree to let me have custody of the kids. I blew it.

I didn't want to take my sister to court. I had hoped and prayed to solve the matter peaceably for the sake of her and the kids. I wanted the best for everyone, even Dean, whom I knew did not really want Emma and Jonah. He had only agreed to it to shut Nicole up. What would happen when there was trouble again and he no longer cared if she was happy or not. The kids would suffer, and it would be my fault because my sister no longer had me to turn to.

As far as my Christianity was concerned, I had tossed it aside at the first sign of adversity. I had prayed but then spoken in haste without waiting for the Father's voice to guide me. I understood more about the Christian charity that Grandma Catherine referred to. Enough to know I didn't have any. I was as guilty as Nicole, talking about the awful things that had happened to us as children, and then turning around and heaping the same disrespect on someone else.

I had to make things right, and it couldn't happen in a courtroom.

Barry called in the middle of the week to ask if I wanted to have dinner over the weekend. My first instinct was to say no. I hadn't yet had time to mull over his words the other day when he found out Nicole was back, and I wasn't sure how I felt about his reaction.

I still liked Barry. I enjoyed his company. Sometimes he talked too much—or maybe he spoke without thinking the way I did—but I felt comfortable and cared about around him. That's all I needed right now.

Every time I thought about my needs my mind went directly to Kyle. Still, I was smart enough to know nothing was ever going to happen in that arena. I might care a lot about him, but I needed a Barry in my life. Not a Kyle.

Barry and I met at the family steakhouse in Genoa after I got off work. I had taken a shower at work and did my makeup and hair in one of the staff bathrooms so I wouldn't need to stop by the house first. I didn't want to answer questions about why I needed to get prettied up to get a bite to eat after work.

Nicole's insistence that I was made of ice and didn't need love still rankled. I sure didn't want to explain to her where I was going or who I was going with.

Barry left work early so we arrived at the restaurant at nearly the same moment. I snagged a better parking space from the early dinner crowd so I was waiting for him near the entrance when he got out of his car.

I saw it coming this time so when he leaned in for a kiss when he reached my side, I turned my head so the kiss landed on my cheek. I liked Barry, but I wasn't ready for kisses every time we met.

If he was discouraged by the lack of physical contact, it didn't show on his face. "I'm so glad you were free," he said. "This is becoming a habit for us. Two weeks in a row."

I let him open the door ahead of me. "How did you manage with Caitlyn two weeks in a row? Don't you alternate weeks with Sue?"

"Sue and her parents are going to a family reunion in Missouri. This is my weekend, but I couldn't balk on letting Caitlyn go with them. We'll just switch weeks. We do it all the time when things come up."

"That's nice. I'm sure Caitlyn will enjoy it." What I was thinking was how wonderful it was that he and Sue had such an amicable arrangement, they were always willing to put Caitlyn first.

Even though it was early, we still had to wait in line behind a family of five and an elderly couple to be seated in the half filled restaurant. I looked around the warm, homey and noisy atmosphere. Uncle Jeb used to bring Grandma Catherine and me here after church on Mother's Day and a few other occasions throughout the year. Since Grandma's death I hadn't been here but a handful of times. I wasn't sure if I associated the restaurant with Grandma or I just didn't to fill up on such heavy meals anymore.

"Nicole is home with the kids tonight," I told him while we waited. "Maybe I'll take some carryout home. Can you believe I've never brought the kids here?"

He cocked his head. "That still going on? I thought Nicole left."

A hostess in her very-early twenties stepped in front of Barry with two leather bound menus clutched to her chest. "Two?" she asked sweetly.

Barry smiled and nodded, holding up two fingers.

The young woman turned and headed into the restaurant. I tagged after Barry. The hostess waved us to a table and Barry took the time to pull out my chair. I wondered if he would ever get tired of doing it.

The hostess gave us one last smile and moved away. I opened my menu but didn't look at it. "Nicole hasn't left," I told him as quietly as I dared. "I don't know when she is or even what's going on in her head."

Barry didn't look up while he studied the entrée selection. "You can't let her take advantage of you, Michelle."

Even though Kyle had told me the same thing, I resented it coming from Barry. "I'm not," I said, though we both knew that was exactly what was going on.

Barry continued to study the menu. "I grabbed a V-8 out of the vending machine for lunch so I'm starving."

I gave him a half smile though he wasn't really looking at me. "I do that sometimes too. No time to eat a real meal."

He nodded absently. He looked at the menu another moment before finally looking up at me. "Do you know what you want?"

I want you to listen to me about my sister. I need to talk about this situation.

Instead I said, "The chicken penne looks good." Actually, it was the only thing I could remember from the four pages of entrees.

"Sure you don't want a steak? I think I'll go for the t-bone. Haven't had one in a long time."

A steak was always a good choice in my book, but I shook my head. The pasta looked like more than enough even though I'd gone light on lunch too.

A waitress came by and Barry gave her our orders. I watched him talk and tried to imagine sitting across the table from him for the rest of my life. Not that he'd given any indication that's where his thoughts were leading. He may think of me as nothing more than decent dinner company and the mom of Caitlyn's bosom friend. He was funny and companionable and ambitious. But what would happen if

Nicole actually took the kids with her. Would I still want a man in my life? Would that man be Barry? Every other week Barry lived the life of a single man while Caitlyn lived with her mother. Without three little kids demanding we cut their meat or open ketchup packets or take them to the restroom, would we have anything to talk about? How would we fill the next forty years of our lives?

I doubted he would be very compassionate or understanding if I fell apart without Emma and Jonah. He would probably tell me to get a grip and get on with my life. It wasn't like they were my kids. I had only been babysitting until Nicole got her act together. Kids belonged with their mothers, not a well meaning aunt who didn't know the first thing about parenthood.

I thought of the conversation I'd had with Kyle about this very topic. He understood better than Barry even though he wasn't a father and didn't seem to have people taking advantage of him at every turn.

"How was work?" Barry asked after the waitress left the table.

"Good," I said automatically. Then I reconsidered. I needed to get honest with him if I ever wanted an honest, from-the-gut response in return. "It's really hard to focus with everything happening at home."

A flash of impatience darkened his eyes. "How old is Nicole?"

I knew immediately what he was getting at. "Twenty-three. She's ten years younger than me, but when we were growing up, we were really close. We were nearly the only family each other had."

Except for Grandma and Aunt Wanda and Violet and all the cousins who periodically reminded me how my parents' irresponsible behavior had ruined Grandma's life, Nicole and I were alone.

"She's a grown woman, Michelle," Barry said. "Okay, so maybe twenty-three seems more like a kid to me now than it used to, but Nicole is still a legal adult. She should be taking care of her own problems."

Was he insinuating Jonah and Emma were problems?

"I agree. But to be fair, Nicole and I were pretty much left to raise ourselves."

"You turned out all right." He arched his eyebrows playfully.

I know he meant it as a compliment toward me, but I couldn't ignore the insult directed at Nicole.

"She's my sister, and I love her. I want to be there for her, but I really don't know how to handle the situation."

My first act at handling the situation should probably be not discussing it with Barry who seemed unable to comprehend what I was going through. I already wished I hadn't brought it up, even though I wanted to know how he really felt.

"Maybe helping her out would be not making her irresponsible behavior so easy to get away with. You know, a little tough love."

I couldn't deny the validity of that suggestion. "You're right. You're absolutely right."

The waitress approached and set a water glass on the table in front of me and a tea for Barry.

After she was gone, I continued. "I'm not doing all this for Nicole. If it weren't for the kids, it would be much easier for me to hang her out to dry. I don't know. Even if the kids weren't in the picture I'd still want to help my sister, whether she wanted my help or not. I want to see her get her life straightened out. And if I could help her do that, I would."

"Of course you would." His voice was as gentle and soft as his gaze. "But it's obvious she's using you. Some people just don't want help. If they're not willing to accept some responsibility in straightening out their lives, sometimes you just have to wash your hands of the situation."

"I can never wash my hands of the situation. She's my sister."

He lifted a shoulder. "That does make it hard."

I sighed inwardly. There were some things you just couldn't talk about with some people. Barry didn't know Nicole. He didn't even know me that well yet. I couldn't expect him to understand the dynamic of my and Nicole's relationship. I had always taken care of her. Whether she was twenty-three or one hundred and three, I would always feel a little bit responsible for her.

"I do have some good news that isn't Nicole-related," I said.

The dimple appeared in his cheek as he rested his elbows on the table and closed the gap between us.

"I got saved at the service the kids did at the church the Thursday before Easter."

His smile tightened. "You did what?"

"I gave my life to the Lord."

Barry was the first person whose eyes didn't tear up at the news. I hadn't told Nicole yet…or most of the people at work. Did that mean I was a bad Christian? Shouldn't I be shouting from the rooftops everything the Lord had done for me?

"Ever since I started taking the kids to the preschool I felt the Lord dealing with me." I exhaled. "I grew up thinking the only kind of people who went to church were the ones who wanted to judge and disparage the rest of us. I let that prejudice keep me closed off from the world. And from God. But hanging out with those people…"

I sighed and leaned back in my chair. "I'm sorry. That makes me sound like a snob. It's just everyone at church and the preschool…" I pushed aside an image of Kyle. "…Miss Billie and the teachers and Angie…they really care about our kids. They care about us. They've shown me what love really is. I wanted to know how to do that. Now with God in my life, I know I can."

Barry's facial muscles hadn't moved the whole time I talked. Finally, he blinked. "I'm happy for you, Michelle."

I exhaled with relief. It felt good to finally talk about what had inspired me to seek a relationship with Jesus. "Really? I wasn't sure you'd understand."

"Why would you think that? I'm all for a person finding peace and joy in whatever works for them."

My heart sank a little. "I guess that means it doesn't work for you?"

"I didn't say that. Religion just isn't that important to me at this point in my life."

"Well, I don't really consider my personal relationship with Christ a religion."

His eyes lit up at something over my shoulder. "Ah, our dinner." The waitress set our plates in front of us. He inhaled deeply. "This looks much more appetizing that a V-8."

It felt a little strange to start our dinner without holding hands while Emma and Jonah recited a prayer over our meal that they'd learned at preschool. But that's what we did. I didn't bring up Nicole or the kids again during dinner. Barry's solution to my problem seemed a little cool and aloof, but maybe he was right. Nicole needed some tough love and I needed to stand up for myself. But washing my hands of my sister and her issues, that was something I didn't think I could ever do.

We didn't talk more about my newfound religion either. Barry accepted the news much like I expected my coworkers would. Like they really didn't care either way as long as I didn't preach to them in the break room.

The only thing I knew for sure was I didn't want to share more dinners with Barry. Whether the kids stayed or went, I didn't think he could ever understand what was important to me. I had always thought Kyle and I were too different to build a relationship together. Now I was beginning to wonder if I would ever find a man who understood me. Maybe Nicole was right. I was closed off and controlling and totally lacking in qualities that appealed to the opposite sex.

Nicole and I barely spoke over the weekend. The county hospital called and said they were short-handed and wondered if I could work Saturday or Sunday. I turned them down. I was terrified of coming home after work to an empty house. I'd have to face that possibility on Monday, but I wanted to put it off as long as possible. I didn't want to let her out of my sight for a minute.

She was still in bed Sunday morning when I got up and got ready for church. Emma woke while I was in the shower. "Is Jonah up?" I asked when I saw her in her own room getting dressed.

She shook her head. "He doesn't want to go to church today."

My first impulse was to go in there where he lay next to Nicole and drag him out of bed.

"In this house we go to church, young man," I heard myself saying. Then I remembered all the times Grandma used those exact words on me.

"He doesn't, huh?" I said instead. "When did he tell you that?"

"A little bit ago. I heard the shower running so I woke him up. He said he wanted to stay home with Mommy."

"What about you? Do you want to stay home with Mommy?"

She smiled innocently and shook her head. "No, I like church."

I tousled her hair. "Good. So do I."

Chapter Eighteen

"You're missing one this morning," Angie observed when she caught up with us after the service.

"Angie!" Emma squealed and rushed into her arms. "I miss you. When can we come back to your house to play?"

Angie knelt down to return the hug. "Whenever you want, Sweetie pie. I miss you too. Where's Jonah?"

"He stayed home with Mommy."

"Oh." Angie looked at me.

Emma smiled bashfully at Angie's daughters. Even though she and the older girls got along famously, she was always shy when first seeing someone outside of their usual surroundings. Fear of acceptance into the group, I supposed. I suffered from the same thing.

"Hi, Emma," Molly, the oldest one, said.

Emma hung back until I gave her a gentle nudge. Molly reached out and took her hand. Katie took the other. The three of them moved off to the fellowship hall where the children usually romped while their parents visited with other members of the church.

"I take it things are a little tense at home," Angie observed.

"Is it that obvious?" I asked.

"Pretty much."

"I didn't want to fight with Jonah this morning about coming to church, especially since he was in bed with his mother. She and I sort of don't see eye to eye on a few issues."

Angie squeezed my elbow. "I'm sorry to hear that, Michelle."

"Yeah, me too. It looks like I'm going to have to hire an attorney."

"Oh, no." Angie turned and looked through the crowd. "There's Chris." She waved at her husband and motioned for him to join us. "I've got a roast in the crock pot at home. Why don't you and Emma come home with us for dinner? We could talk there."

I would like nothing more, but I didn't know if it was a good idea. "I don't want to be an imposition, and Nicole will be wondering where we are."

"You know it's no imposition. You can call her on the way. Besides, you don't need her permission. Come on, Michelle. Kyle will be there."

"Then I'm definitely not going."

I was sure she was matchmaking, but she looked truly perplexed. "Why? You need to talk to someone, and who could offer better advice than a man of God?"

"Angie, this makes me really uncomfortable. I feel like all I do anymore is broadcast my troubles. I'm sure people have better things to do than listen to me moan about my family."

"Nonsense. That's what friends are for."

Chris appeared at her side. "Michelle and Emma are joining us for dinner, honey. Isn't that nice?"

Chris grinned broadly. "The more the merrier. Let's go. I'm starved."

Nicole didn't answer the phone when I called on my way to the car so I hung up and left her a text, telling her where we could be reached. Surely she wouldn't take off without Emma.

If she did…oh, I really would wring her neck. I comforted myself with a reminder she usually stayed up late watching old movies and then slept in. She probably hadn't rolled out of bed yet even though it was nearly one o'clock.

I had accepted the invitation so I could talk to Angie about what was bothering me, but my problems seemed distant seated around the table with Angie, Chris, their girls, Emma, and Kyle. The girls did most of the talking, telling us what had happened in Sunday School. We laughed and enjoyed the pot roast and each other's company. After dinner and store bought apple pie, the girls took Emma upstairs to their rooms to play.

I pushed my chair back. "Let me help with these dishes, Angie."

"No, no. Chris can help. You and Kyle go into the living room. You can talk in there."

From the smile on her face I wondered whether she was more interested in putting us together than for me to benefit from his Godly counsel. "But I—"

"Just go." She put her hand on my shoulder and turned me toward the door. "I can't think of a better person to talk to when you're having problems, except my Chris here," she added with a wink, "and you can't have him. Now go. We'll be in after the dishes are finished."

"There's no use arguing with her, Michelle," Kyle said. "She's formidable once she gets something in her head."

"Tell me about it," Chris said as he turned on the tap in the sink.

"Watch it, you two," Angie warned.

I followed Kyle into the seldom-used living room and sat down on the long, coffee-colored sofa. Kyle settled into an oversized recliner and put his hand on his stomach. "I think I overdid it in there. It isn't often I get such delicious home cooking."

"Me either. I'm afraid most of mine comes out of a box or the microwave."

We relaxed into our seats and listened to the sounds of the house. Dishes clinking and soft laugher came from the kitchen. Muffled sounds of the girls playing drifted down the stairway.

"Angie says things aren't going so great at home with Nicole," Kyle said after a few moments of silence.

I snorted. "That's the understatement of the year. We got into it pretty good the other day. I'm afraid I didn't handle things too well. I threatened Nicole with a lawyer."

"Ouch."

"I guess I have to follow through with it now. She's getting back together with her old boyfriend. He could show up any day." I leaned forward and gazed earnestly at Kyle. "I can't sit still and let her take the kids."

"Of course you can't."

"But what am I supposed to do? I don't have any legal right to them. And as mad as I am at Nicole right now, it doesn't seem right to alienate my own sister. I don't have much family to speak of. The only close relatives are Aunt Wanda and Uncle Jeb. Uncle Dewitt's next-door, but he's been a stranger to his own brothers and sisters since the day he was born. I love Nicole. I hate to think I'll do something to drive her away forever."

Kyle put his fingertips together like a teepee and rested his chin on them. "I don't envy the position you're in, Michelle. On one hand, if you fight Nicole for the kids, you could be saving them from a life of pain. On the other, even if you win, you may drive a wedge between you and Nicole that her kids will someday resent you for. Really, it's only you who can make this decision."

I slumped into the couch cushions. "That's not what I wanted to hear, Kyle. I wanted you to say something wise and profound that would put everything into perspective. I almost wish I could go back to last year when none of this was my concern."

"You don't mean that."

"Sometimes I do." I was instantly ashamed for putting my thoughts into words, but I needed to explain. "My life was so simple before all this happened. When all I had to worry about was me."

"Sometimes we're called to move out of our comfort zone for the sake of someone else. To sacrifice ourselves."

My temper flared. "You've got to be kidding. What do you think I've been doing for the past nine months? I've made nothing but sacrifices, and all I got in return was a lecture on what a jerk I am."

The patient, pious expression on his face only fueled my anger.

"Do you have any idea how much money I've spent on those kids since they got here? I'm not begrudging a dime of it," I hastened to add. "I want them to be safe and with people who care about them. Not like Nicole who let them fend for themselves. They miss the neighbor lady more than they do their own mother. I would never do anything like that to them. But, Kyle, come on. To imply I haven't sacrificed is insulting. I've sacrificed everything. Money, time, independence—everything I have. And what have I gotten back for it?"

He still wasn't talking. His expression remained unchanged. I had half a mind to reach over and change it for him.

"Nothing," I practically shouted in response to my own question. "That's what— absolutely nothing! I give and give and give and all I hear is how I should do more. That sacrifices have to be made."

I blinked tears away and crossed my arms over my chest, even though I knew I looked like a petulant child. I wouldn't cry. I wouldn't let him think his words had wounded me. They only demonstrated his ignorance of the situation. Most of the time when people made barbing comments, they had no idea what they were talking about. Well, now he knew.

Kyle leaned back in his chair, but didn't take his eyes off me. I wished he'd stop staring at me like that, as if he knew everything going on in my head. Just because he claimed to be a man of God didn't mean he could see into my soul.

When he finally spoke, it was so soft I had to strain my ears to hear. "Do you really think you haven't received anything in return?"

I blinked. "What? What are you talking about?"

"I'm talking about everything you received in the past nine months. I'm not suggesting you haven't given a lot to those kids. You've done more than most people would think about. You didn't have to accept them into your home that first day, and I commend you for doing it. But…you received a hundred times more than what you gave."

My anger boiled back to the surface. There he went again. Making his ignorance apparent. I opened my mouth to give him a piece of my mind. Then I remembered.

An image of Emma's face when she spotted the black chunky shoes on the store shelf during that first trip to Walmart flashed through my mind, followed in rapid succession by Jonah standing on stage singing his heart out. The two of them running across the field in pursuit of Gypsy. Emma perched on a kitchen stool, a smear of flour across her cheek, as she helped Aunt Wanda roll out homemade noodles. I saw Emma and Jonah on the bank with Uncle Jeb fishing. I could see them as plain as day in my mind's eye on Christmas morning when they came downstairs, squealing with delight and wonder at the packages under the tree.

Tears sprang to my eyes again. This time they were not out of anger or indignation.

Kyle got up from the chair and joined me on the couch. He took my hand. "Sometimes it's worth the risk of loving someone, Michelle."

I studied his face through the veil of tears and tried to decipher if he was referring to the kids, God or himself.

Everything was so simple a year ago. I went to work every day, was paid well for my efforts, took care of the farm and Gypsy. That was enough. I was happy. Fulfilled. I didn't miss having someone to come home to. I didn't have to clear my schedule to make room for another's needs. I ate what I wanted. I stayed up late to watch old movies if I wanted. I slept as late as I wanted on my days off and didn't have to worry about a little someone waking me up at seven demanding breakfast. The only wet towels I retrieved from the bathroom floor were mine. Compromise was not in my vocabulary.

I was living the dream.

So why was it so hard to face the possibility of things going back to the way they were?

"It's too hard," I admitted, my voice an unattractive croak. "It's easier never to have something than to try to get along without it once it's gone."

"Tell me about it."

I sniffed hard and looked at him. "What?"

"Nothing." He kneaded the back of my hand. I turned my hand over and curled my fingers around his.

It was several moments before he spoke. "You deserve to live your life however you want, Michelle," he said finally. "No one can tell you what you need to make you happy. You have a job you love. I know it brings you great satisfaction. The question is, is that all you want? Will that be enough when you look back on your life in fifty years? For millions of people, it is. No one will judge you if you decide that's all you need to make you happy. But does it? Is there nothing more you want?"

It almost sounded like he was talking about something other than Emma and Jonah. Nicole said I didn't know what it took to please a man. Maybe she was right. Maybe Kyle was still interested in me because he was too dumb to realize I was a controlling ice queen like Nicole said.

I pulled my hand away from his and pinched the bridge of my nose to quell the threat of tears. "I never thought about what I wanted before. All I thought about while growing up was moving past whatever stage I was in at the time. Getting it over with so I could move on to something else, hopefully something better. I never really enjoyed the moment I was in no matter what I was doing. Even in nursing school, though I loved everything about it and met some really great and interesting people, it was just another step I had to complete before I could move on.

"I thought after I had work experience, I could move up and earn more money. With more experience and education, I kept working toward higher seniority and better benefits. I never had many expenses living on the farm so my bank account kept growing. I remember thinking how cool it would be to save ten thousand dollars. That was my goal. It was such a big amount of money at the time. I thought if I could save that much, I'd be happy and secure. Then it was twenty. When I realized my IRA reached a hundred K, all I could think was, 'What good is a hundred thousand dollars going to do a person in this economy?' That was a pittance if something happened and I couldn't work till retirement."

I plucked a tissue out of a box on the end table. I looked into Kyle's kind face and smiled. "I never thought about having someone in my life. Relationships were so much work. Spouses, kids, mortgages. Who needed it? Whenever somebody would bellyache at work about their rotten marriage, credit card bills or whatever, I felt kind of superior, like, 'You should've thought of that before you got into this mess. You should be more responsible like me.' Life was just plain easier back then."

"But were you happier?"

I shrugged. "I told you, I didn't think about it."

"I don't believe you."

"Why would I lie?"

"I don't know. To protect yourself?"

"From what?"

"From opening your heart to someone."

He thought he had all the answers, but he didn't get it.

"That's not it at all. I told you, I was too busy moving ahead with whatever I was doing at the time. I never gave myself a chance to think about a relationship."

"Is that what you did with us?"

"What? When?" We didn't have a relationship. I couldn't deny it would be wonderful, and I had been thinking about it, especially since my eyes had been opened concerning Barry.

"In high school," he explained. "You always held back. You never truly opened up to me. After we broke up and I joined the Air Force, I realized I really didn't know you at all. You gave just enough of yourself to let people know they shouldn't expect anything more. That's where it stopped. You didn't open up to me or Nicole or anyone. You cheated us, but you cheated yourself more."

My jaw clenched. I was sick of people reminding me what a cold, unfeeling mess I was. I wasn't Grandma Catherine. I had feelings. I had love in my heart. I took care of strangers for a living. Hadn't I taken in my abandoned niece and nephew and given them everything their own mother withheld?

"If I held back, it was because no one, including you, ever made me feel like I could be myself. Any time I wanted to open up and show part of the real me, I was let know it wasn't a convenient time. I was always a burden to someone."

"Give the world a break, Michelle. You held back because you wanted to. You wanted to protect yourself. You said so yourself. You can keep on blaming the rest of us for what a rotten life you had or you can make the best of what you've got left. You don't have to feel like you're a reed beaten down by the wind anymore. You have a choice. It isn't too late to let someone love you."

My heart nearly stopped in my chest. What was he saying? I didn't really want to know.

"Yes, it is," I insisted. "It's too hard." I leaned forward in the chair and hugged my knees.

He pulled me against his chest and tilted my face up to meet his. "No. It's not."

My breath caught in my throat. I didn't want him to let go of me. I forgot about Angie and Chris in the kitchen and the girls playing upstairs. It was just the two of us. I prayed the moment wouldn't end.

"Michelle," he said, his voice husky. He brushed his lips across my cheek and my nose. I wanted to tangle my fingers in his hair and force his mouth to mine, but I didn't. What if he wasn't saying what I thought I saw in his eyes? What if he was still talking about the kids? Or Nicole? I wanted to believe he meant it wasn't too late for him and me. But I couldn't take the chance. I couldn't risk the rejection.

He was right. Nicole was right. I held the world at arm's length to protect myself. What choice did I have?

"Michelle," he repeated. He didn't speak again until I was looking into his eyes. "I love you. I've never stopped. Not in the last fifteen years. I realized it the first day you showed up with the kids at the preschool. I kept telling myself it was the memories of us I loved. Something lost in youth. It was easier believing that than accepting there could never be anything between us."

My heart didn't know what to think. All I heard was, 'I love you', and 'There can never be anything between us'.

I pulled out of his arms and cleared my throat awkwardly. I needed some distance between me and Kyle Swann. He loved me. So what? What good did love do? I would have preferred he not confess his feelings if there would never be anything between us.

I pulled away from him so I could reach the box of tissues. I took one and dabbed at my nose. "I—um, I need to find Emma..."

Kyle grabbed me before I could finish my sentence. He pulled me against him and pressed his lips to mine. I could feel the barely suppressed passion in his embrace. There was nothing chaste or cautious this time. I melted into his arms in shock. My head was reeling by the time he released me.

"Kyle, I..."

He put a finger over my lips. "Don't say anything. Except that you love me back."

I put my hands against his chest and pushed him away. Tears sprang to my eyes. "Why? Why do you want me to say that? It's bad enough you already did."

He yanked me back against him. His gaze was hard, almost angry. "Then tell me you don't. Either tell me you love me, or tell me you don't, but you have to say something."

"All right. I don't love you. Now, will you leave me alone?"

His gaze softened. "You're a terrible liar, Michelle," he whispered. Pain clouded his gray eyes. Pain I had put there.

I jerked away from him, angry with myself this time. "All right, fine. You win. But what difference does it make? You said yourself there'll never be anything between us. We're two different people. Nothing will change that."

He caught hold of my hands again. "God has changed it. Remember? You're a new creature. Old things have passed away and all things have become new. I don't know what kind of future either of us have, but I believe we have a chance to pursue it. If you want to, that is."

I couldn't think. What he said couldn't be that easy. Just apologize to God for denying Him my entire life, and then 'poof', my past was eternally forgotten? Even if God could forget it, I couldn't. I was an ice cold mess. I could never be the wife Kyle needed and deserved.

"Kyle, I don't know if I'm ready…"

"I don't know if I am either. All I know is how I feel right this moment."

When he pulled me into his arms again, I went willingly. I knew Angie and Chris were in the next room, their hands in the dishwater, within earshot of everything we said. And I didn't care.

Chapter Nineteen

Emma had her car seat straps off her shoulders and unhooked before I got the car into park. She knew I didn't like her to do it until the ignition was turned off. Today I didn't lecture. My mind was on other things.

She bounded out of the car as soon as I raised the back of my seat to let her out. She had an exciting afternoon and couldn't wait to rub it in Jonah's nose about all the fun he missed. I gathered my purse and Bible from the passenger side of the front seat and followed her into the house.

Emma had joined Nicole and Jonah in front of the TV in the living room by the time I got in the house. Hamburger grease was congealing in a skillet on the stove. I dumped my things on the kitchen table and went straight to the sink to run dishwater. While I was never thrilled to come home to a messy kitchen, at least cleaning up Nicole's mess gave me something to do as I processed my tumbling thoughts about Kyle.

I could still feel the heat of his lips on mine. My hands shook a little as I lowered a stack of plates into the dishwater. What was I going to do? So he loved me. That didn't change anything. My life was the same mess it had been this morning.

Yes, God had come into my life and changed me from the inside out, just like Kyle said. But my future happiness hung on the whims of my irresponsible sister who seemed to relish the control she had over me.

I didn't know how I'd survive if she walked out of this house tomorrow with Jonah and Emma. God might be there to turn to for the first time in my life, but my heart would still rip right out of my chest.

I thought of how Barry couldn't understand my conflicting anger and frustration for Nicole and my love and defense of her. Whether she needed tough love or not, I couldn't turn my back on her. As mad as I got, she was still my sister. And I couldn't ignore the needs of the kids.

I hadn't called Barry since the other night. He texted me twice after our dinner but I hadn't got back with him. I didn't know what to say. He was right in a lot of ways, but his words of advice had been hurtful and unfeeling. I wondered if he had anyone in his life he loved who sometimes treated him badly.

I would have to talk to him. Even if nothing worked out between Kyle and me, I couldn't be with Barry. With the warmth of Kyle's kisses on my lips, I had realized I would never be satisfied with a man I didn't love passionately. But passion and kisses aside, I needed someone who understood me. Or at least tried to understand. Life was tough. If you were going to share it with someone, it needed to be someone who knew what made you tick, at least most of the time.

After the dishes in the sink were washed, I started working my way around the kitchen with a wet sponge. The stove and countertops were splattered with grease, fingerprints and everyday grime from a family who never took the time to clean up properly. By the time I cleaned a swath to the refrigerator, I decided now was as good a time as any to defrost the freezer in the twenty-plus-year-old Kenmore.

I turned off the fridge and emptied the freezer's contents into my clean sink. Working in Grandma's domain got me thinking about her. What had happened to Catherine Barker in her youth that turned her into the woman we all knew? Had her husband, my grandpa, made her life so unbearable she had to defend herself by hiding behind a gruff façade? Or had she been like that since childhood? I never knew Grandma's parents and never heard her talk about them. I wondered if her mother was hard and critical and impossible to please no matter how hard she tried.

Something in Grandma's life must have contributed to her mean dislike for everyone and everything. Even Aunt Wanda, who had seemed a mirror image of her when I was a kid, had been a source of great irritation to Grandma. When Mom wasn't around, Grandma turned on Aunt Wanda. I had overlooked it at the time, thinking Aunt Wanda deserved it. But no one deserved to be put down over things they couldn't change. Now that I thought about it, even Violet took almost as much shame and ridicule as I did.

Actually Grandma's situation wasn't so different from mine, although I hated to admit it. Her children were raised and out of the house when the daughter she always expected to mess up her life with a loser came home with no husband and two kids. Two kids who ruined any chance she had for a peaceful old age. She didn't want to raise her grandkids. Even when Mom was here, much of the responsibility for three added people in the household fell on Grandma.

I couldn't excuse the way she handled it, especially how she took out her frustration on me, but I finally understood it a little. For the first time since Grandma passed away, I almost wished she were here to talk to. I suddenly wanted to know her better. I wanted her to know me better too. While we may never have become friends, with a little understanding and empathy, we might have at least been able to appreciate the other.

.... ❀ ....

On Monday morning I didn't say anything to Nicole about getting the kids up for school. I left at my usual time with the three of them still asleep, hoping she'd do the right thing but not expecting much.

During my lunch break I went out to my car and called my caseworker's office. She wasn't in so I left a brief message telling her I needed to speak with her. I left my number and asked that she please not contact me on my house phone.

I thought about calling Kyle just to hear his voice. I called the preschool instead and asked Billie if the kids were there. They had arrived at eight-thirty and just finished their lunch. At least that phone call lifted my spirits. If only I knew what Nicole was planning. I wanted to enjoy the memories of Kyle and our afternoon in Angie's living room, but I couldn't shake the eerie feeling something terrible was brewing inside Nicole's head.

When I came in from work Nicole thrust a slip of paper into my hand. "Call this number."

"Why? Who is it?"

"It's Mom. She wants to talk to you. She said she'd be home all night."

It took a moment to get over the shock. I hadn't talked to Mom in years. I didn't even have any idea where she was living. How had Nicole found her?

"Mom? Is everything all right? What does she want?"

"She's fine. She wants to talk to you."

My concern turned to suspicion. "Why? What did you tell her?"

"I told her what was going on around here."

"You mean how you left your kids here for eight months without letting us know if you were dead or alive? I bet she's so proud."

Nicole's lip curled in disgust. "She knows all about it, Michelle. Only unlike you, she is capable of understanding a person with problems."

"You're kidding, right? Wasn't it you just the other day telling me how she and Dad had ruined our lives by taking off on us? How we were both wrecks because of what they did."

"Everyone makes mistakes. We all deserve second and sometimes third chances."

I resisted an eye roll. I squared my shoulders. "Nothing that goes on in this house is any of *her* business. How'd you even find her? She hasn't had anything to do with this family for years."

Nicole raised a finger into the air. "Not exactly true. She and I have been in touch for quite some time. We both have come to the point in our lives to let go of the past and move forward. I've tried to understand what Mom was going through when she left us here with Grandma. Sometimes you have to be the bigger person, Michelle, and forgive."

"Forgive?" I spat. "You were the one telling me how your biggest dream was having parents who loved and were proud of you. Now you're telling me you've forgiven them."

"Life is too short to harbor bad feelings toward our own family."

"And life is really too short to be turning to our mother for advice."

"Are you going to call her or not?"

"No." I shoved the paper back into her hands. "I'm going to take a shower, and then I'm getting something to eat. It's been a long day. Have the kids eaten?"

"Aunt Wanda sent over a meatloaf."

"Thank heavens for Aunt Wanda." I started upstairs.

"Mom will be very upset if you don't call, Michelle," Nicole hollered after me. "You can't leave her waiting all evening."

"Let her wait," I hollered back. "I waited for her for eighteen years."

My conscience immediately pricked at my attitude. I stomped that much harder to drown out the little voice in my head. I didn't want to hear the familiar lecture on Christian charity.

The instant my phone rang, I knew it was Mom. It was nine-thirty. I was in my pajamas in the rocking chair in Grandma's old sewing room. Since I never sewed a stitch and had no inclination to start, I had converted the sunny room into a sort of study/retreat for myself. I had given Grandma's Singer to Aunt Wanda, but held onto the old pedal style one, much to the dismay of Uncle Bill's wife Mabel. She swore only someone who actually liked sewing should have the antique machine. I disagreed, and since possession was nine-tenths of the law, it sat in a sunny corner of my study. I cleaned it up and used it as a centerpiece for the room. I surrounded it with antique lamps and lace curtains. I threw an ivory, lace coverlet over the old rocking chair and set a porcelain doll in it when I wasn't occupying the spot. The room was the only one in the house that would make a robber think he had broken into a house that belonged to someone with grace and a flair for decorating.

I closed the Bible in my lap and pulled my phone out of my pocket. I resented Nicole giving Mom my number, but I didn't expect any less. I had been praying for the last little while for some forgiveness myself for Mom. I was born again, and it wasn't right to hold any ill feelings toward my own mother. I could already see honoring her was going to be a major test of my Christian faith.

Mom got right to the point. "What's this I hear about you taking Nicole to court to get her kids?"

"Nice to hear your voice too, Mom."

"Don't get smart with me, Michelle. Your sister called this morning all tore up over this. She said you're trying to steal her kids. You know her kids are all she has. If she lost them, she wouldn't have a reason to live."

"Kind of like you, Mom?"

"Michelle, there's nothing to be gained by dredging up the past. All we need to worry about is the here and now. I want you to get off your sister's back and stop threatening her with court. Your Grandma—God rest her soul—never saw a need to take me to court. She just did what needed done and kept it between the family."

"Things aren't that simple anymore, Mom. Kids get sick, but a doctor can't treat them without consent from a custodial parent. Emma starts school next year. I can't enroll her until I've done something legal. All I'm doing is trying to protect her and Jonah."

"Then let them go with their mother and mind your own business. Nicole told me Dean is coming to get her, and they're getting a place in the city."

"Did she also tell you Dean was the one who convinced her to dump the kids in my front yard in the middle of the night? Did she mention they didn't even have shoes on their feet? Or that she was passed out drunk and didn't know it had happened till she sobered up?"

"Stop being so melodramatic. Everything worked out fine, didn't it? Now she's back and ready to accept her responsibilities."

"What happens the next time she decides she isn't ready to be somebody's mom the way you did? What if she's a thousand miles away from here and it's too inconvenient to dump them on me? Where is she going to take them then, or are you worried about that? They're your grandchildren. I'd think you'd care about their well-being."

She sighed so hard into the phone it nearly vibrated in my hand. "I can see things haven't changed. I was hoping you'd mellowed with age, but I see that hasn't happened. You're still the one with all the answers. Little Miss Doomsday. Why can't you leave Nicole alone to make her mistakes? That's how we grow, Michelle."

Just once I wished I didn't have to be the adult in every conversation.

"We can't leave Nicole to her own devices, Mom," I growled into the phone. "She has two kids who depend on her. She's already proven she can't be trusted to put their needs in front of her own. I, for one, won't risk giving her another chance."

"Well, I've already decided to send her the money to defend herself. I'm not going to make her accept the help of some public defender when keeping her kids is at stake."

"Where are you, Mom? I didn't recognize the area code. For someone so interested in her daughter's life all of a sudden, you sure don't keep in touch."

"Because I can't talk to you, Michelle. I gave up on trying to be a mother to you long ago. You're so full of yourself and this grudge you won't let go of, I just can't take it."

I stared at the phone in my hand, incredulous. Surely I'd misunderstood.

"You gave up trying to be my mother long ago? Nineteen years to be exact! You walked out on Nicole and me when I was fourteen. Fourteen, Mom. No explanation. No apologies. Just cowardice—just like Dad."

I was so mad I wanted to throw something, preferably at her head.

I checked my anger and tried to calm down. If I told her I wasn't the same, that I'd been born again and was a new creature, she would laugh in my face. And rightly so by the way I was acting.

"I'm not even going to dignify that with a response," she retorted. "What happened, happened—period. If you want to spend your life eaten up with bitterness, that's your choice. But I won't let you drag your sister down with you. As far as the kids being better off with you, I'm not so sure about that. Nicole has her faults, but at least she is willing to admit them. You see nothing but what suits you. I feel sorry for you, Michelle."

Her end of the phone went dead. I couldn't believe she hung up on me.

Chapter Twenty

Tuesday morning I was in front of the bathroom mirror capturing my still damp hair into a ponytail when Nicole pecked on the door casing and stuck her head into the room. She looked as bedraggled as I felt.

"I didn't sleep very well," she said. "Can you drop the kids off at preschool on your way to work?"

I swallowed my frustration at the thought of how long it would take me to get them up and ready to go and not be late for work. Whatever the aggravation and rushing around, I was relieved they were going today, and at their usual time. They hadn't arrived at the right time for as long as Nicole had been home.

I maneuvered my ponytail into place. "Sure. Are they still asleep?" As if I didn't know the answer already.

"I think so." She turned and stumbled, still bleary-eyed back to bed.

I finished up in the bathroom and hurried across the hall to get them moving.

As expected I arrived at the preschool with barely enough time to drop the kids off and still get to work a moment before

I was due to clock in. Emma and Jonah had been sleepy and cranky at the house, but now that they were near the school, they were excited about arriving at the same time as their friends instead of walking in as the others were finished breakfast, or worse, when class time was half over.

I groaned inwardly when I saw Barry's car sitting in the parking spot just outside the main door. I slid into the spot next to it and ushered the kids out of the backseat and into the preschool. He had just turned away from the sign-in sheet when we walked in.

His face lit up. "Hi, guys," he said to Emma and Jonah. "It's good to see you here on time for a change."

I bristled. "We do the best we can."

Emma and Jonah ran to the hooks to hang up their jackets, oblivious to any tension.

Barry looked taken aback. "I was just kidding," he said.

"Hey. Kisses," I reminded Emma and Jonah as they turned toward the play area. I wondered if Nicole bothered to kiss them goodbye when she dropped them off.

They dutifully exchanged kisses and hugs while keeping their eyes turned toward the fun going on in the play area. After they scampered away I turned my attention to Barry. We headed for the door together. "I'm sorry. I'm just in a hurry. I didn't realize I had to drop the kids off this morning."

He didn't roll his eyes, but I could tell it took a lot of effort not to. "So I guess that means Nicole is still at your house."

I wished I hadn't said anything. "She's still there. The kids are happy."

We reached our cars. I took my keys out of my pocket.

Barry went around his car and looked at me over the top of it. "Just because kids are happy doesn't always mean something is good for them."

I didn't know what to say. He was right again, but that didn't mean it applied in every situation. Was this what Mom had been talking about last night? I was so sure I was right and the situation was black and white, I was incapable of seeing the other side of the coin?

"It was good seeing you, Barry. I gotta run."

I opened my door and dropped into the bucket seat.

"I didn't mean to offend you," he said.

"I know. I'm running late."

I flipped my hand up to wave goodbye and put the car into reverse. In the rearview mirror I watched him climb into his car. From the distance I couldn't tell if he believed me or not."

My phone buzzed almost immediately to alert me to a text. I knew without looking it was from him. I didn't check to make sure. Whatever he had to say could wait. I wasn't kidding about running late, and I didn't have time to defend myself to a man who couldn't try to understand my situation.

Just as I grabbed a yogurt out of the mini-fridge in the nurses' station my phone buzzed. My heart sank. I didn't want to check the text, but I couldn't keep avoiding Barry. I was sure he wanted to apologize again for any misunderstanding this morning. There hadn't been a misunderstanding. We were just two people at two different places in our lives. I didn't know if we'd ever be at the same place. I wasn't sure if he thought I was stringing him along, but it became more apparent with each encounter that we weren't a good match. I didn't want to waste more of his time, and I kept thinking he was wasting mine.

Kyle had called me Sunday night to ask how I was since I hadn't gone to the evening service. I quickly explained there was so much drama around the house with Nicole back I was hesitant to leave more often than I had to. I didn't want to argue with the kids about going to church, but I didn't want them to think all they had to do was pout and dig in their heels and they'd got their way. So I hadn't brought it up at all.

The excuse satisfied Kyle. He made some sympathetic sounds and told me he hoped to see me soon. I didn't tell him the other reason I hadn't gone was I didn't think it was appropriate to attend church with the sole purpose of making googly eyes at the pastor. I'd never been good at hiding my emotions. I didn't want everyone there to know I was nuts about him.

It felt good to finally accept that I loved Kyle. It was amazing to know he loved me back, but I still wasn't sure what it meant. None of it changed who we were or meant there could be anything between us. I wasn't even sure Kyle wanted anything to develop. We were so different. Not to mention set in our ways. At least I was, and I was certain he was too.

In romance novels love was always strong enough to overcome any obstacle. Differences like ours ratcheted up the tension in a book, but I wasn't sure how they were resolved in real life.

I swung the refrigerator door shut as I slid my phone out of my scrubs pocket. My breath caught in my throat, and what I assumed was a dopey grin covered my face.

Kyle.

Thinking of you, he wrote. *Call me when you get a chance.*

My fingers were moving across the keypad before I even finished reading his text.

Unfortunately he didn't pick up.

"Hi, Kyle," I said breezily into his voice mail as if my heart wasn't trying to pound its way out of my chest. "Just got your text. It's crazy here at work. I'll try to get back with you later. Maybe on my way home."

I hung up, hoping I didn't sound desperate or giddy. But Kyle probably already realized I was both those things. I couldn't wait till the ride home.

At the end of my shift my phone was in my hand checking for messages before I even stepped onto the elevator. I didn't want to be one of those annoying people who couldn't spare a glance at the world around her because her attention was constantly on her phone, but tonight I couldn't help it.

It only took one disappointing moment to see Kyle hadn't called back. My thumb hovered over his number for a moment before I decided I wouldn't call. Not right away anyway. Yes, we had professed our love for each other, but we hadn't made any moves toward a relationship. He was still the pastor of my church, and I was his old girlfriend from high school. Whether we were head over heels in love or not, that alone couldn't bridge the abyss between us.

I climbed behind the wheel of my Mazda and hoped he'd still be at church when I got there to pick up the kids. That way I could see him without it looking like I was going out of my way to see him. Michelle Hurley might grovel to her sister in order to see her niece and nephew, but she would not go chasing after a man.

I still had a little pride.

Unfortunately my pride wasn't as resolute as I liked to think. My heart soared at the sight of Kyle's truck at the other end of the building. I had freshened my lipstick at the last traffic light. Now I scrubbed my finger across my teeth in case I had got any on them in my haste.

I took a deep breath to calm the pounding in my chest. "You're not walking into his office," I said aloud inside the car. "You're not going to look pathetic. The only way you'll see him is if he sees you and comes over."

I squeezed the steering wheel as I pulled into an empty slot halfway between the preschool door and the portico over the church's main entrance. I hoped no one would wonder why I parked so far away from the preschool doors when there were plenty of empty spots right in front.

I was halfway out of the car when I saw movement down the sidewalk. My heart took a little tumble. Kyle stood at the far corner of the building talking with an older man I didn't know. Based on the other man's clothes and the fact he was standing in the mulch surrounding a grouping of bushes, I assumed he was a groundskeeper or landscaper.

I thought about jumping up and down or yelling to get Kyle's attention. But I wasn't going to look desperate. Instead I headed very slowly toward the glass doors of the preschool.

I was nearly to the doors—and trying to think of a valid reason to go back to my car, thus increasing my chances of getting noticed—when Kyle called my name. I nearly did a fist pump in the air.

I turned casually and looked around as if I didn't know exactly where he was. I couldn't help grinning when I saw him headed my way. I started toward him and we met under the portico.

He stuffed his hands in his pockets and rocked back on his heels. "Here to get the kids?"

My grin widened. So I wasn't the only one trying to appear casual and aloof, and failing miserably. "Why else would I come to this end of town?"

He removed one hand from his pocket and brushed my chin with his index finger. "I thought you might be here to see me."

I sniffed. "I see you all the time."

"Is that right? I never see you."

"Maybe it's intentional."

"It better not be. If you see me, I expect you to stop and say hi."

I leaned around him to look at the man in the bushes. "You looked busy."

"I'm never too busy for you." His hand slid down my arm and caught hold of my hand.

I hoped he couldn't see the flush on my cheeks in the shade of the portico. "Are you flirting with me, Pastor?"

He frowned. "If you have to ask, I must not be doing it very well."

I couldn't believe I was standing here with Kyle Swann, feeling as silly and tongue tied as I had the first time I saw him freshman year. I took a trembling breath for his benefit. "Oh, you're doing it very well."

"Glad I haven't lost my touch." He glanced at his watch. "Do you have a little time to get something to drink in my office?"

I looked at my watch. The preschool would be open for another forty-five minutes. "I don't think the kids will miss me for a few minutes," I said. "But we'll have to make it quick."

"Of course."

He held open the door and I stepped into the cool, hushed interior of the church. I moved ahead of him toward his office. The secretary's desk in the outer office was empty. I wasn't sure what time she left or how many days a week she came in. I was pretty sure it wasn't a full time position, but I'd never asked. I was always more interested in Kyle when I was on this end of the building.

Kyle opened the mini-fridge and handed me a bottled water without asking what I wanted. There probably wasn't much of a selection in there anyway, which was fine with me. Instead of circling his desk to sit in his office chair, he dropped into the chair next to mine.

"How's everything at home?"

No time for niceties, I supposed, or maybe he had been worrying about me.

"Mom called the other night."

His eyebrows arched. "Your mother? Wow. How long has it been since you heard from her?"

"Years. She only called because Nicole called to tattle that I'm being mean. She told me to stop trying to run Nicole's life."

Kyle shook his head in sympathy. Or maybe it was disbelief. "I'm sorry to hear that, Michelle. What about your dad? Do you ever hear from him?"

I stared at him for a moment trying to identify the person he was talking about. "Dad? You mean my dad?"

He chuckled. "Well, I'm certainly not talking about my dad."

I shook my head to clear the cobwebs. "I'm sorry. I just haven't thought about him in even longer than I thought about Mom. I don't...I haven't...I don't even know if he's still alive."

I was surprised how hard it was to say out loud. I hadn't thought of Dad in so long, it hadn't crossed my mind until this moment he might not even be living. Did he ever think of Nicole and me and wonder if we were alive and healthy and happy? Would he be sad if he found out we weren't?

I thought about the life he had now. There could be a new family, a new wife to replace the one he walked out on. He may even have another daughter. Though I hadn't given him much thought in years, it still stung to think I had missed out on so many years with him, and he had missed out on so many with me. He didn't know what I did for a living. He didn't know how tall I was or that I had outgrown most of my freckles or that I was the fastest girl on my high school track team. Insignificant things to be sure, but stuff most parents cared about.

Did he care that he didn't know anything about Nicole or me? Did he ever wish he could fill in the blanks?

Kyle didn't say anything for a minute. He twisted the cap off his water bottle and took a long drink. I followed suit. I hated it that my hands shook a little and I was suddenly dry mouthed.

After my drink, I licked at the moisture on my top lip. "I can't believe the only time you drag me in here is to talk about my dysfunctional family."

A corner of his mouth twitched upward. "I didn't drag you in here."

I forced my gaze back to his eyes and away from his mouth. "I don't really want to talk about my parents. Neither of them mean anything to me."

He put the cap back on his water and set it on the desk. "Of course they do. They're your parents."

"I'm sorry, Kyle, but I don't have the same relationship with them that you do with yours. They abandoned me when I needed them most. For years, they made me think their leaving was my fault. There's no worse thing to do to a kid."

I stopped talking and shook my head. "There's no point in even talking about it. It doesn't even matter anymore."

"It does matter, Michelle. It always will." He put his hand on my chin and brought my face around to his. "I want you to do me a favor."

I stiffened. I could pretty well guess what he was going to ask.

"I want you to think about forgiving them."

Forgiveness. Nicole had used the same word on me the other night. It sure was easy enough to tell other people how they should feel about stuff.

I exhaled, tired of talking before I even started. "I have forgiven them. I'm fine. I've moved on. I barely give either of them a second thought."

"Moving on isn't the same as forgiving them."

I knew he was right, but I didn't want to think about it right now. I didn't want to ruin our few moments together thinking about my parents and how they failed me my entire life.

"Moving on is all I'm ready to do right now." I straightened my shoulders. The room suddenly felt very small and tight. I glanced at my watch. "It's nearly time to get the kids. They haven't been to preschool for this long in weeks. I'm sure they're ready to go home by now."

He took my hand. I wondered if I'd ever get used to the way his casual contact warmed me all the way to my toes.

"I'm sorry, Michelle. I don't mean to push you." He sat back in his chair a few inches, giving me enough space to take a breath. "I didn't invite you in here for a counseling session. I love you. I want you to be happy. Free. Free of all the weight you've been carrying around for so long. I hope you'll let me alleviate some of that someday."

My heart swelled. What I wouldn't give to let someone else shoulder the burden for a while. But I knew what Kyle meant. He was talking to me like a pastor talked to a congregant, not the way a man talked to the woman he loved. It was his job to teach me how to lay my burdens at the cross and leave them there.

I really wanted to, and someday I would. Just not today.

I reached for his hand. "I appreciate that. But I'm just not ready. Everyone in my family has used me all my life. I finally feel a connection with Aunt Wanda. I have the kids and it's like I'm part of a real loving family relationship for the first time. I don't want to ruin it by thinking about how Grandma resented me or how Mom and Dad so easily walked away from being my parents."

"I don't want you to think of that either. I want you to someday think of them with love and patience and understanding."

I thought of what Mom said the other night about how she couldn't talk to me because I always had to have my way. If she thought about the ludicrousness of the statement, she'd take it back. I'd never had my way in anything. I never asked to be abandoned on Grandma Catherine's porch. I never asked Mom and Dad to walk out of my life. I hadn't even asked Nicole to leave Emma and Jonah under my lilac bushes.

But that part had worked out better than I ever could've imagined. I loved those two kids more than I thought any person could love another. I would willingly lay down my life for them. I was better off now that the kids were in my life.

With Kyle staring at me, I considered how Mom and Dad had shaped me into the person I was, even if they hadn't intentionally done so. Leaving me with Grandma had made me strong and resilient. My life had never been easy, yet I had been able to get through every situation life threw at me, and come out the other side stronger than ever. There was no way to tell what would've happened if Mom and Dad had stayed together. They obviously hadn't loved each other. For the first time in my life I considered how I might have turned out had I grown up in a home with two parents who only stayed together for the sake of Nicole and me.

Sure, leaving us had not been the right choice, but staying out of obligation wouldn't have worked out much better.

I looked into Kyle's eyes. "I'll think about it. And I'll pray about it," I added quickly.

He squeezed my hand and kissed the end of my nose. "Good. You've got a long road ahead of you, Michelle, and I want to be here for you."

I didn't know what to say. I couldn't remember anyone ever being there for me. I almost couldn't wrap my brain around the concept.

He took my hand. "Are you free tomorrow night? I haven't seen much of you. Not since…"

He arched his eyebrows. I knew what he was thinking of. Since Sunday dinner at Angie's when he told me he loved me. When I told him I loved him back.

I wasn't working at the county hospital this weekend. I had told Meg in scheduling I wouldn't be available for the foreseeable future. Not as long as Nicole was in town.

My gaze softened. I watched as his tanned fingers entwined in mine. "I'm free as a song. If Nicole isn't around to watch the kids for whatever reason, I'll get Aunt Wanda to do it."

"Good." The word was soft and breathy and made my insides go soft. "I'd like to have you to myself for a while."

I giggled nervously. "I trust your intentions are honorable, Pastor."

His gaze pierced mine with blue clarity. "Always."

Holding my gaze, he leaned toward me. I followed suit and wondered what had taken him so long. After a long kiss with only our mouths touching, we sat back in our chairs. I desperately needed another drink of water, but I didn't want him to notice my hands shaking. I couldn't believe he had such an effect on me.

"I should get the kids. They'll be wondering what's keeping me."

We stood up together. Kyle put his hand on my elbow. "Can I walk you up front?"

I considered it for a moment. "You better not. I don't want the kids associating us together too much too soon."

He cocked his head and gave me an innocent look. "Too soon for what?"

"Leave me alone."

I started to step away. He tightened his grip on my elbow. "I love you, Michelle," he whispered.

"Why?" I whispered back. "I'm a mess."

"You're my mess."

Chapter Twenty-One

I heard a car outside and hurried to the window. It had been three days since my phone call from Mom. On the days I worked I couldn't get to the mailbox to see what came before Nicole got to it first. As far as I knew there had been no money sent. I finally got hold of my caseworker who suggested I hire a lawyer. I had a good case, she assured me. It was only a matter of time before a judge awarded me custody. Sadly the wheels of justice moved slowly.

I couldn't shake the dread each time I thought of suing my own sister. I prayed every night for God to reveal to me if I was making the wrong move. I wasn't sure if God wasn't speaking or I wasn't hearing, but it seemed to me there was no other way. I just wished it were someone else doing it.

I never answered Barry's text from the other day. He had apologized and assured me he hadn't meant to stick his nose where it didn't belong. I wasn't sure if I believed him or not. I couldn't overlook the similarities in his insistence that he knew the right way for another person to handle their problems and my own. Even though I was offended that Mom was dropping everything to help Nicole when she had never lifted a finger on my behalf, my way of looking at things wasn't always necessarily the right way.

I slipped into my flip-flops and hurried to the road. I hoped Nicole wasn't watching from the window. I wanted time to sort through the mail before she accused me of invading her privacy, even though this was my house and all the mail expected bore my name.

I flipped through the mail quickly. An electric bill and four pieces of junk mail for the kids to play with. Last of all, a letter addressed to Nicole Hurley. No return address, yet I still recognized Mom's handwriting after all this time. She obviously didn't want me to know where to find her.

As if I wanted to.

Wrong. I did want to. That's why I looked for a return address. Even after everything we said the other day, and all the years with no contact whatsoever, part of me wanted to know where my mother was—where to send a Christmas card...or a wedding invitation.

I turned the letter toward the sun to see what I could find out about its contents. The envelope bore a faded Las Vegas postmark. One question answered. I squinted against the sunlight and made out the imprint of a personal check partially exposed between a fold of paper. I could imagine the quickly scrawled note wrapped around the check.

"You take this money, Nicole, and make your high and mighty sister eat her words. She thinks she should always get her way. We'll show her this time she doesn't rule the universe."

How much money had Mom sent? Where did she get it? I didn't know if she was working or living with someone or married again. No one had mentioned her in years. I almost regretted not asking when I had her on the phone.

"So, Mom, how's work? Anything good on the horizon? Do you have a special man in your life?"

Questions typically unnecessary when talking with one's mother.

I tilted the envelope to one side and then the other. I could make out a scrawled signature. I glanced anxiously at the house and then tapped the envelope against my free hand to make the check slide out of the letter. Another quick peek and a few zeros became visible. I pinched the envelope between my finger and thumb with my right hand and tapped the opposite corner hard against my left hand. I glanced again at the house before raising the envelope over my head.

A one followed by five slanted zeros came into view—one thousand dollars! I'd never known my mother to have that kind of money at one time, especially money she could afford to give away to a very dumb cause.

Bitterness filled my heart. Mom could come up with a thousand dollars for Nicole to fight me in court against the best interests of her own grandchildren, but she couldn't send me one dime the whole time I was struggling through nursing school.

Once near the end of my final year when money was especially tight, Mom showed up on the doorstep and stayed for a few weeks. It was the first time we'd heard from her in two and a half years. I was thrilled to have my mother back during a very stressful time in my life. Within hours though, I realized her presence was not going to alleviate any stress. She was one more responsibility added to my already long list.

Besides tuition, books and living expenses, I had a licensing test coming up that was going to cost me an extra two hundred dollars. At the time two hundred dollars may as well have been twenty thousand.

I got up my nerve and approached Mom. I sat her down and painted a bleak picture. I left out the part about how, if she thought about it, she sort of owed me since she hadn't paid one nickel toward my rearing in five and a half years. It was implied. I wasn't through painting my picture when she saw what was coming and interrupted me. By the time she finished her own hard luck story, I wished I had money to give *her*. I never asked her for money again.

Yet somehow she managed to scrape together a thousand dollars for Nicole.

I headed through the house and out to the back porch where Nicole was reading a paperback she'd found on the bookshelves. I dropped the letter into her lap without a word and turned and went back into the house. Rude and childish, yes, but I couldn't bring myself to speak to her. If Mom had been here, I wouldn't have spoken to her either.

That night I heard Nicole in the kitchen whispering into her phone. When I walked in, she quickly ended the conversation. I was over my aggravation at Mom for sending the money. Mom was simply being a mother. Seeing what she wanted to see. She so desperately wanted to believe Nicole would get her life together and do the right thing by her kids it was worth a thousand dollars to make it happen.

As far as Nicole was concerned, I imagined she saw things the same way. Her intentions were good. At this moment, she didn't plan on dumping her kids off again on an unsuspecting relative or friendly neighbor. Consequently, it blew her away that I was being so hard on her when she wanted nothing more than her family together again.

I pulled out a kitchen chair and sat down to face her. "I don't want either of us to waste money arguing over your kids in a courtroom in front of a bunch of strangers," I said. "Why don't we forget the whole thing?"

Her eyes widened in surprise. She opened her mouth to speak. I could see she misunderstood me, so I hurried on. "You signed the kids over to me once. Do it again. This time do it with my attorney. Let's make it permanent."

Her eyes narrowed and her jaw clenched.

It was too late to stop now. I kept talking. "You will always be Emma and Jonah's mother, but whether we admit it or not, they're better off living here. Just because I have permanent custody doesn't mean anything will change. You'll still be Mom and I'll be Aunt Shell. You'll be welcome to come for holidays or to visit anytime you want. It doesn't have to get complicated. We need to put our egos aside and think of the kids."

I presented my case as well as I could. I wasn't sure how smart it was to offer an open invitation for holidays and unannounced visits. I could see it causing all kinds of problems down the road, but for the first time since deciding to keep the kids here, I felt a peace in my spirit. This is the way things were supposed to be. Not perfect, but doable.

This had to be what real Christian charity felt like. Not the ideal situation for myself, but a sacrifice that put another's needs ahead of my own. A true sacrifice meant doing something for someone even while knowing there would be no recompense.

Nicole didn't see it that way.

"What an ego you have, Michelle," she said. Her cheeks flushed and her sparkling blue eyes flashed. "It's a wonder you can fit through a doorway with that big head of yours. You are so sure a judge will take your side over mine. It hasn't even crossed your mind he might actually think children are better off with their mother."

"Yes, it has. I know how…"

She raised her hand in front of her and cut me off, her anger building steam. "I can't believe you actually have the nerve to sit here and tell me you're doing this for the kids' own good, or even mine. We both know you'll do anything to prove how right you are and how wrong I am. I am their mother. Yes, I've made some mistakes. But I'm willing to try and do better. I'm not a drug addict. I've never been in jail. You won't have as easy of a time as you think. I'm not saying I shouldn't have to pay some kind of penance for what I did, but I'm paying it every day. I want my kids back. I'm ready to take care of them."

She slumped into the kitchen chair next to mine. "I'm going to do whatever it takes to get on with my life, a life which includes my kids." She put her arms on the table and dropped her head into them so I couldn't see her face.

My stomach tightened. She looked so destitute, so defeated. Had I judged her too harshly? Just because I thought the kids were better off here didn't necessarily mean Nicole couldn't provide a decent life for them either.

The kids had never been in real danger when Dean left them under the lilac bushes. It was summertime. The farm was located down a quiet back road with little traffic. He knew Gypsy's barking would rouse me within minutes and I'd find the kids before any real harm came to them. It hadn't been the most responsible way to handle the situation but not as bad as what other children went through everyday. Maybe the sacrifice God was calling me to make was to let the kids go.

Is this what you want me to do, God? I prayed silently as I watched my sister's shoulders tremble while she cried.

I got up and went around the table and put my hand on the back of her head. "Nicole," I said through my own tears, "I never meant to hurt you."

She raised her head to look at me, her eyes hopeful.

"I won't fight you," I continued before I could change my mind. "Whatever you want to do, I'll help you out as best I can."

She gasped. "Do you mean it? You won't fight me in court? Oh, Michelle."

Her chair scraped against the cracked linoleum as she jumped up and wrapped her arms around me. She pulled me into a hard hug. "Thank you. You don't know what this means to me. You actually believe in me. That's the best part."

I wasn't sure I did, but I hugged her nonetheless. "I've always believed in you."

Thinking her own family thought of her as a loser had to have taken its toll on her. No wonder she had no confidence in herself and allowed men to talk her into anything. None of us could really understand the burden carried by another.

Was I doing the right thing? I still believed the kids were better off with me. That didn't mean they weren't meant to live with their mother. Maybe Nicole had learned from her mistakes and was ready to move on.

I didn't need to control everything. Sometimes there were more important things than being right.

"I'm sorry," I murmured into Nicole's hair. I stepped back to look into her eyes. "I felt really put upon when the kids appeared out of the blue. I never thought about having kids, especially someone else's. It took a lot of time to realize they were a blessing instead of a curse."

I dropped my arms and chuckled. "I had to learn in a hurry how to be somebody's mother. In the beginning I didn't want to learn. I wanted my freedom back. The next thing I knew, I couldn't bear the thought of you coming to get them."

"I'm sorry, Michelle. I was wrong to put this on you with no warning or consideration for what it was like for you."

"I'm the one who's sorry. I was wrong. By the time you got back, I was so sure I knew what was going on in your head, I wasn't willing to listen to what you were saying."

"It's all right, Michelle. I put you in a terrible position. It's my own fault you didn't react the way I wanted you to."

"So, what do we do now?"

"Well, Mom sent me some money. I guess I should give it back to her since I won't need to hire a lawyer."

"That's between you and Mom. Whatever you decide to do is fine with me. I wish you would stay here long enough for Emma's preschool graduation in a couple weeks though."

"Well—" Her voice trailed off, and she looked away. "I'd really love to see her graduate. I know she's put a lot of work into it and everything, but Dean is coming. I don't know what he'll want to do."

I wanted to tell her Dean didn't deserve any say in the situation. This concerned the family, of which he had no part. I bit my tongue. My perception of the man had nothing to do with whether Nicole wanted to include him in her life or not. While I saw nothing redeemable in him, it wasn't my decision to make.

From now on I would keep my opinions to myself unless they were specifically requested and stop trying to run Nicole's life. We began preparing dinner together, chatting like old friends for the first time since her return. I pushed my reservations to the back of my mind. I wanted Nicole to be happy. I needed to give her the chance to find happiness, even if it wasn't my version of happiness. It was her life. She could live it the way she wanted, and I could get back to mine.

I thought of Kyle and the possible future we might have together. Without Emma and Jonah here, we would be free to pursue whatever we wanted.

Somehow my freedom didn't hold the allure it once did.

I prayed I hadn't made a grave mistake.

Chapter Twenty-Two

Saturday was my thirty-fourth birthday. If I had my way it would pass unnoticed like every birthday before it. Nicole and the kids had other plans. Emma and Jonah woke me up by bouncing on my bed and singing off key. Nicole stood in the doorway smiling. I gave her a nasty look. After breakfast she sent Jonah and me to the store for ice cream and hotdogs—the kids' menu—so she and Emma could bake a cake and decorate the house in honor of my ongoing journey into decrepitude.

I ran a few errands while I was out and did the weekly grocery shopping. With Nicole in the house, it seemed all I did was shop for food. But Jonah and I had a good morning together. I hadn't spent much time with him since his mother came back.

I tried not to grimace when the cashier gave me the total for our groceries. While sliding my debit card through the terminal and thinking this might be the last time my bank account would take such a hit, I saw Barry walking past the bank of registers on his way to the exit.

I stiffened. The polite response would be to call out. I really didn't want to talk to anybody, him especially. My emotions were already a little raw and uncertain with everything going on with the kids. I wasn't in the right frame of mind to make idle chitchat, or worse, explain why I hadn't returned his last few calls.

Before I could decide one way or the other, he looked over and saw me.

He stopped at the end of the register next to my rapidly filling cart. "Hey, Michelle. Hey, Jonah."

Jonah grinned and waved. Barry eyed my overflowing cart. "Did you need to stock up on every item they carry?"

"Pretty much." I motioned toward the bags he held in each hand. "It looks like you weren't being too greedy."

He lofted the two bags and grinned. "This is all it takes when it's just me for the weekend."

I nodded, remembering those days as if they'd been a lifetime ago. They might be back in my future before I was ready. The bagger set the last bag into my cart and thanked me for shopping there. I smiled in return and pushed my cart into the aisle next to Barry.

"You should come to our party," Jonah piped up.

I jerked my head around to look at the little boy at my hip. How was I going to get out of this?

Barry arched his eyebrows in question.

"The kids are throwing me a little party," I said.

"It's Aunt Shell's birthday," Jonah explained. "We're gonna have hotdogs and cake."

"Not together," I clarified. "It's the kids' menu."

Barry smiled and bumped my arm with his elbow. "Well, let me wish you a happy birthday."

"Thanks."

"Can you come?" Jonah asked again. He looked back at me for confirmation as I maneuvered my cart through the crowd with Barry keeping pace. "Right, Aunt Shell? You gotta have lots of people to have a good party."

I gave up trying to formulate an answer and cocked my head apologetically at Barry.

He took the hint. He shifted the bags to one hand and dropped his free hand on Jonah's shoulder. "Sorry, buddy. I can't make it today. But thanks for inviting me."

Since your aunt obviously wasn't going to, he probably added at me.

Jonah appeared to take it harder than I did. We reached the sliding exit doors. Barry hung back to let me and Jonah and my overloaded cart go out first. I looked at him over my shoulder. "It's just a little family thing."

"Sure, I get it. With your sister and everything, you need time as a family."

I swallowed a sigh. He didn't get it. He never would.

"I left you a couple messages," he said, his tone mildly accusing.

I had been wrong to ignore him. If I didn't want to see him anymore, I should've come out and said it instead of pretending I hadn't gotten the messages until he finally stopped calling.

"I'm sorry I didn't get back with you. There's just been a lot going on at my house."

I didn't want to make excuses for not calling him, but I felt I owed him a little explanation since I'd been rude. "I haven't really wanted to talk to anyone about it."

That much was true.

"I appreciate that," he said. "Listen, I'm sorry about the other day. I didn't mean to be insensitive about your situation."

"I know."

I think he really meant it. Barry was the kind of person to say what he believed without sugar coating it. Maybe he was too much like me.

"It's really been bugging me," he continued. "I wanted to apologize for being a jerk. I had no right to talk bad about your family."

I managed a little laugh. "I wouldn't say it was that bad."

"I would. And I am sorry."

"Thanks," I repeated. To be honest, so much had happened in the last few days, I couldn't even remember everything he said. I hadn't given Barry more than a passing thought since I last saw him, but it would be insensitive to admit that.

"I'm the one who was acting like a jerk by not returning your calls and making you wonder if you hurt my feelings or not. Seriously, it's fine. In fact, Nicole and I sort of made up the other night."

"What does that mean?"

I lifted a shoulder. It wasn't an easy thing to explain to anyone who hadn't lived my life for the last thirty-four years.

"We've both made mistakes. I think we finally reached the point where we can try to understand each other."

I took a deep breath before telling him the rest. There was no point in keeping it a secret. He needed a chance to tell Caitlyn, especially if Emma and Jonah weren't going back to preschool.

"It doesn't look like the kids will be with me much longer."

Barry closed the gap between us so Jonah wouldn't overhear. He shifted his grocery bags to one hand and gave my elbow a squeeze. "I'm sorry to hear that, Michelle. I really am. I know how much they mean to you."

Tears clogged my throat. Over the top of the cart, I looked at Jonah's head bouncing along as he danced to a tune only he could hear. How long before I could have a normal conversation or buy groceries or watch another little boy playing on the sidewalk without feeling like I was moments away from bawling my eyes out?

Barry pulled me against him for a quick one-armed hug. "It's okay," he whispered.

My resolve not to cry faltered at his astuteness. Maybe he did understand, at least a little.

I nodded. I couldn't speak.

"If there's anything you need…anything at all."

We walked through the doors together. I didn't know where he was parked, but he headed the same direction as me.

"I want to be there for you, Michelle. You mean a lot to me, and I don't want to see you go through this alone."

It sounded kind, but I knew where he was going with it. "Thanks, Barry, but I'll be fine."

"No, I'm serious. You've got some tough times ahead of you. I want you to know I'm here, even if I am sometimes an insensitive tool."

He was being so helpful, so compassionate, but I knew he would think our relationship was headed some place I knew it couldn't go. I hit the trunk release on my key fob. We were close enough that I didn't call out to reprimand Jonah when he let go of the front of the cart and ran the rest of the way to the car.

Barry set his bags on the pavement and started loading mine into the back of the car.

"I appreciate the offer," I told him. "It means a lot. You were there when I needed a friend."

He looked up and smiled, the skin around his dark eyes crinkling in his easy manner. "Of course. You mean a lot to me."

"You mean a lot to me too, Barry. I've decided to get more involved with the church. They have a New Converts Class I've been meaning to check out."

Disappointment was written all over his face. "Ah."

"The teachers at the preschool have taught me a lot the last few months. They helped me through this entire process. More importantly, they showed me my need for a Savior."

He straightened after depositing the last bag in the trunk. "I guess you don't have room in your life for all of us."

I opened my mouth to tell him it wasn't that. I just needed friends who understood my faith and why it was so important to me. I didn't want to lecture him, and I didn't want to tell him more than he needed to know.

"There will always be room for you at the church. Maybe someday you'll even see a need for the New Converts Class."

He lifted an eyebrow like he didn't see that happening anytime soon. "I'll see you around. I hope everything works out with, you know…" He wagged his head at Jonah. "Happy birthday. Have a nice time at the party, Jonah."

Jonah had already climbed into the backseat and was strapping himself in. He turned as best he could within the constraints and waved. "Bye, Barry."

Barry waved, then gave me a little nod as he picked up his grocery bags and headed across the parking lot.

I felt a little bad about brushing off his attempts at consolation. I knew they wouldn't come without conditions I didn't want to meet. I hoped I had sounded gracious and sincere. I never wanted to offend him. I climbed into the car with Jonah, relieved the whole thing was over.

"Is Barry coming to the party?" Jonah asked.

I managed a smile in the rearview mirror. "No, honey, he's not."

Jonah turned his face toward the window, any regret quickly forgotten. I prayed the next few weeks would be as easy for me.

"There's Dean," Jonah said when I slowed to turn into our driveway.

I looked up in dismay at the battered car sitting in my spot. What was he doing here already?

I kept my face impassive. "Do you like Dean?" I asked carefully as I climbed out of the car.

Jonah shrugged as he followed me out. I remembered how he looked when he first got here. So tiny and uncertain. "Mommy does."

"Do you want to live with Mommy and Dean again?"

He twisted his mouth thoughtfully and gazed up at me through his fringe of dark blond bangs. "You mean Dean is going to live here?"

I swallowed my frustration at Nicole. I couldn't believe she hadn't discussed Dean's eminent return with the kids or the fact they were all leaving as soon as Dean gave the word.

"No," I told Jonah. "You and Emma will go someplace else to live with Mommy and Dean. I'll keep living here."

His eyes widened in alarm. "What about Uncle Jeb?"

"Uncle Jeb will keep living with Aunt Wanda." I put my hand on top of his head and brushed his bangs back from his face. "You can visit us whenever you want."

He worried his lip again with his teeth. Finally he shook his head. "Nah. I think I'll just stay here. When Mommy misses us again, she can come visit. That's the best idea."

My heart ached. I wanted to pull him into my arms and tell him I couldn't agree more. Instead I took a deep breath to keep the tremor out of my voice. "Now you know, Jonah, when Mommy decides to leave, you and Emma are going with her. She's your mommy and kids need to be with their mommy."

"Not Emma and me. Remember, Aunt Shell? You promised. You said if Mommy wanted us to live with her, you'd tell her we wanted to stay here. Remember? You said, 'Don't worry. She'll be okay. She won't mind.'"

Tears stung the backs of my eyelids. In all the confusion of the past few weeks, I had completely forgotten the promises I made the kids on two separate occasions. Last September when I found them huddled in bed crying, I promised I would make Mommy understand they wanted to stay on the farm with me. Again when Emma was going through her separation anxiety, I had promised I would make it so Nicole wasn't mad. I was the big sister and she had to listen to what I said.

How could I have forgotten those promises?

Worse, how would I explain to Jonah and Emma why I had to break them?

I closed the car door and squatted in front of him. I ran my hands up and down his arms. He was so beautiful. What would I do without him? How could I get through one single day without seeing his sweet face?

"Mommy and Dean want to move back to the city," I began gently. "When they go, they want to take you and Emma with them."

Jonah froze. His face hardened into a mask of confusion and dread. "Tell them we don't wanna go. Tell them you promised. We can't miss school. Miss Jennifer will be mad at me. We gotta stay here."

"Miss Jennifer won't get mad at you, sweetheart. We can tell her when we go to pick up your stuff."

I hated myself before the words were even out of my mouth. I was such a rat. A lying rat.

Jonah's face crumbled. "You mean we're not going back to preschool at all? What about Emma's graduation?"

"If Dean is here to take you, Emma and Mommy back to Memphis, you won't have to go back to preschool." I rubbed his arms again. "You'll live there with them."

I tried to smile like it was the most exciting prospect going.

He jerked away from me and stomped his foot. "I hate Memphis. Don't make me go. Gypsy won't know what happened to me. Uncle Jeb won't have nobody…to help him in the fields…or go fishin' with him," he finished quietly, his indignation melting into unshed tears.

I reached for him again. "Oh, sweetie, don't worry about Gypsy. And Uncle Jeb will be excited for you." I cringed inwardly at the lie. Aunt Wanda was going to kill me. "All that's important is you and Emma…" My voice trailed off at his expression.

He was staring at his feet. The toe of one shoe dug a hole in the gravel driveway. Finally, he looked at me and asked in a small voice, "Are you gonna get another boy to stay in my room? Are you gonna give him all my toys?"

"Of course not, Jonah. You can take your toys with you. Or you can leave some of them here for you when you come to visit."

"Nuh uh." He clenched his fists. "You're mad at me. That's why you're not keeping your promise. You're mad cause I wouldn't pick up my toys. Now Emma and me'll never come back. You'll find another boy."

Tears rolled down my cheeks. I wrapped my arms around him. "Jonah, no. That's not it at all. I'm not mad at you. I love you. But Mommy needs you with her now. I'll always keep a place here for you and Emma—forever. I'll leave your rooms just like they are now. You can come back whenever you want."

He lunged into my arms and latched onto my neck. "Don't make me go. Please. I'll be good. I promise I will. I'll pick up my toys from now on as soon as you ask. I won't play on the kitchen floor and get in your way. Please don't make me leave."

I couldn't keep my own tears in check. They streamed freely down my cheeks. *I'm doing the right thing,* I chanted over and over in my head. *I believe in my sister.*

I sank to my knees and pulled Jonah against me. His feet came off the ground as I rocked him back and forth. He wrapped his arms around my neck and pressed his face against mine. Our tears blended together.

I couldn't tell him this wasn't my idea. If I had my way he and Emma would live here forever. Nor could I let him think I didn't want him because he'd been naughty. I never should have promised him and Emma I'd make sure Nicole let them stay. I never should've told Nicole I wouldn't take her to court and fight for them.

My biggest mistake was falling in love with them in the first place.

I had probably ruined him and Emma forever. They would never trust anyone again. Aunt Shell had taught them a promise meant nothing. It was as easily broken as an old toy.

I cried for Jonah and Emma and the lessons the adults in their lives were teaching them. I cried for myself that they were about to walk out of my life, probably forever. I cried for Aunt Wanda who would be devastated when she found out I wasn't fighting for them. I even cried for Gypsy who would lay in the driveway for days after Dean's car pulled away and wait for her two playmates to come back.

When Jonah finally got too tired to cry any longer, I released him. He didn't look at me as he dragged his feet all the way into the house. I went around the car for the groceries and to pull myself together. As I popped the trunk lid, I thought I saw a face disappear behind the curtains. Had Nicole or Dean overheard our conversation? At this point, I didn't even care. I wanted to strangle them both.

Chapter Twenty-Three

I've had some lame birthday celebrations in my life, but this one took the cake...literally. I don't know if Jonah told Emma what I told him in the driveway, but both of them barely looked at me all evening. Even Uncle Jeb couldn't lift their spirits with games or jokes or lopsided birthday cake.

They spent my party on the sofa in front of the TV with Gypsy lolling against the couch. Even she wasn't speaking to me. Nicole tried half-heartedly to add some life to the party, but she didn't have a lot of patience for party-poopers. Aunt Wanda didn't need to be told why Dean was there. She immediately deduced his reason for sitting at the table. Even though she spent the evening shooting daggers out her eyes at Nicole, Dean, and me, it was evident she was directing the biggest part of the blame at me.

To his credit, Dean had brought candy and a couple of cheap toys for the kids. I smiled at his attempt to make Emma and Jonah happy. Maybe there was hope for this group after all. I tried to forget the times Nicole had called and told me Dean had slapped or pushed or otherwise degraded her. As far as I knew he never laid a hand on the kids. I hadn't pressed for the truth, though, afraid of what I'd hear. Regardless of his history, it was possible he had truly changed the way Nicole claimed. Maybe he would even marry her someday and provide the kids with the stability and security they deserved.

I stood patiently while Nicole made a big deal about the party she and the kids put together for my birthday. I wanted to be happy for her. I really did. All I could think about was how they were leaving me and how empty my life would be without them.

After dinner and cake, which most of us barely touched, the kids went back to the TV and I went outside. Uncle Jeb followed.

"What's going on, Peanut?" he asked when he found me yanking weeds from the flowerbeds. Since it was early in the season, the weeds hadn't had time to take root and they came up easily in my hands, along with a few of the annuals we'd planted. Maybe I was putting more muscle into the chore than necessary.

I sat back on my haunches and blew a wisp of hair out of my eyes. "The kids are leaving." My voice cracked. "Dean and Nicole are moving back to the city and they're taking Emma and Jonah with them." I shrugged. "I guess."

He upended the five-gallon bucket I was depositing the weeds into and sat down on it. "I figured it'd be just a matter of time before this happened."

Tears pressed at the backs of my eyes again. I swallowed hard to keep them in check. I'd been crying most of the day. I figured I would dry up soon. "What am I supposed to do? I can't keep Nicole away from her kids. But how can I let them go?"

I turned a hopeful gaze up at him. I expected him to offer some great advice. Something I hadn't thought of yet that would solve everyone's problems while keeping our family together. Or at least consoling words that put the whole thing into perspective.

"Sometimes things don't work out the way they're supposed to. We just have to let things happen the way they're meant to happen and pray it all works out."

My heart sank. This wasn't what I wanted to hear. I didn't want to pray. Nor did I want to throw my hands into the air and concede defeat. I wanted something concrete I could clamp my teeth onto.

"Who'll take care of them?" I said around the lump in my throat. "Who'll be there the next time Nicole falls apart?"

Uncle Jeb laced his gnarled, calloused fingers together and stared at them. I wanted him to say something. Give me hope or comfort. All he did was sit there. He'd been spending too much time around Uncle DeWitt.

Finally, he looked at me. Tears had pooled in his eyes. "I don't want to put those young'uns in Nicole's hands anymore 'n you do. But they're her kids. Short of taking her to court and having a judge declare her unfit, there's nothing we can do."

I clenched the garden trowel in my hand. "Is that what we should do? Fight? I promised her I wouldn't. But I promised the kids I'd make her see this is the best place for them. I don't want to hurt Nicole, but I don't want the kids to leave here thinking I don't keep my promises. They trusted me all this time. I feel like I'm letting them down."

"You've done the best you could, Peanut."

I dropped the trowel and hammered my thigh with my fist. "No, I haven't. I let everyone down. Even you and Aunt Wanda. I have to trust Nicole. I have to let her know I'm on her side. But why does it have to be at the kids' expense?"

I didn't expect an answer. I was only venting. Venting and grieving and wishing everything could be different.

Again, Uncle Jeb was quiet for too long. He sighed and wagged his head from side to side. "Only God can see into the future, Peanut. He's the only one who knows what's best for those little 'uns, and for Nicole and the rest of us. All we can do is pray everything works out for the best according to his purpose."

How could it? I wanted to ask. God wasn't in Nicole and Dean's relationship. Nicole hadn't acknowledged God's existence in years. There was no way anything good could come from Nicole driving off tomorrow with my kids in the back of Dean's car.

Uncle Jeb put his hands on his knees and groaned aloud as he got to his feet. He dropped a hand onto my shoulder and squeezed. "Have faith, Michelle. We don't have to like the way things turn out. We just have to believe it will be okay."

With those less than inspiring words, he turned and walked away. I watched after him as he trudged across the yard looking every bit his sixty-plus years. I let my head drop forward until my chin rested on my chest. If Uncle Jeb didn't believe things would work out in the best interests of the kids, what hope did I have?

A few minutes later Aunt Wanda and Uncle Jeb came out on the back porch with the kids. I stayed where I was in the flowerbeds as Aunt Wanda hugged the kids goodbye as if she'd never see them again. I knew she still blamed me, and I didn't want my presence to add insult to her injury. With barely a backward glance she hurried down the porch steps and across the yard as fast as she could go. Uncle Jeb gave the kids one last hug and a wave and then took off after her.

I knew she didn't want the kids to see her cry. I hated it that she was so upset. I hated it more that it was my fault. How would I face her once the kids were gone for good? She would probably go back to seeing me as she had all those years when I was living here with Grandma. The love and kinship that had blossomed between us over the last few months would dry up and blow away like a hot, dry Arkansas summer.

Losing Aunt Wanda would be nearly as hard as losing the kids.

I had to convince myself this was the right choice. It would be hard to be sure, to let the kids leave with Nicole, but it didn't necessarily mean it was an end. Most kids didn't live with their aunts, yet they enjoyed loving, strong relationships.

This wasn't goodbye. We wouldn't go back to a time when they didn't recognize me and I didn't remember their birthdays. They'd come back. Aunt Wanda would get over being mad at me. All of us would get used to seeing each other only on holidays and summer vacations like we did the rest of the family. It wasn't a permanent thing, just a little goodbye.

I only hoped I could convince my heart of that.

My fingernails were caked with dirt and my back ached, but the flowerbeds looked pristine by the time I unbent my cramped knees and headed with the bucket of weeds to the back fence. I washed my hands at the spigot in the barnyard and air dried them as I walked to the porch. I was nearly there when I heard voices coming from around the side of the house. Agitated voices not going to a lot of trouble to keep from being overheard.

I knew I should mind my own business, but I couldn't help myself. This was my business if it affected me or the kids.

I tiptoed to the edge of the porch and trained my ears to listen to the conversation going on in the driveway. The only voice I could make out belonged to Dean. Since he had only spoken to Nicole since I first laid eyes on him a few weeks ago, it was a safe bet he was talking to her now.

"Do you think I care what she thinks?" he demanded, making no effort to keep his voice down.

It didn't take a genius to figure out whom he was talking about.

I couldn't make out Nicole's response, but it sounded like she was defending me.

"I've taken about all I'm going to take," Dean said. "We were getting along fine before you involved your family in our lives. They might push you around, but I'm not going to sit here and let them do it to me."

Who was he kidding? Couldn't he see Nicole had been the one pulling our strings since the moment she appeared?

"She's just trying to help," Nicole said.

My heart lifted. Nicole finally seemed to have realized I only wanted the best for her. I was trying to help, if only she would let me.

"No, she isn't," Dean snapped. "She's treating you like a kid. If you can't stand up to her, I will."

I clenched my fists, almost anticipating an altercation with Dean. I would love to show him there was one Hurley woman he couldn't push around.

I caught a few more snatches of conversation as the two of them drifted out of earshot. I wanted to run to Nicole and tell her she didn't need a man who didn't respect her. I wanted to point out her family truly loved her while Dean apparently only cared about how her decisions and opinions affected him. I wanted to remind her she was strong and capable and she'd be better off alone than with someone who couldn't understand what was important to her.

I didn't do any of it. She would only accuse me of being the one who didn't understand. Maybe I didn't.

Uncle Jeb was right. All I could do was pray she'd make the right decision by her kids. Even if it wasn't the right decision at the time, I'd pray everything worked out for the best.

I spent the rest of the night doing exactly that.

Chapter Twenty-Four

Gypsy's incessant barking woke me Sunday morning. I raised my head from the pillow with a groan. Six fifteen. Ugh! That dog. Every time I planned to sleep in, she decided it was the perfect morning to bark her head off. I swung my feet over the edge of the bed and stumbled to the window. I hit the pane with the heel of my hand to get it to move upward. The spring rain had caused the wood to swell, and it was even more resistant than usual to the upward motion. One of these days I would get new windows. At the price the guy had quoted me on the phone, replacing windows was something I figured I'd put off until I was dead and buried. Let the next generation worry about it. But I was getting too old and impatient to keep banging away at wood windows.

One of these days…

I couldn't see Gypsy from my position at the window, but I could certainly hear her. She was directly below me on the porch where she'd spent the night. She liked to do that on nice nights when the weather cooperated.

A vision of last summer flashed through my mind. I jerked my head toward the driveway. I could barely see the backend of my Mazda from my vantage point. The only thing behind it was empty driveway. Dean had parked there last night after coming in from town and not speaking to anyone, including Nicole. Now his car was gone.

My heart lurched. I forgot about Gypsy and the open window through which I had planned to yell at her. I ran out of the room. My bare feet grew cold against the hardwood floor as I hurried across the hall. I threw open the door to Emma's room. She and Jonah lay curled together in the double bed. I let out a sob of relief.

"Thank you, God," I whispered.

I moved down the hall. I rapped lightly on the door to Nicole's old room before pushing it open. I advanced into the room and gazed down at an empty bed. Dean wasn't the only one missing. Where was Nicole? I slid a couple of drawers open. They were also empty.

I ran downstairs and opened the front door. "Gypsy, get in here," I ordered. I didn't want her waking the kids, not until I found out what was going on. I turned on lights as I moved through the house, looking this way and that for a note or some indication about where Nicole had gone and if she was coming back. I was sure I'd find something in the kitchen. I didn't. Nicole had vanished again without a word.

How typical!

What was I going to tell the kids?

Monday morning the kids were back in preschool. I pulled Miss Gail aside and told her the latest development as Emma and Jonah trudged to the play area.

"I don't know how they'll do today," I told her. "They haven't said a whole lot since yesterday morning when I told them Nicole was gone. I don't know what they're thinking."

Gail shook her head. "I'm sure they think she left because of something they did."

"Maybe they're blaming me. Nicole and I exchanged words more than once during her stay. I know they overheard a lot and picked up on the tension."

She put her hand on my arm. "Honey, don't blame yourself. We all knew this would happen eventually. It's not very encouraging, but isn't it better that she left them with you before she took off? How much worse would it be if she moved them somewhere else, and then pulled a disappearing act?"

For the hundredth time since yesterday morning I thought of the argument I had overheard between Dean and Nicole. In hindsight I realized they must've been talking about Nicole's resolve to take Emma and Jonah with her when she went back to Memphis. Dean obviously wasn't happy I had supported her decision. I knew Nicole was easily influenced by the men in her life and she usually chose the path of least resistance, yet I was still in shock she had left the kids with me again.

"There's nothing I can do, is there?" I asked Miss Gail dismally.

"I wish I could say the kids'll bounce right back and you'll all live happily ever after. Even if a judge awards you permanent custody, Nicole will always be in your lives. She is their mother. She will most likely flit in and out of here whenever the mood strikes her, play Mommy for awhile, and then be gone again, leaving you to pick up the pieces."

I drove to work with a heavy heart. It was a long twelve hours.

I picked up the kids at Angie's that evening and headed home. They still weren't talking. Emma was quiet. I noticed her fingers in her mouth several times. Jonah stared out the window the whole way home. Any questions from me were met with one-word responses. At least the kids were familiar with me this time. I knew they wanted to stay on the farm. But it had to be like getting dumped.

Even when you knew a relationship was doomed, it still hurt when he stopped calling.

The phone rang just after dinner. Emma and Jonah were on their knees behind the coffee table watching television, an armload of coloring books in front of them. As soon as I heard Nicole's voice, I hurried from the room and out the back door.

I glanced over my shoulder to make sure I hadn't been followed. I growled into the phone. "Where are you? Didn't you learn anything from the last time?"

"I'm sorry, Michelle," Nicole said with a whine in her voice but no discernible contrition. "I thought it would be better this way."

"Better for who?"

I tightened my grip on the phone. I didn't want the kids to hear me, but I wanted nothing more than to chew her out good and proper. "I can't believe you did it again, Nicole. Just up and disappear without a word. What do you think it's doing to your kids?"

"And what do you think it does to me to hear my son cry and beg his aunt to let him stay with her so he won't have to go with his own mother? After everything I've done for him."

Just as I thought, Nicole had been the one listening at the window Saturday. I tried to empathize with her pain. It was getting harder and harder to care what she was going through.

"I'm sorry, Nicole, but you can't blame Jonah. All he knows is living here isn't a constant struggle. He knows he'll wake up in the same bed he went to sleep in. Everything's the same. Routine. Kids need that. They can't handle the alternative."

"Well, I can't give them that right now, Michelle. I'm sorry but I can't." Her voice rang with self-righteous tears. "Dean and I are headed to Vegas. We're going to stay with Mom for a while till we get on our feet. I'm going to use part of her money to have an attorney draft a permanent custody agreement with you. I'll send it and you can sign it and give a copy to your attorney, or however it works. I think that's best for everyone."

Tears of gratitude blurred my vision. Whether she knew it or not, she couldn't have given me a better birthday present. There was no point in yelling at her. The deed was done, and nothing was going to make my sister feel the least bit responsible for the way things turned out. In her mind things couldn't be peachier. She knew the kids were safe and cared for. She had Dean back and apparently our mother. I would take care of her kids. She could concentrate on getting her life figured out, which I had a sneaking suspicion would never completely happen. She was free and I…

I had come out the winner.

It hadn't seemed that way last August. For the longest time I thought God was punishing me for some terrible sin, much like Grandma Catherine had felt when Mom walked away, leaving Nicole and me for her to worry about. Unlike Grandma, I realized before it was too late Nicole's kids were the best things that could've happened to me. They were a blessing, not the curse I first thought. If they hadn't showed up under the lilac bushes, I never would've recognized how empty my life was. I never would have met Kyle again. More importantly, I may never have met my Heavenly Father.

Yes, I definitely won hands down.

"Nicole, I wish you and Dean all the best," I said. As the words left my mouth, I realized I meant them. They weren't just selfish words because I had gotten what I most wanted.

I wanted my sister to be happy. I wanted her to find her purpose in the world. I wanted her to be free like I was. Free to forgive Mom and Dad. Free to love the kids and put aside the bitterness and anger I held onto for much too long.

Fresh tears stung my eyes as I realized I had forgiven Mom and Dad. I had even forgiven Grandma. I would never understand how Dad could walk away from his family. I would think of him sometimes and wonder if he ever thought of me. But I was through holding on to the pain and anger that had characterized my life. The weight was too heavy. I realized now I couldn't forgive Dad on my own. No matter how hard I tried, something would happen to remind me of the pain he put me through. Like Nicole with the ceramic ballerina Mom sent her for her birthday, I would get angry and hate him all over again.

Regardless of whether or not Mom or Dad ever called to apologize or admit guilt, or even if they ever recognized their guilt for what they'd done, I had forgiven them. It was only possible through God's grace. My parents' rejection of me no longer defined who I was. I was a child of God. He would never leave me. Nor would I have to carry a burden again by myself.

"Thank you for that, Michelle," Nicole said. "I really appreciate everything you've done this past year. I know I don't always act like it, but I do. You've always been the only person I could count on, no matter what."

"I'm your sister, Nicole."

"Well, I'm your sister, too, and I've been nothing but trouble from the beginning."

"I'm not going to disagree with you if that's what you're waiting for," I said with a chuckle.

"Michelle, I love you. Take care of my kids, will you?"

"You know I will."

"Tell them I'll be back to visit as soon as I get settled and get some money together. Maybe you could keep Christmas open for us. We could bring Mom for a visit. Wouldn't that be nice, the family together again?"

"That'd be great," I lied easily since both of us knew it wasn't likely to happen.

For the first time I understood Mom a little. She had always been afraid. She hadn't been able to stand up to her domineering mother. She couldn't stand up to Dad either. She probably hadn't been that surprised when he left. She was alone and scared and without choices. At least that's the way she saw her situation. Like Nicole, she chose the path of least resistance.

How could I stay mad at her for giving in to her fears? I remembered my impatience with Emma those first few weeks on the farm when she cried every time I looked at her. She was in a brand new world and hadn't known how to react. Mom was the same. She wasn't strong enough to handle the changes in her life. It was scary. There had been no one to turn to. If she had been a Christian then, maybe things would've been easier.

Standing up to Grandma Catherine was probably similar to the early Christians thrown to the lions. They had marched into those coliseums singing God's praises. God would've given Mom strength to face her lions if she had only known how to ask.

The Lord had bestowed mercy on me and saved me from my dreadful past. I would make it a point to begin to pray for Mom and Nicole to come to the realization they needed him too.

I'd even pray for Dad, wherever he was.

"Thanks for everything, Michelle."

"You too, Nicole. I mean that. Give Mom my love."

"I will. We'll see you in December."

I hung up the phone and wondered when and if I'd hear from my baby sister again.

Chapter Twenty-Five

"Hold your head still, sweet cheeks," I said with my teeth clenched around a mouthful of bobby pins. "I'm having a hard enough time getting this ponytail in the center of your head without you wiggling all over the place."

"Wait till Aunt Wanda gets here," Emma suggested patiently as I pulled her head into the angle I needed. "She always gets it straight the first time."

I removed the bobby pins from my mouth. They were too big for her head anyway, and they stood out against her blond hair. Didn't these things come in white? "Oh, she does, does she?" I gave the ponytail a playful yank. "I think that'll do it. Yeah, that's better. Turn around and let me see."

Emma turned to face me, her jaw clenched in pain. "You got it too tight. It hurts when I close my eyes."

That was the least of her problems. The ponytail tilted to the left. The delicate blond tendrils I'd purposefully left down to frame her face looked scraggly and tangled. The angelic look I'd been going for had somehow fallen short. She looked more like a scarecrow at the end of summer. I grinned at my ineptitude. I spun her around, let the ponytail down and combed my fingers through her long hair. "How about we wait and let Aunt Wanda do it? She has a knack for that French braid thing across the top of your head."

"Yay!" she cheered.

I agreed too much to be insulted by her enthusiasm.

"Is Pastor Kyle gonna be at the church to see me graduate?" she asked as I brushed out the damage I'd done.

My hands paused in their work. An image of Kyle's gray blue eyes looking at me from the pulpit yesterday while he read the part he had prepared for the graduation, flashed through my mind. "Didn't he practice his speech last night at the dress rehearsal?"

"Yes."

"Then you know he'll be there."

She turned in the chair and tucked her feet under her bottom. "Do you think he'll come here after the graduation for our party?"

Heat rushed into my cheeks at the prospect. Even though I'd made it a point to help out last night at the dress rehearsal just so I could see him there, I still blushed at the thought of seeing him again tonight. "I'm sure he'll stop by."

"Does he like you, Aunt Shell?"

I smiled and tweaked her nose. "Why do you ask that?"

"I think he does. He looks at you an awful lot. Uncle Jeb said he looks at you like a puppy with a—with a—"

"A new bone?" I offered.

"Yeah, that's it. A puppy with a new bone."

"That sounds like something your uncle Jeb would say. He shouldn't be talking like that in front of you. Don't forget Kyle is our pastor and we have to treat him with respect. I don't want you asking him any questions like that at our party."

Emma's eyes grew wide. "Oh, I won't."

My reminder was unnecessary. As shy as she was, she wouldn't say anything to him, or any other adult in the room for that matter, if the house caught on fire.

A party for a preschool graduation seemed a little pretentious to my old cynicism, but I couldn't resist. Emma was my preschooler—soon to be kindergartner—and I wanted to make a big deal of her accomplishments.

I heeded Aunt Wanda's advice to keep things simple and had decided against hiring a caterer. While I spent the day cleaning and hanging party decorations, Aunt Wanda had baked and whipped up hors-d-oeuvres to suit a five-year-old palate. She, Jonah and Uncle Jeb were due home any minute to set things out for the party before we headed to the preschool for the graduation ceremony. Hopefully there would be enough time to repair the damage I'd done to Emma's hair. At least she was clean. That was one maternal job I could handle.

I still couldn't believe the kids were mine. At least until the next familial blowup. Adoptions within a family were seldom uncomplicated. My caseworker warned me to expect disruptions until Emma and Jonah married—and even after. Nicole would never be completely out of their lives. She was their mother and I would always be Aunt Shell. I wouldn't want it any other way. Deep down I couldn't help wishing Nicole would stay in Vegas with Mom and leave us alone.

"Yoo-hoo, where is everybody?"

"We're up here, Aunt Wanda." I reached for Emma to give her a kiss before our hectic evening began, but she was already gone.

"Aunt Wanda, I need you," she called on her way down the stairs. "Aunt Shell messed up my hair."

She reached the bottom of the stairs and headed toward the back of the house so I couldn't make out the rest of the complaint. I'm sure my ego was better off. I headed to my own room to finish getting ready. Emma would be fine now that the cavalry had arrived. I could spend some time on myself. As Emma pointed out, Kyle would be at the graduation and later at our party. Since our afternoon at Angie's, we barely had more than a few moments together, and never alone. Kyle saw to that. I knew he didn't want to hurt his witness with people who might think the worst. I kind of liked being treated like a lady.

This time last year, I thought my future held nothing more than the same old same old. Like Grandma Catherine, I imagined living here the rest of my days with Gypsy for company and my job and the garden to occupy my time. I couldn't have imagined how two little people under my lilac bushes would change everything.

Jonah and Emma didn't deserve all the credit. I had a Heavenly Father with a sense of humor who knew exactly what I needed when I needed it. Now I had an abundance of what I sorely lacked before. A house that knew the sound of children's laughter, a much-improved relationship with my family and a man who loved me. More than that, I knew the Creator of it all loved me too.

Thundering feet sounded on the stairs. "Aunt Shell, Jonah said I looked like a grape in my purple dress."

"I did not. I said she looked 'great'."

I smiled again at the reflection in the mirror and opened the bathroom door. I wondered how many years it would be before I could enjoy five uninterrupted minutes in the bathroom again. Funny how at this moment it didn't matter.

I barely had time to do more than smile at Kyle where he sat at the back of the stage during the graduation ceremony. As usual Uncle Jeb had snagged a seat near the front to get the best camera angle. He didn't plan to miss a moment of Emma's big night. The younger kids opened the ceremony with a couple songs and memory verses before joining us in the pews. Jonah didn't have a solo this time. I was a little disappointed at the missed opportunity to show him off to the congregation.

Tonight was about Emma. I had a feeling there would be plenty more chances to see Jonah behind a microphone in the years to come.

It would be strange next year dropping Emma off at the Christian school on Olive Branch Road after leaving Jonah at preschool. I wondered how they would react to the separation. Probably better than me. Months ago one of the teachers had reminded me kids were resilient and adapted to nearly anything. If only it were that easy for me.

Back at the house Uncle DeWitt handed Emma a flower and balloon bouquet and a lavender teddy bear. I blinked away fresh tears as Emma stretched her skinny arms around his neck and hugged him tight. It was the first hug I ever saw them share. I imagined it was also the first bouquet Uncle DeWitt ever paid hard-earned money for.

"It's hard to believe that's the same little girl I saw sucking on her fingers last August when you brought her and Jonah to the preschool."

I looked over my shoulder and saw Kyle's face a few inches from my own. I turned back to watch. "I can't believe I'm the same old curmudgeonly aunt who didn't want them here."

"You were never curmudgeonly." He moved closer and rested his chin on my shoulder. I tilted my head and let it rest against his. "You just didn't know how beautiful life could be."

His breath was warm on my neck. A shiver worked its way down my body. I snagged my bottom lip with my teeth.

Kyle slipped an arm around my waist, and I snuggled against him. "I'm still not sure I know."

"But you're getting closer."

We watched as Emma sniffed the flowers and set them on the edge of the table that held her cake. She clutched the teddy bear to her chest as she took off to show it to her friends.

Kyle took my hand and led me to the bench in the foyer used for taking off shoes and hanging up jackets. The bench was meant for one so it was a tight squeeze for both of us. I didn't mind. Kyle didn't seem to either.

"Have you heard from Nicole?" he asked once we were settled.

"She called from Mom's to tell me she and Dean had arrived in one piece."

"That was thoughtful of her."

"It's more than she ever did before. We seem to be on friendly terms for the first time in years. I didn't berate her this time for taking off without warning. What's done is done. At least she didn't take the kids with her."

Kyle stroked my hand. "You're learning to pick your battles."

I gave an exaggerated sigh as I watched his hand caress mine. "It's not easy."

I wondered if anyone would come looking for us if we sneaked out onto the front porch. I wanted to kiss his mouth, touch his hair, breath in the scent of him. I didn't know if Kyle wanted the same from me though. I believed him when he said he loved me. I just wasn't sure yet what that meant.

"Nicole wasn't completely wrong when she called me a control freak," I said in an effort to rein in my wandering thoughts. "She is who she is. So are Mom and Dad. I need to get it through my head I can't change the world or even my little corner of it. All I can change is the way I react to what happens to me."

"Sounds like the kids aren't the only one who've grown since that first day the three of you walked into the preschool." He wrapped his finger around a tendril of pale hair that grew near my temple.

"You make it hard to concentrate on what you're saying when you look at me like that."

He leaned closer until his lips were nearly against my cheek. "Like what?"

"Like…" I took a deep breath to still the rapid beating of my heart. I wondered if I'd ever get used to the affect his close proximity had on me. I wasn't sure I wanted to. "Like a puppy with a new bone."

He tilted his head and cocked an eyebrow.

I laughed. "It's just something one of the kids said earlier tonight."

"About me?"

"It's a long story."

He snuggled closer. "You can tell me. I'm not going anywhere."

"Promise?"

He nuzzled my neck. "I promise. I waited fifteen years for you, but I'm about waited out."

"What does that mean?"

"It means…when you're ready…"

"Ready for what?"

"Ready to trust your heart with what you've wanted your whole life."

"Do you mean you?"

He nodded. "Me. I love you. I want you in my life forever."

Was he saying what I thought he was saying? Or did I just want it too much?

I wanted to ask. I wanted to make a joke so he wouldn't see how uncomfortable his words were making me, especially if I was wrong. But I didn't feel like joking. I wanted to be honest with him. I wanted to be myself without trying so hard to matter to someone as much as they mattered to me.

"A few weeks ago I didn't think anyone could ever love me."

"And I told you a person can't earn love. You just have to reach out and accept it."

I looked through the doorway to where Jonah was playing on the floor with two boys from preschool. I couldn't keep from smiling. "It's the best blessing I ever received."

"Michelle," Kyle said as if snapping me out of a trance, "I'm not talking about the kids."

I turned my gaze away from the boys in the next room. The playfulness was gone from Kyle's face.

"Neither am I."

"I was hoping you'd say that." He shifted on the narrow bench and drew a velvet box out of his pocket.

I gasped and my eyes filled with tears. I was going to be in an embarrassing situation if the box contained an old lapel pin his mother asked him to get rid of.

I brought my questioning gaze up to meet his. My doubts vanished at the intensity in his expression. Kyle raised the box. "Marry me, Michelle."

"But, we just…How long have you—"

He kissed me, cutting off my words. "I've carried it with me for the last month, waiting for the right moment. I wanted it to be romantic. Something you can tell our kids about someday. I figure any moment with you is the right moment."

"Our kids?"

He smiled gently. "You have to give me an answer first."

"Oh, Kyle." I put my hands on either side of his face and pulled him to me.

After our kiss, he dried my cheeks with his thumbs. "Is that a yes?"

I nodded, crying and laughing at the same time and wishing I could think of something romantic and profound to say worth repeating to future generations. "Oh, yeah," I said instead. "It's a yes."

Jonah ran into the hallway. He skidded to a halt at the sight of my face. "Aunt Shell, are you crying?"

I wrapped an arm around him and pulled him against me. "I'm crying, buddy, but it's a good crying."

Jonah looked from Kyle to me, clearly not knowing what I meant. Voices in the next room quieted as everyone clustered in the doorway. The kids looked equally concerned, confused or disinterested while the adults held their breath in hopeful suspicion.

I kissed Jonah and then rested my forehead against Kyle's. "Are you sure you know what you're getting into?"

Kyle wagged his head toward the waiting crowd. "Are you?"

I nuzzled my head into the crook of his neck. "I've never been surer of anything in my life."

Epilogue

"Hurry up, you two. You're going to miss the bus."

"Coming."

The thundering of feet on the stairwell to my left rattled the windows in the panes. One of these days I needed to replace those old, drafty windows. Gypsy barked in rhythm to the pounding footsteps as she hit the landing two strides ahead of Emma and Jonah.

I gritted my teeth against the noise. "I told you not to run on the stairs. Somebody's going to get hurt, not to mention you'll wake your brother."

"Don't worry about this little angel," Aunt Wanda said, coming through the living room door to the hallway. She bounced the sleeping baby in her arms as one hand patted his bottom. "He can sleep through anything."

"He has to in this house," Uncle Jeb quipped. He raised the video camera in front of him. "Now, everybody look at me. I need to capture every moment of this morning."

I didn't want to rain on Uncle Jeb's parade, but I was already stressed about as far as I could go. "We don't have much time for capturing. The bus will be here any minute."

Uncle Jeb lowered the camera and smiled at me. "Don't fret, Peanut. I've known Greg Smalley since he was littler than Jonah here. If he pulls up in that bus and we ain't ready, he'll just have to wait a minute."

"Aunt Shell," Emma shrieked. "I can't find my backpack."

"Did you put two juice boxes in my lunch?" Jonah asked. "We're supposed to bring two juice boxes every day this week on account 'a we're donating them to the homeless shelter. I don't want to be the only kid with only one juice box."

I snagged Jonah's shoulders before he could rush past me. "We packed your lunch last night. Remember? We packed an extra juice box so you'll have some to donate like everybody else. And Emma, your backpack is hanging right there on the rack where we put it last night. We're staying organized this year."

As I removed the backpack from the rack and handed it to her, I marveled at how it had been over a year since Kyle proposed to me on this very bench. What a hectic, exciting, blessed, and eventful year.

Our engagement only lasted six weeks. Neither Nicole nor Mom attended the ceremony, though I sent invitations. I would've invited Dad, too, if I had known where he was. Life was too short and too precious for holding onto unforgiveness.

"Not like last year when every morning was chaos," Aunt Wanda said with a smile as she continued to pat the baby's bottom.

"Last year was a crazy one all right, huh, Mama?" Kyle came in through the kitchen and stopped to kiss my cheek. "But the Lord saw us through."

"Yes, he did. I don't think we'd be standing here right now if he hadn't been with us from the very beginning."

Kyle kissed me again, this time a lingering one on the mouth. "He knew what the kids needed. Most of all, he knew what we needed."

Even though I was stressed that the kids might miss their first ever bus ride together, I smiled and relaxed into my wonderful husband for a moment. Last year had been a year of chaos with all of us adjusting to life together. After a short honeymoon on the Gulf in Galveston, while the kids stayed with Aunt Wanda and Uncle Jeb, we returned home and started combining Kyle's life with ours here on the farm.

Emma had excelled in kindergarten, though her teacher said she was the quietest kid in her class. She was coming out of her shell more and more every day. I hadn't seen her sucking her fingers in over a year. She still studied her feet sometimes when she was in a new situation, but that was okay. She would probably always be a shy person. Given time, she would find her own way of dealing with a reticent personality.

Yesterday had been her first day of first grade and Jonah's first day in kindergarten. There had been little concern on my part about Jonah fitting in at Big-Boy school. I was more concerned that Harrison County's only Christian school might not be ready for him. We had driven the kids to school yesterday, but today was the first day they'd ride the bus. They could barely contain their excitement. I was focusing on getting through the day tear-free. Over the last few months I had been a hormonal mess, and sending two kids to school was nearly more than I could take. It was a good thing I had Kyle and Aunt Wanda and Uncle Jeb to lean on.

Nicole and Dean were no longer together. They had barely hit Las Vegas when Dean met someone new and disappeared into the neon landscape. Nicole survived the break better than any of us figured she would. She continued to live with Mom while she found work. Maybe getting rid of Dean was exactly the catalyst she needed for getting her life together.

Over the winter she moved to St. Louis and started working at a home improvement store. She was taking classes at a community college and talking about getting a degree, though she still hadn't decided where to focus her studies. The last week of June we drove the kids north to spend a few weeks with her. Her apartment was cute, though small. She seemed really happy for the first time in her life. I held my breath every time I thought about her getting together with a new man. I hoped she took her time and focused on more important things first.

Before Kyle and I left for the night Nicole thanked us for everything we'd done for her and the kids. It looked like my sister had grown up a lot in the last year, much like I had. I knew she loved her kids, and they had a wonderful visit, but I think she was enjoying her freedom like any twenty-five year old who finally realized she had leaped into adulthood much too early.

Aunt Wanda and Uncle Jeb had to go to St. Louis to pick Jonah and Emma up after the visit. I was getting much too big by then and having some difficulty with hypertension, which I knew was common for a woman my age in her last trimester carrying multiples.

"Okay, you two," Uncle Jeb said with false gruffness in his voice. "Enough smooching. Let's go out on the porch so we can get shots of the whole family before Greg comes tearing down the road on that bus."

Aunt Wanda shifted the baby to her left arm and wrapped the other one around me. "Oh, Michelle, it seems like just yesterday you and Violet were going out this door to catch the bus. Now it's our Emma and Jonah's turn."

Tears pooled in her eyes.

"Aunt Wanda, don't." I sniffed hard at the tickle in my nose. "You're going to get me going again."

"I can't help it," she said tearfully.

"Let's go. Let's go," Uncle Jeb ordered. "Kyle, get the door. I don't want to miss Emma and Jonah getting on the bus."

The mewing cry of a newborn sounded behind Aunt Wanda. I tensed and started around her.

"No, no, you take Trevor. I'll get his little brother." She thrust her charge into my arms and turned toward the living room where two bassinettes had been set up for daytime naps.

I smoothed a lock of dark downy hair away from my sleeping son's face. Trevor was a spitting image of his father with black hair and gray-blue eyes. Tyler, nine ounces lighter and four minutes younger, was identical to his brother except for a pale cap of strawberry blond hair just like mine and Emma's pale skin that would freckle mercilessly under the Arkansas sun.

James Trevor and John Tyler Swann were born on the two-year anniversary of the day Gypsy found Emma and Jonah under the lilac bushes. Every time I breathed in the soft velvety scent of my babies, I marveled at the changes my life had seen in those two years.

I was going back to work in the cardio-care unit in six weeks but only for three twelve-hour shifts a week in order to maintain my seniority and health benefits. A few years ago I wouldn't have been able to imagine my life without work. I didn't know who I was without that part of my identity. Now work seemed so insignificant compared to everything else.

I had planned to take the babies to Angie's on the days I worked and Kyle had commitments at the church, but Aunt Wanda put an end to that nonsense right away. She reminded me, rather tearfully, that years had a way of getting away from a person, and she didn't plan to miss a moment of cuddling babies if she didn't have to.

How could I argue with logic like that?

At my age, and with an already overflowing house, I wasn't sure there would be more babies for Kyle and me.

Emma and Jonah were growing up so quickly I could barely keep track of the changes. Like Aunt Wanda, I didn't want to miss one more moment of my life.

I smiled at Kyle over my three-week-old bundle. He smiled back as he held the door open for the kids to go out ahead of us.

Uncle Jeb was barking orders about where we should stand on the porch to avoid the glare from the rising sun. Aunt Wanda came out last shushing Tyler. "Let's make this fast. This one's going to want breakfast soon." She arched her eyebrows at me.

I heaved a sigh, though I couldn't be happier. "Again? He ate an hour ago."

Uncle Jeb laughed and ruffled Jonah's sandy blond hair. "They're trying to catch up with their big brother."

Jonah beamed. He and Emma loved their little brothers. It was all I could do to keep them from kissing them black and blue all day when they weren't running through the fields with Gypsy.

Uncle Jeb stepped off the porch and turned to face us. "Okay, now. Everybody smile."

Emma thrust her arms out to Kyle. "Hold me, Daddy."

Kyle bent his knees and lifted as she jumped expertly into his arms. The kids started calling Kyle Daddy as soon as they found out we were getting married.

Daddy. A word I imagined they had dreamed of calling someone their whole lives.

I looked at Emma beaming at Kyle with her skinny arms wrapped around his neck. Like her, I had a new Daddy in my life as well. I finally knew I was loved and cherished by a Father who would never turn his back and walk away as though I never existed. Emma's Daddy loved her and would always do his best with her. But he was human. He would make mistakes. He would forget important days and sometimes say or do the wrong thing.

My heavenly Daddy wouldn't. I had what I'd been looking for all those lonely years.

For the most part, Emma and Jonah still called me Aunt Shell, though I was called *Mommy* more and more often. I figured by the time the twins were talking, it would be second nature, and I'd be Mommy to everyone in the house.

Even though our custody order was allegedly permanent, I wasn't sure how Nicole would react the first time she heard her kids call me Mommy. I couldn't worry about that now. I would always refer to her as Mom to Emma and Jonah, and I wouldn't let them forget who she was.

Our family was complicated, just like every other family in the world. Nicole would have to get used to it. I prayed she learned to pick her battles and not find offense in the simplest things.

Mom was just a word. A word I was proud to bear.

In the distance we heard the distinctive rumble of a school bus lumbering down our rural road. The Christian school had acquired two old buses from the county and painted them to match the school colors. Greg Smalley and a couple other parents drove the routes in exchange for reduced tuition rates for their kids at the school.

Kyle and I were thrilled we were able to support our Christian school while providing a stellar education for our kids. Yes, our kids.

Emma slipped out of Kyle's arms and jumped off the porch steps after Jonah.

"Hey," I exclaimed, startling Trevor out of his sleep. "Kisses."

Emma ran back up the steps and kissed the three adults and her two baby brothers. Then she ran to Uncle Jeb and wrapped her arms around his neck as he lifted her into the air. Jonah heaved a kindergarten sigh at the ridiculous realization he was going to have to kiss half a dozen people before he got on the bus. He hurried through the process before the bus rolled into view so no one outside the family would see.

Uncle Jeb straightened after receiving the last of the kisses and trained his camera on the kids as they hurried down the path to wait for the bus. The thirty-year-old lilac bushes had bloomed months ago. Now they stood, tall and bushy, nearly concealing the opening in the fence where a gate once stood.

The bus creaked to a stop next to the mailbox, and the doors swung open. Jonah jumped onto the step first but turned to wave. Emma turned, too, and waved. "Bye, Mommy. I love you." she called out.

I waved back. "I love you, too. Sweet Cheeks. Have fun. Learn stuff."

The last part came out as little more than a whispered croak only I could hear as tears clogged my throat.

Kyle put his arm around me and pulled me against him. "Drive carefully," I whispered for the benefit of the driver, though I knew he couldn't hear, and I had every confidence that he would.

We watched, Uncle Jeb filming the whole time, as Jonah and Emma moved through the bus and found their seats.

Kyle kissed my cheek. "We did it, Mama."

I laughed through my tears. "Are you kidding? We're just getting started."

The End

Story Behind the Story

Preschoolers have always been my favorite group of people. I taught at a real life Noah's Ark Preschool in Waverly, OH with the teachers mentioned in the Tender Blessings series. I still teach the Beginners' Sunday School class at my church.

Maybe that's why writing a story that illustrated some of the difficulties facing families today was so important to me.

Readers began asking for more of Michelle's story—and more romance—nearly from the first day of publication of *A Tender Reed,* the original paperback. I was happy to comply and hope *A Little Goodbye* met all your expectations.

My goal with everything I write is to make you laugh out loud at least once. Doing so in a book with such serious subject matter can be tricky. Life is tough. But I still believe laughter truly is the best medicine.

Michelle was an intriguing and multi-faceted character who will always hold a special place in my heart.

I would love to know what you think about Michelle's story, as well as my other novels. Please consider posting an online review. Authors live to hear what readers think and what they want to see more of. Your input and advice matter and may show up in a book someday.

Thanks so much for reading and stay in touch.

Before You Go

If you enjoyed this book or any of my other titles, please consider recommending them to a friend or posting a review on Amazon, Goodreads, your blog, or any other online site that allows reviews. It's the greatest compliment you can give to an author you love. Even short reviews show booksellers there is interest in the books and they will display them to more readers.

To stay up to date with new releases or special promos sign up to sign up for my Newsletter and receive a free book.

Thanks so much & happy reading.

Also by Teresa Slack

Runaway Heart: A Sweet & Clean Contemporary Romance

Kyla Parrish has never held onto a relationship for more than a few months. She's quit more jobs than most people have applied for. Until Will Lachland. He's the first man who ever made her think of getting serious about something, about putting down roots.

What if she's wrong? What if Will's wrong for her? To avoid a decision, Kyla does what she always does. She runs. Back to the one place where life was simple—the family farm. But no matter how far she goes, she can't outrun her heart. Can she find peace and the love she longs for? Or is something else, something greater, calling her heart toward home?

Joy Redefined: A Novel of Suspense

"An unlikely hero…"

When Joy Kessler's neighbor and best friend Dorothea Westlake disappears and a long-lost nephew takes over her house, Joy's suspicions go into full alert. Where is Dorothea, and why is no one else suspicious?

As days turn into weeks with no sign of her friend, Joy must become the woman of courage she always wanted to be to uncover the truth to save Dorothea—and herself.

The Ultimate Guide to Darcy Carter: A Sweet, Small-Town Romance

Comfort food and romance. Ultimate Guide guru Darcy Carter has no time for either until she meets the subject of her next book.

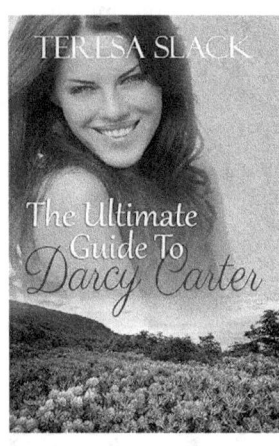

Darcy is an expert at everything--except her own life. She has written over twenty how-to books on every subject under the sun, but she can't guide herself out of a paper bag, especially when it comes to romance.

When her editor suggests a new book idea, *The Ultimate Guide to Finding Mr. Right*, Darcy wants no part of it. She heads south to research an idea of her own. She soon discovers Mr. Right might be hiding in the last place she thought to look.

Don't miss this contemporary Christian romance, a feel-good, laugh-out-loud story that reminds us how fun--and complicated-- falling in love can be.

About the Author

Teresa Slack's down-to-earth writing style and endearing, true-to-life characters can be attributed to her upbringing in rural Ohio. Writing from her home in the southern Ohio hills, she is thankful for the opportunity to do what she loves while sharing her faith with readers.

"I write stories to entertain first. Reading should be fun—an escape. Secondly, I want my stories to inspire and edify the reader. If we're breathing, we're going to face conflict in our daily lives. I want to create characters my readers can identify with and learn from. Life isn't easy. But it's good to know we don't have to do it alone."

Teresa is the author of nine other novels including *Love Begins*, the first book in the Tender Blessings series. Check out her website http://www.teresaslack.com/ or her author page on FaceBook & Twitter to stay abreast of what's coming next. Readers are encouraged to contact her at teresa@teresaslack.com